ENOUGH

ROPE

SUSA CAPO

Published by Book Writing Pioneer

Cover design by Book Writing Pioneer

ISBN: Printed in the United States

Table of Contents

Dedication 5

Chapter 1 6

Chapter 2 12

Chapter 3 40

Chapter 4 49

Chapter 5 63

Chapter 6 80

Chapter 7 95

Chapter 8 107

Chapter 9 114

Chapter 10 122

Chapter 11 127

Chapter 12 133

Chapter 13 140

Chapter 14 153

Chapter 15 169

Chapter 16 183

Chapter 17 193

Chapter 18 199

Chapter 19 206

Chapter 20 216

Chapter 21 229

Chapter 22 237

Chapter 23 248

Chapter 24 257

Chapter 25 268

Chapter 26 275

Chapter 27 284

Chapter 28 292

Chapter 29 299

Chapter 30 308

Chapter 31 318

Chapter 32 323

About the Author 329

Dedication

To My Daughter, Nora

Eyes shining

Smile radiating

Heart warming

You are my sun

Arms holding

Hands comforting

Love nourishing

You are my earth

Laugh twinkling

Mind illuminating

Competence rising

You are my moon and stars

Chapter 1

"**H**anged, Hung? Which is correct?" Carol's voice shattered the silence, echoing off the high living room ceiling with its false beams and skylight. She gazed upwards, her eyes tracing the beams as if seeing them for the first time. Suddenly, her heart shuddered. "You used a beam in your offices. Why, Ed?" She was whispering now through her raspy throat.

The late afternoon July sun slanted through the skylight, casting sharp angles of light but offering no warmth to Carol's chilled frame. Lack of sleep, dread, and sorrow had sucked out her warmth, leaving her systems unregulated, cold. She heard the uncompromising ticking of Ed's grandfather clock, which seemed to mock her with each somber tock. "Tell me, Ed," she murmured, her voice a blend of despair and defiance, "How could you?" The words hung heavier than the silence, unanswered. Time moved on, but Ed did not.

Carol envisioned her life without Ed. It wasn't going to be too different alone, would it be? Not quite—with two loving, grown-up daughters and her best friend from high school who newly moved to town, plus two other close friends. Financially, the sale of her business left her with substantial investments and a healthy bank account. Well, no thanks to 'Ed and his gambling.' She dodged a bullet by not investing in the dubious stock scheme he and Charles cooked up. The rapid beating of her heart now matched the clock's ticking, mirroring the urgency and disquiet she felt inside. Their last few weeks together were fraught with turbulence, like small boats helplessly caught in a media storm.

That tenacious TV reporter kept hounding them relentlessly, and each encounter was more invasive than the last. Other columnists followed suit, their calls frequent and their tones insinuating. Bribes? Gambling? Corruption? The whispers grew louder; they even intimated Mafia involvement. Is that true? Have you put us in danger? What happened to you? I used to be so proud of your dedication as a city councilman. How did it come to this?

Her current numbness was almost a relief, a break from the unyielding exhaustion they'd both felt these last weeks. The press were like hounds, always sniffing for a new angle to catch photos. The attention had been building each week, reaching a crescendo when the governor asked for an investigation based on that damn reporter's information. One even knocked on the door early yesterday morning.

Was it yesterday? No, the day before? How can time pass quickly and so slowly all at once?

She didn't get up when she heard the knock. She didn't look for Ed.

You were gone even when you were home. You stayed in your study alone or with your stupid lawyer, Charles. You were floating in a leaky boat of addiction named Gambling.

Carol clasped her hands around her throat, squeezing tightly as her fingers pressed inward tighter and tighter now. She could feel her neck swelling under the pressure; she wanted to breathe, but she kept increasing the pressure. The clock's chime startled her, breaking the suffocating silence. She released her grip and took six deep, shuddering breaths, each one matching the ticking of the clock. *Six in the afternoon already. You got up at 6:00 every morning, like clockwork.* Now, the clock seemed to mock her with its steady beat; he was not getting up again.

His breath had always been refreshingly sweet when he kissed her goodbye. Each morning brought a soft kiss, and she could feel the slight smile playing on his lips—a tender ritual that she cherished deeply. She really did love him. Yet, last night, she hated him; in the morning, she mourned him. Tears streamed down her face as she gasped for air, the sorrow overwhelming her. The grief was intense, enveloping her like a dense fog, making it hard to see past the pain. *You're so pathetic. Whining, that's what this is, pathetic whining.*

Am I to blame? I have plenty of money. I could have bailed him out... again. I wanted to protect my money for the girls. Who are you fooling? You knew he would gamble it away, and you didn't want to lose your lifestyle. True, well, partly, I worked hard. I tried to help him. Didn't I? Oh, Ed, I'm sorry.

"Get up!" Shouted Carol, her voice cutting through the silence as she pushed herself upright. She scanned the room for the ringing phone that had jolted her from her thoughts. It was on the end of the couch, right where she had thrown it after yet another invasive call from a reporter. Looking at the name on the screen, she paused. A wave of relief washed over. She took a deep, calming breath and relaxed some, feeling the tension in her shoulders ease, and smiled slightly before picking up the call.

"Stevie, glad to hear your voice. How are you doing?" her voice softened as she greeted her oldest daughter. "I'm fine, I am. Nothing I need right now. Is Kay okay?"

Carol listened intently, a part of her marveling at how Stephanie (Stevie is what she liked to be called) handled the conversation with such composure. She was discussing her younger sister and her husband, Tony, her voice steady and filled with a practical tone. She commanded herself to focus as Stevie described funeral arrangements with a calm that Carol herself used to embody. She spoke about the phone calls that needed to be made and the food that had to be arranged. Carol was usually the one who took charge, the organized force in their family. However, Stevie was logical and pragmatic. It was a comforting realization for her that the roles could shift, and Stevie was more than capable of managing under pressure.

"That all sounds perfect. Really, it does," Carol said, her voice carrying a mix of gratitude and exhaustion. "Of course, it's okay if you take care of the funeral arrangements. It is good Charles offered to help. Please tell him I didn't mean to be so abrupt on the phone. He's right; we don't know when the coroner will release the body. So don't prepare too soon. I know you know; I was trying to… oh, never mind, Hun," she trailed off, her words tinged with a hint of regret as she settled back onto the couch.

As Stevie continued to outline the plans, Carol reached and pulled a couch pillow close, her grip clearly showing her need for comfort, "Tomorrow morning, yes, that works for me. Not too early, okay? I do need my morning time," she added, trying to inject a light tone into her voice. "Love you too," she whispered before hanging up. Then, slowly, Carol curled into a fetal position on the couch.

"I need a mother," she whispered to herself. She knew Stevie sensed that. "Just not my mother," Carol mumbled into the pillow. Her muffled words were laden with a lifetime of complex emotions.

Uncurling, she thought about her girls. They had accepted their dad's death. They were so young when the cancer took him so quickly. They had accepted Ed with love and affection.

Oh, poor Stevie has been going through her private grief since her girlfriend left. At least Kay seemed to be happy with Tony and their new home. This has been a long day! Damn. Okay, just breathe. Focus on your breathing. Get up! Eat something! Yuck. Okay. Get up. One leg at a time, girl. You can do this.

Her legs resisted. Fighting with herself was a battle she could win; she usually did; the bloodshed would be minor… hopefully. She was strong. She was resilient. "Damn, you. Ed, how could you?" she shouted. "Up!"

Hand pressed against her diaphragm, she rose and moved to the wide Tara-style stairs. She encouraged herself with each step, climbing up to their shared bedroom and bathroom. "Okay, shower, then clean panties and a favorite jazz concert tee shirt; you don't even need a bra," she coaxed herself. "You survived Tom's death. You survived your uncle's abuse at 12. You can survive ah, ah what? Another husband's death? A betrayal? Okay, I can say it: suicide. Suicide," Carol repeated over and over as tears streamed down her face as fast as the water in the shower.

Chapter 2

———— • ● • ————

"**O**k, passengers, you know the drill…seats, tray tables up!" The lively air steward announced into the microphone, his voice carrying down the aisles.

"Nice to know some people still enjoy their work," Jimmy's wife commented, her tone light yet observant. "Jimmy, 'hello,' we are landing in Tampa. We are home. You know, Florida, not North Carolina anymore."

Jimmy stared out the plane window, his mind only half on her words. He was deep in thought about the investigative report that awaited his full attention back on the ground. As the lead detective, he had to come home and solidify the charges against a prominent Tampa figure. *Edward T. Wallin seemed so smug while running for Tampa City Councilman. He loved to discuss his development in Plant City … for the people… code for cheaply made for the poor. Buy here, pay here with outrageous mortgages. My poor Dad was paying a ridiculous price to smell the Sulphur from the phosphate mines. He did love searching for fossils around his land, known as Bone Valley.* Jimmy's heart clenched. He thought of his Dad crippled with osteoporosis. Jimmy was sure the groundwater from Wallin's land caused his dad's suffering.

"Jimmy! Listen. I don't like cutting our North Carolina vacation short any more than you do. But you are the chief fraud investigator. Be happy you have a job that appreciates your talents. C'mon, Jimmy, don't brood. I hate it when you brood."

"Talents? I'm happy to have such a lovely wife." Jimmy teased.

"Ten points," Dayna replied. "You are almost out of the red. A few more, and I'll have to go to Victoria's Secret and get a new nightie."

Jimmy looked lovingly at his wife of ten years. Dayna was truly special: energetic, understanding, and tougher than any guy in the Florida Department of Law Enforcement (FDLE). This vacation was supposed to fix their broken relationship. Dayna had drifted, but it was partly his fault. He always felt he wasn't enough for her family… especially her big financier father who frequently belittled him, which only fueled his resentment toward Dayna. It had made their relationship toxic for a while, but now, as they neared home, he hoped they could finally start to heal.

He focused on his work, perhaps to a fault. Meanwhile, she had found someone else who paid attention. Someone who offered her the attention and the prestige she craved, someone with money. They both tried to forget the painful fact that she couldn't have children. The counseling they underwent was a temporary bandage, barely covering the deep wounds—what they needed was something stronger than any antibiotic to heal what had become systemic issues in their marriage.

This investigation of Wallin's 'apparent suicide,' as labeled by the Tampa Tribune, was, unfortunately, placing him right back in the wrong place at the wrong time. Even with the loan fraud, the investigation would be mostly routine—he hoped. Maybe then they could return to their retreat in Highland, NC retreat—yeah, right, as if that would solve anything. He needed to keep himself away from ruining his family further, to keep Dayna away from her special friend. He clung to the hope that this recent vacation had rekindled something in her, drawing her back to him. Maybe this investigation would break the spell the other women had on him.

Damn, damn, idiot, he chastised himself. *Focus on the here and now! Why did I have to come back?* But deep down, he knew why. He was the right person for this investigation. It was a privilege to have been personally requested by the governor. *Man up!! After all, my CPA and double master's, one in forensic accounting and the other in psychology do allow me a special perspective as an investigator. Things have to add up. Things were not adding up in his life right now.*

"Maybe we could take a ride up to Tallulah Gorge in Georgia when we get back. We could hike into the Gorge. Swim in one of the beautiful waterfalls that are in those pictures I showed you," Dayna suggested, her voice mingling with the rhythmic thud of the plane's wheels hitting the pavement. The idea floated in the air, a pleasant fantasy amidst the stark reality of their return.

As they moved through the bustling Tampa International Airport, Jimmy was only half-present in the conversation. He was mentally making notes. The investigation's tasks followed him like a shadow onto the tram, through the concourse, and down the escalator of the Airport. At the same time, Dayna chatted away about the new shops sprouting up around them. He found himself gently guiding her through the crowd. His psychology degree always paid off during the interviews. "Yes!" A realization hit him amidst the flow of his thoughts, a nagging concern that refused to be quiet. Wallin did not fit the suicidal profile. Wallin was a fighter—friendly but arrogant, not the picture of a broken man. "Who knows what evil lurks?" Jimmy mimicked absorbed in the coming requirements.

"What did you say? Don't look like a kid who broke something. Run off to your downtown 'rocky' playhouse. I'll manage," Dayna said as they retrieved their luggage.

Jimmy couldn't help but smile at Dyna's reference to the Regional Operations Center (ROC) of the FDLE as his 'rocky' playhouse. It was an apt description for the seven statewide centers of the Florida Department of Law Enforcement. Sometimes, they were fighters like Rocky and at other times, they were on 'rocky' footing with local and public officials as the agency tasked to investigate public officials. Then, sometimes, they stood as a stabilizing force in Florida's intricate web of law enforcement, charged with domestic security and the apprehension of sexual offenders and predators.

Jimmy ensured their luggage was securely loaded into Dayna's cab. Before he got back in line for his own, he made a quick call to his partner, Salvador Carducci. As he waited, his thoughts reflected on how easy it was for him to detach from being a family man and jump to 'cop' stuff. He had been very detached before their vacation in more ways than one.

Highway I275 was clear as the taxi maneuvered its way downtown. You couldn't see the Tampa Skyline until you got close, and there it was. *Growing city, growing crime, job security,* Jimmy mused darkly to himself as he unfolded his 6'2" black and beautiful form from the cab. His instincts cried that this high-profile case would have no winning tickets. He was sure it was more than the $150,000 in gambling debt Wallin left behind, and that was the money they knew about.

"Hey, Carducci, how's my vehicle?" Jimmy boomed as he strode into the bustling office area of the investigative division of the FDLE in downtown Tampa. He made a conscious effort to disguise the twinge of regret he felt for having lent his prized car to his partner.

"All repaired, keys in the desk. Listen, I am sorry my wife tore it up. She just got distracted by your car phone ringing. Quite a fancy gadget. Anyway, I'm not the only one who ruined your vacation," Sal teased.

"Got that right!" Jimmy shot back acknowledging the complexity of their friendship and partnership. Sal was older than Jimmy with an extensive background. His proud Detroit street kid senses mixed awkwardly but effectively with his Einstein logic and a Shakespearean soul.

"What are your instincts on this one, Carduch?" Jimmy asked, leaning in slightly, his tone serious.

"You don't want to know," Sal responded, his expression grave. His deep knowledge of Mob activity made Jimmy's stomach turn. Jimmy knew Sal had been consulting on a big mob sting operation that involved a myriad of agencies in south Florida. He had already spent a lot of time in south Florida, New Jersey, and New York. "This Year, 2000 is not going to be a good year for the Mafia," Sal quipped. "Want a donut, Mr. GQ?" he teased, offering a light-hearted jab at Jimmy's always impeccable appearance.

What a pair they made: Sal, the insightful detective with a non-cigar smoking Columbo vibe sans raincoat, and Jimmy, Mr. Neat. Just as Jimmy was about to reply, his beeper vibrated against his hip, breaking his train of thought. Looking at the number, Jimmy's clean façade slipped briefly. His mind raced. *How did she know I was back?* He mumbled while he pulled back his composure.

"Sweet talking trouble?" Sal said, using his uncanny perceptive powers to read the room—or, in this case, his partner's troubled expression.

"Huh; no. We need to get a look at the scene before there is nothing left," Jimmy said, his voice tight with urgency as he struggled to maintain his composure.

"I'm ready. You need to make a private call first?" Sal asked, his tone laced with concern as they left the bustling FDLE offices, which buzzed with the constant influx of new responsibilities each day. Just recently, they had been tasked with the responsibility for investigating Public Assistance Fraud, adding another layer to their already hefty workload. "You know, the Chief received a letter from the Gov to investigate Wallin on Wednesday? Same day as the suicide."

"You were already investigating Wallin, weren't you? In your other life?" Jimmy's voice was flat, directed at the windshield more than to Sal as they moved through the traffic on Kennedy Blvd toward the crime scene. But for which crime?

"No comment at this time," said Sal.

July in Tampa, Florida, was oppressively hot and muggy, the air thick with humidity that seemed to cling to everything. They were going to Jimmy's favorite part of Tampa, Ybor City—a place steeped in his family history. Jimmy's grandfather, Jose, an unskilled Afro-Cuban immigrant, had worked as a street cleaner there. He would often tell stories of the Yellow House Bar. It was at the center of Bolita gambling until it shut down in the 1960s.

Jimmy was double pissed at Wallin. Hanging himself from one of the columns of the Ybor Factory Building not only ended his life but also disrespected the historic integrity of the building.

"Hey, did you know that the Y columns on the first floor of the Ybor Factory were each from an individual tree?" Jimmy mentioned, trying to shift his focus from his frustration.

"Fascinating," Sal responded with a smile as they made their way around the urban projects and into the heart of Ybor, the historical echoes of the area mixing with the present challenges of their investigation.

"The projects are getting worn down. More crime each day. Ybor could be a real hot spot if the powers that be would just pay attention. So much history here," Jimmy lamented as they drove through the deteriorating streets of Ybor City.

"I do have a favorite story of the building where our buddy hanged himself. Remember, it's the famous cigar that started the Cuban revolution for freedom from Spain. I can imagine these guys writing their declaration to start the revolution," Sal shared with a hint of reverence in his voice.

"That's right, they took the message signed by Jose Marti, el activisto importante, and rolled it in a cigar. Then, some guy travels to Havana with it in his pocket. Viva Cuba Libre!" Jimmy exclaimed, his voice rising with excitement as Sal playfully raised his fisted arm in solidarity."Do you think it was a suicide?" Jimmy then shifted the conversation, his tone turning somber.

"Normally, I would say yes. Don't know if I mentioned the double hanging ruled suicide in May in New Jersey. It was Giovanni Ligammari, 60, and his son, Pietro, 37. They hanged themselves, face to face, in separate nooses with… **nylon packing cords**. Then we have a jail hanging of a Mafia guy in June…**nylon packing cord.** Now this one…**nylon packing cord.** My Spidey senses are tingling," Sal detailed, his voice laced with skepticism and a hint of foreboding.

"Damn, this one is going to be impossible to prove either way. Have we heard anything from forensics?" Jimmy pondered aloud as he maneuvered the car into a space in the Community College parking lot about three blocks from their destination.

"Our job is to follow the money. Forensics promised a fast turnaround since this is such a high-profile case," Sal reassured him, his voice steady and focused.

"This guy is set to be cremated according to his Will and the note that his son revealed. There's no need to be too hasty. They need to reconstruct the scene, examine the direction of the fibers of the cord, and get all the blood work to determine if he was incapacitated…" Jimmy detailed their next steps, his mind already racing ahead to the myriad of forensic details that could potentially unveil the truth behind the apparent suicide.

"Whoa there, Jimbo, or should I say Mr. Coroner. Slow down. May I repeat, we follow the money," Sal quipped, mopping his sweating forehead with a handkerchief as they approached the imposing structure of the Ybor Factory building where Wallin was found hanging. "Damn, did ya have to park a mile away? Look for spaces right next to the building. Oh yes, excuse me, you don't park on the street," he teased, his tone a mix of irritation and jest as they trudged toward the building.

Jimmy ignored his partner's ribbing as they climbed the stairs to the grand entrance. He paused at the top, his gaze sweeping over 15th Street. He could almost hear the echoes of José Martí rallying the Cuban sympathizers from the stage-like platform where they now stood. A shiver ran through him, and for reasons he couldn't explain, he held his breath as they entered. Inside, Jimmy's eyes methodically scanned the space, and he examined the tin ceilings and each visible column. Each of the Y-structured stately trees had one square branch on either side. *It wouldn't be hard to throw a cord over the side branch, climb on the chair then kick it away, not hard at all.*

"Remember, you are the CPA. You are not investigating a suspicious death," Sal reminded Jimmy with a stern tone as they went through the building. "Captain said we need to prove or disapprove Florida Ethical Law violations and any misappropriation of public funds. We can look at his private business. I suspect the FBI and Securities and Exchange Commission (SEC) will want to take over any of that even if it is connected to our case."

"You think there is something that the FBI and SEC will want to see, don't you? Will LoScalzo's name come up? I know you won't answer that," Jimmy pondered aloud, his voice laced with curiosity and a hint of frustration. As far as he knew, LoScalzo was the current boss of the Tampa Mafia. He had taken over from Trafficante, Jr. back in 1987. Jimmy was sure that whatever Sal's consulting job was with Miami, he was not going to discuss it right now. He knew he didn't go undercover anymore, not since he was almost killed years ago because of an FBI screw-up.

"Wasn't Wallin's lawyer buddy, Charles Atoll, involved in Tampa's bank scandal with all those mortgage issues? More Mafia garbage. As I remember, that was so poorly handled everyone got off," Jimmy added, his tone dripping with disdain as he recalled the chaotic handling of the case.

Still puffing from the walk and wiping the persistent sweat from his brow, Sal responded, "Yup, major keystone cop fiasco. FYI, the Feds got eighty-five indictments here in Tampa this June; that should keep them busy with the Mob. Maybe they won't run us away so fast."

A moment of silence fell between them as they both pondered the implications. They examined the crime scene photos they brought along, their eyes lingering on the beams.

"This guy's suicide is much too convenient," Jimmy broke the silence, his voice a mix of skepticism and determination. "I know; I know; focus on the money. We need to interview the wife and his associates. Any snitches who can help? What about the reporter who broke the story about his gambling, money borrowing, and use of public resources?" asked Jimmy. They spent the next hour rummaging through Wallin's office, meticulously gathering all financial documents that could be relevant to their investigation.

"I have the reporter lined up for five at his station on Kennedy. My crazy Spanish informant thinks he has something. I need you with me. He slips into Spanglish, and I lose some of what he says. He is always hyped up," Sal said, the urgency in his voice reflecting the gravity of their investigation. "We still need to make set arrangements with Wallin's wife, Carol. I gave you notes about all this."

"Oh, those were all the yellow sticky notes stuck to my computer," Jimmy said with a grin, acknowledging the clutter that had taken over his workspace.

"You can put them in your 'o so organized' spreadsheet or stick them wherever," Sal teased, poking fun at Jimmy's penchant for perfectionism.

"You mean this?" Jimmy retorted, waving a sheaf of papers in his hand with a playful smirk. "Don't pout. I read your report on the plane. What about Nan Hamber? I think that's her name. His secretary? And the report you sent me says that everyone loyal to Wallin got raises several times a year. Then, he borrows the money right back from them and probably goes to the dog track," said Jimmy.

Sal's reports were always thorough. He was careful not to go past the facts while his gut instincts spilled out onto little scribbled notes. "Her name is Nancy Hamlin. I don't think she realized that the loans would have been against the Ethical Codes. I am not sure he did, either. Not that it mattered. I put my notes about her and others on your desk. He manipulated over $150,000 in employee loans, which I could see—no telling what other funds he re-directed. I know you will find the money trail," said Sal as they left the building.

Jimmy walked slowly, feeling the oppressive heat of the Tampa streets even as they made their way through the bustling downtown. He stopped looking down an alley just to let Sal catch up, the sweat beading on his forehead.

"Did you have a chance to look at his corporation, GatWin? It was supposed to be this big deal technical company. Sure went public quickly. Bought by HarborTech, Inc., a publicly traded company," Jimmy mused, his skepticism apparent.

"Left most of that one for you, Mr. Numbers. I contacted Roger Barnes to get a bead on the accounting stuff, but he was on vacation with his family in Ocala. I did take a ride to Ocala," Sal admitted with a slight chuckle, hinting at his need to escape the city's confines.

"You just wanted to get out of the city. He's the CPA for Wallin's wife, right?" Jimmy joked, stopping again and bending down to pretend to fix his shoe; which gave Sal a moment to catch up. His mind was ticking off the people involved: Wallin, Atoll, Wallin's wife, and Roger Barnes, her accountant. Not to mention Wallin's buddies in the city council offices and…

"What are you doing down there? I thought Barnes might know something about the businesses. He might still be important. I figured Carol Wallin might have talked with him, or Ed Wallin might have discussed some business with him, but I didn't get much. You might get more from him, accountant to accountant. I think it's time to go talk with my snitch, Toco," Sal suggested.

"What's with that name?" Jimmy asked.

"The meth head thinks he's the last Chief of the Tocobaga Indians who lived around here. From what I can gather from his ramblings, his great, great, great whatever was captured by Spaniards but escaped with a beautiful Spanish lady and hid in the swamps surrounding the Hillsborough River. None of that could be true. He was an FBI informant when I first met him," Sal explained.

Jimmy knew he had to tread lightly about Sal's informant days.

"That's right. You knew him in your other life. Can we get anything that makes sense from him? You've known him quite a while," Jimmy probed, his tone laced with a blend of concern and curiosity.

"He seemed to spiral some when we were doing the Miami-New Jersey connection. Went off the rails after that. You do know he once saved my life, then just vanished for a while," Sal recounted, a hint of nostalgia and gratitude coloring his voice.

Jimmy detected a certain depth in Sal's tone when he spoke about this informant. "Saved your life? Oh, that's right, your other life, the undercover life. Right? You trust him?"

"Even now, as crazy as he's become, I get good information from him. I think some of what he does is an act. Truthfully, I don't think he's a meth head. He talks like one, but he has none of the physical signs."

Sal was sweating buckets when they returned to Jimmy's SUV. Collapsing into the seats, they both sat silently, allowing the air to blast on them. Even the hot air was better than nothing.

"Maybe he's schizophrenic?" said Jimmy.

"He seems to know stuff. Always did. Saved my life. We go way back to the early to mid-nineties. Always had spot-on intel." Sal mused, reflecting on his long-standing connection with Toco. The car was growing uncomfortably warm, prompting Sal to remark somewhat irritably, "Never mind that. Does that AC even work?" said Sal.

"If you trust him, then I do. So where are we going?" Jimmy responded, reaching over to crank up the AC fan to its maximum setting. The cab of the SUV was silent for a moment. *Always quiet about that time. Must have been a tough undercover assignment,* he thought.

"He already told me that Wallin and Atoll, his attorney, were negotiating to buy the Ybor Factory Building for HarborTech. Also, they had bought some other buildings around Ybor," Sal disclosed, joining together the pieces of their investigation.

Jimmy gazed out at the surrounding buildings as they drove through the edge of the historic district. The area was steeped in history, both good and bad.

"He could be federal drug enforcement or gun undercover. What do think Toco knows?" Jimmy's mind was turning. So many unanswered questions: *Where would Wallin get the money to buy buildings? Might be a money laundering operation. I haven't looked at HarborTech's books yet, but I suspect there is strange money there. Maybe our Tampa Councilman, Mr. Wallin, not only borrowed money from employees but maybe he used Mob money intended to be laundered. Now, that would be worth following.* Jimmy speculated; his detective instincts fully ignited. "Where do we find Mr. Toco?"

"We can head down 7th Avenue, then over to Adamo Drive under the overpasses to the parkway. He's got a camp set up there," Sal directed, mapping out their route to Toco's current whereabouts. His tone held a hint of sarcasm as he added, "Are you going to get nostalgic on me as we go down 7th?" he asked rhetorically.

As they cruised down 7th Avenue, Jimmy's thoughts momentarily wandered. He couldn't help but notice the Italian Club, which now boasted an updated facade. Many of the other historic buildings had also received facelifts, each now gleaming under the Florida sun. The area had transformed into a hub of activity, with trendy bars and gourmet restaurants pulling in the downtown Yuppie crowds at lunchtime. On Friday and Saturday nights, 'take the lady' outers felt smug walking through Tampa's version of New Orleans's Bourbon Street with coffee houses and struggling galleries.

The musical offerings were as diverse as the city itself, catering to every conceivable taste. On the weekends, the avenue was closed to traffic as it was morphed into a pedestrian-only zone, bustling and vibrant. Cameras were installed along with mounted police along the avenue to make the 'new' Tampa residents feel safe enough to spend their dollars and take the ride from North Hillsborough County for a night out. Yet, despite these efforts to sanitize and secure, the proximity of the rows of project apartments, drug and gun deals on the side streets, and impoverished surrounding neighborhoods cast a long shadow over the area and kept the majority away – not to mention the gay clubs, heavy metal dudes and dudettes, and other assorted wild ones.

The crime stats showed that the chances of being assaulted in Ybor are still higher than in the rest of Tampa. Since the bloody days of Mafia rule, Ybor City has continuously grappled with its dual identity, oscillating between its rich cultural heritage and the ongoing challenges of ensuring safety and security.

"Look, they changed the name of that club where the Goya Male Revue performs to the Pleasuredome," Jimmy observed, pointing out the neon-lit sign to an uninterested Sal as they headed toward the Crosstown Express overpass.

"Hey, watch it! Remember, 20th is one-way," Sal teased, his voice light with familiarity, knowing full well that Jimmy was well-acquainted with the streets of Ybor.

"Is that your guy hopping around by the concrete pillar?" Jimmy inquired, squinting toward the shadowy figure that seemed to be waiting for them.

"Looks like we were expected," Sal responded dryly, noting the informant's less-than-subtle positioning.

When they returned to the SUV, Jimmy rifled through his notes and tried to make sense of their last 20 minutes of explosive chatter from Toco. "Okay. Let's review the CI's ramblings. Toco says he saw Wallin that morning. Claims he was hanging around because some big deal was going down with out-of-state 'guys.' That's almost sunrise. Then he said he saw four 'guys' go over to the Ybor Factory Building. He waits outside to see if he can get some information," recounted Jimmy as he took out his notebook.

"Thinks he can make a deal with them, so he waited it out. According to him, they never came out," Sal added, folding his arms as he leaned back against the leather seat.

"Right then, around 6:30 am, he was about to look around inside when a reporter and his cameraman showed up. Damn, scum won't come down to the office for a statement. He claims the guy or guys are still in town and looking for trouble," Jimmy said as he expanded his notes.

"He may be right. Do we have surveillance cameras around the building?" asked Sal.

Jimmy completed making notes and then said, "I'll check on the cameras. I didn't see any. You are probably right about Toco faking it. He talked about seeing Wallin at the racetrack and the dog track. For a bum, he gets around," his tone half-amused, half-perturbed. He did some quick mental math, calculating the distance between the tracks—about 20 miles apart. "The guy didn't have a car, or did he?" he wondered aloud, the puzzle pieces not quite fitting together in his mind.

"Wallin claimed he hardly ever went to the track, according to the news stories. What else?" mused Jimmy as he continued making notes. "Oh yeah, he mentioned that GatWin was Wallin's corporation. How's a CI so well-informed? I had to delve into the papers you sent me to understand all that myself. He also knew that GatWin was purchased by HarborTech. Did you pick up anything else on that?"

"You got more than me. What's with the name GatWin?" asked Sal, his curiosity piqued.

"Oh, I figured that out when I reviewed the papers on the plane. Wallin's lawyer, Charles Atoll, went to the University of Florida. Their football team is the Gators, sooo…Gators Win," Jimmy explained, connecting the dots with a slight chuckle as he maneuvered his SUV onto Adamo Drive, heading toward the news station's offices.

"There is definitely something with Wallin's corporation, his lawyer, AND his supposed suicide. By the way, did you hear him caution us 'Cuidado, Cuidado' and something about a woman from New Jersey?"

"New Jersey is tied to the Gambino family, internet gambling, and the track. Gambino's brother rules the Jersey Shore. Glad we're headed over to the news station. The reporter said he'd give us the full tape they took," Sal added, his tone hinting at the anticipation of uncovering more layers to this unfolding mystery.

Jimmy cranked up the AC but knew the drive wouldn't even be long enough for the SUV to cool down in Tampa's unyielding humidity.

Both Sal and Jimmy were lost in their thoughts, the weight of their investigation pressing down. They didn't need to plan their interview. Their technique was like a dance they'd practiced for years; sometimes they waltzed, sometimes they tangoed, and sometimes they danced alone.

"Let's stick with the facts, Stevens. You followed Wallin on his walks with a cameraman?" Jimmy stated, his voice firm and direct, as they finally arrived at the news station.

"He walked early every morning along the bay down Bayshore Drive. I was looking for him. I was going to ask him about the loans - get a comment for the early report. I also had some intel that the City's waste-hauling contract got him some kickbacks. I hadn't been able to catch up with him. I went to the house, but no one answered," Stevens explained.

"That was what time?" Jimmy asked, trying to confirm the timing of events.

"Six AM," Stevens replied succinctly.

"Go on," said Jimmy.

"His wife didn't answer the door," Stevens reported.

Jimmy raised an eyebrow, his expression incredulous. "You knocked on the door at 6 in the morning? You're a piece of work. Ok, you didn't see him on Bayshore. Then what?"

"I went over to Ybor City to see if he was in his office at the Factory Building," Stevens responded.

"AND?" Jimmy prodded, leaning forward slightly, his eyes narrowing as his impatience was evident in his sharp, clipped tone.

"We went to the courtyard entrance and looked in the window," Stevens continued, his voice lowering slightly.

"AND? You are dragging this out, Stevens."

"It's all documented on the film," whined Stevens.

"I want your version, please. What time exactly did you look in the window?" Jimmy insisted.

"Okay, we looked in the window. It was around 6:40 am by the time we looked up and down Bayshore and rode by his house on Swan again. As I looked, I thought I saw something moving. I tried the door, and it was unlocked. We went in, and well there he was hanging there. It was awful," Stevens elaborated.

"Did you see anyone else around? When you found him hanging, did you walk up to the body? You only took film? Did you touch the body?" Jimmy asked.

"Of course, I didn't touch him. I called 911. I made a copy of the whole tape for you so you can see I didn't break in or touch the body. Oh, I did see a homeless guy on the street. He isn't in any of the footage. We edited the tape for the news. You don't understand how horrible it was. His coloring, the smell," Stevens's voice trembled slightly, the horror of the moment resurfacing as he recounted the details.

"All right, let's go over this again," Sal asserted, his tone firm as he took the reins of the conversation, giving Jimmy a moment to retrieve the tape from their collection of evidence.

"Listen, I answered your questions. We gave you the tape. What have you found out about the loans? What about kickbacks?" Stevens shot back.

"I ask the questions," Sal snapped back authoritatively, his gaze steady and commanding.

"Only a few more questions since you seem to think you had the right to harass the councilman."

"He was dirty; the public had a right to know. The suicide proves he knew he would be caught this time. I know he's connected to Gamboni. C'mon guys, look at his record. Just because I investigated doesn't mean I am responsible. My responsibility is to the public and their right to know," Stevens retorted, defending his actions.

"Let's define terms. Investigated means hounded. Responsible means 'anything I have to do to get a story.' So now, Mr. Responsible, are you going to turn over your investigative notes and save us some time?" Sal countered, his voice cool but pointed.

"Get real, Detective Carducci," Stevens dismissed, not buying into the interrogation tactic.

"If this turns out to be murder, it will be very real," Carducci said softly with his best 'you bastard' grin.

"That's out; the coroner has already confirmed suicide. Why don't you watch my news report and learn what's happening," Stevens said arrogantly.

Both Jimmy and Sal turned and left without another word, their expressions signaling that this was far from over, the tension palpable as they exited.

"Son of a bitch! How can the department leave us holding our dicks like that?" Sal exploded as they climbed into the SUV, his frustration boiling over at the lack of support they felt from their own department.

"Let's not play 'shoulda'; media guys were sitting at the coroner's office and annoying everyone," Jimmy countered calmly as the car phone suddenly rang. Sal snatched it up.

"It was Sally letting us know the coroner ruled a suicide, and the report is on my desk—bad timing. I got a headache—enough for today. Drop me off at my car. Maria will kill me if I'm late for dinner with her nephew, Benny, who, by the way, is from New Jersey. So wonderful," said Sal.

"Do you hear a squeak in the front end?" Jimmy suddenly asked, shifting the subject as he tried to tune out the troubles for a moment.

"We can take it by the shop in the morning. Could be a joint that needs grease. I know you didn't like Wallin. But, maybe, just maybe, he was protecting his family from a long-drawn-out ordeal when he checked out. The mob can be rough, and a lot is going down right now," Sal speculated, his voice softening as he considered the personal toll such circumstances could inflict.

Jimmy mulled over the facts so far, his mind racing. *Sal knows more than he is letting on.*

"So, our friend on the FBI Tampa force, Donnie Castillo, gave you a heads up? You're right, I didn't like Wallin. 'Segue el dinero' or 'segui i soldi' in Italian. This is starting to get interesting," Jimmy mused, the pieces beginning to align in a larger, more ominous picture.

"Those are our orders. Follow the money. Donnie can be helpful. Remember, they will protect their butts over our backs. They've done it to me before," Sal reminded him.

Jimmy considered what Sal was telling him—time to rely on facts. "Wallin's addiction sets the motive for the investigation. Willing to throw everything away. Think there could be a bigger fish on the end of this hook than we know. Dayna may have to follow waterfalls next summer," Jimmy said, half-joking as they pulled up next to Sal's sensible '89 Volvo, the day's revelations weighing heavily on their minds.

"Waterfalls, huh? Well, stay out of Hyde Park. I hear they have pretty addictive stuff there," Sal quipped with a knowing smirk, a hint of irony in his voice as he climbed into his car.

SOB's good. Jimmy thought as he drove down Bayshore, directly towards the area Sal had just warned him about. *Addictive was a good word for it. Why can't he stay away? What was it about this lady?* His thoughts berated him more intensely as he looked at Tampa Bay and the joggers along the 'world's longest sidewalk'.

The new moon had left everything black. Streetlights and the ambient glow from the homes cast shimmers across the bay, painting a serene yet haunting picture. The mansions along the way intrigued Jimmy and spoke of old money and new money, each staking its claim along the waterfront. He turned down Bay to Bay Blvd and tried to convince himself to keep going west and not make the last two turns into her alley.

"I only have about an hour, Joanne," Jimmy stated as she opened the back door. His tone was a mix of urgency and resignation, betraying the conflict within him.

"You know what they say about older women—grateful. Why do you insist on using the back door?" said Joanne.

Chapter 3

· ● ·

"**Joanne**, thanks for coming. It is so good to see you. Tell me something that has nothing to do with my mess," Carol's voice was heavy with exhaustion and desperation.

"Oh Carol, don't you want to talk about things? Come on! Tell me. I'm a good listener," Joanne offered gently.

"I know you are, but I want a way back from hell right now. Talk, please. By the way, you look radiant. I would almost suspect a new man in your life. You used to glow like that as a teenager,"

"Well, you could say that. But he's not mine. I'm borrowing him for a while. Picture this," Joanne started, her voice dipping into a playful tone.

"OHH, good, one of your sensual stories."

"Not too young, but the perfect body, a lot of stamina, a great passion. He brushes against you, his scent fills your nostrils, you get that ache, you remember," Joanne described, her words vividly drawing Carol into the fantasy.

"You should write romance novels. Tell me more," Carol urged.

"Lots of strokes, soft kisses, and then his beeper goes off."

Carol stifled her laughter in her hand, the sound muffled but genuine. The girls would think her crazy to be having this conversation a few days before she was to bury her husband. "No more," she snorted, shaking her head.

"More wine?"

"Now you," Joanne said as she handed Carol a glass.

The two walked onto the lanai. The cricket's rapid rasping added a mild tension to their conversation.

"What can I say? It is a nightmare that never ends. The FDLE has subpoenaed all our financial records. Everyone says it is suicide, but I can't believe it. I DON'T believe it. He was upset. He was even angry. And there were financial woes. But he was a fighter, Joanne. He never gave up," Carol confessed, her voice breaking as she pulled the ever-present box of tissues closer.

Joanne was concerned about her friend. She wanted to be there for her and make sure that she knew it. "Well, so are you. You will get through this with your usual grace and style. Did you say to the

FDLE? Have you spoken with them?" Joanne's tone was encouraging and attentive.

Carol was silent for a moment or two, her gaze drifting as if lost in a turbulent sea of thoughts.

"Talk, Oh. His son and I talked with Detective Carducci. They want to interview me again and discuss blocking any cremation. We will know more once the preliminary Coroner's report is issued. They promised tomorrow afternoon at the latest. Oh, you're right. I'll survive, and eventually, the media will move on. Right now, it is so…" Carol's voice faltered, the weight of the situation pressing down on her.

Carol sat up from the lounge chair and grabbed more tissues. Tears came streaming down her cheeks like hot lava. She dabbed her eyes. Joanne got up and sat next to her, her presence offering a comforting pillar. She held Carol's hand, giving it a gentle squeeze.

"Painful? I remember. You feel naked and abused. Your body hurts all over. You drift, thinking of the most ridiculous things. Part of you isn't even here. Some parts have already run somewhere, and you can't find your core. You're fragmented, sometimes purely numb. You stare, and people stare at you. Am I close?" Joanne's voice was kind, her words painting a picture of Carol's internal chaos.

"Yes," Carol answered through her tears.

"Tears are the healing. Let them come," Joanne encouraged softly, her voice soothing.

Carol leaned into Joanne, then sat up straight, gulped down her wine, and continued her staccato refrain.

"Sometimes, I wish I wasn't so strong. I wish I could fall apart. But when they rape you young, they cannot do much else. I thought Ed was THE man. After Tom's death, I had almost given up. For a while, it was perfect. He was so strong, so sure of himself." The raw emotion in Carol's words clearly showed how she was dealing with not just her current grief but also the struggles from her past.

Carol remembered him as a confident Councilman and businessman, someone who really had his life together. When he asked her to marry him, she thought, "Finally, a man that can match my strength and be comfortable with my independence. All he asked for was loyalty. He was good to the girls."

"What happened?" asked Joanne.

"Reality hit. It was little things at first. His time at the track, the dwindling finances, and this underlying anger that seemed to follow him kept me at bay. You know?" Carol's voice carried a mix of disappointment and resignation.

"Oh yes. My husband John was like that. The anger was almost palatable. I thought his WASP background protected me. I thought, marrying him, I would not have to put up with the Italian macho emotional bullshit. But that silent anger was worse. I longed for a good fight. It was the silence that killed him, I'm sure," Joanne shared, a note of sadness threading through her words.

"God, Joanne, I am suddenly very tired."

Joanne stood up and grabbed their glasses. Carol checked to see that the French door was latched behind her friend. Joanne put the glasses in the sink.

"You're tired, so I have done my job. Now I know there is a family viewing, the cremation, then the public memorial. What can I do to help?" Joanne asked.

"You're doing it. I don't need you to come to the services if you don't want to. I do need to know you're at the end of a phone line if I need you," Carol replied.

"I'll be there, my friend, I'll always be there. You were always there for me. I'm going to go now. You get some rest. Need some pills or something? I always have a collection. Anything I can do for the funeral?"

Carol checked her list on the kitchen counter.

"No, I'll manage. Oh, there is something. You could get here a little earlier and open the house for the caterers. Let me give you the key."

Carol grabbed a key off the hook in the laundry room. As she walked back to the living room, she jotted down the alarm code on a scrap of paper, a thoughtful frown crossing her face. She stopped staring at Joanne, hesitated for a moment, then cocked her head to one side and said, "May I ask you something, ahh, personal?"

"Sure!" Joanne exclaimed.

"Was your family involved with the Mafia?" Carol's question hung in the air.

"Why do you ask? You know, with an Italian name and living in a small New Jersey town, we were always suspected. There were family members that were in deep. My Dad was in construction and did know some of the wise guys," explained Joanne.

"Well, rumors and that damn reporter is saying Ed was involved. What does that mean? He was married to an Italian. I suppose that could have sparked the rumors. Do I need to worry about the girls, me?" Carol questioned. Her concern for her family's safety was evident.

"I don't think so. But I'll check with a couple of 'connected' uncles and see if there is anything you should know. Owing them money isn't a good idea. The Mafia isn't as organized as you might think. WASPs, on the other hand, are deadly. I was married to one, as you know. Of course, he did SEC investigations like I do," said Joanne.

The two women walked to the front door. Carol stopped halfway, a new thought interrupting her stride. It was Joanne's turn to move her head to one side. As Joanne raised her eyebrows, she said, "And?"

"Well, there are some things. I'll be damned if I am going to turn them over to the police. I found them in our walk-in closet. I would appreciate it if you would look at them. It has to do with a stock deal," Carol confided.

Joanne nodded, understanding the delicacy of the situation. "You're not alone in this," she assured. Then she walked back to Carol and gestured that they should sit in the living room. Carol was wringing her hands and then wiping them on her thighs. Joanne sat close to her.

"Okay. Tell me," encouraged Joanne.

"Well, the papers appear to be transaction information, not really accounting. People's names with numbers. Company names with numbers. Also, things like Garbage, Cable, and such. The numbers could be money. I really can't tell. That's why I haven't given them to Roger, my accountant, Charles, Ed's lawyer, or even the police. I did tell Roger about them over the phone," Carol explained.

"You think they're important? Why?" Joanne probed, her eyebrows knitting together.

"I am sure it's Ed's supposed big deal that got traded on the OTC…Over the Counter Market. What am I doing explaining that to you? Stocks are your specialty. I guess John taught you all about that, or maybe you taught him," Carol mused, acknowledging Joanne's expertise in financial matters. "Some of the spreadsheets may relate to Ed's Councilman work. The strange thing is that there are some cassette tapes with the papers. The only place I have a cassette tape player is in my old BMW."

"No problem. I have one. You can just give everything to me. I can review it…and," said Joanne.

Carol stood up, a sudden worry taking hold as she paced toward the door, then paused and turned back to look at Joanne, who was still seated on the couch. "Let's deal with this next week. Let me ask you something. I remember reading that the Mafia was involved with the stock market, especially OTC. The article talked about small caps; I think that is what they called it. I read something about four years back in Business Week. Is that true?" asked Carol.

"Wow, lady. We are talking about a major conversation. Do you want to discuss that now or give me the tapes? I can stay as long as you want," said Joanne.

"I'm too tired. I'll let you know after the funeral. I need to get through that, and then I can think about other things," Carol responded, her voice weary.

"Of course, you get to bed," said Joanne softly.

They hugged, holding each other for a moment longer than usual. After saying goodbye, Carol locked up, put on the security alarm, and made her way to bed.

***

Outside, Joanne was already on her cell phone as she pulled out of the driveway, her tone switching to one of quiet urgency. "Benny, me. I've got a lead on what we're after. I'll let you know as soon as it is in my hands. Relax. I've got it under control."

Chapter 4

— • ● • —

"Thank God for Joanne," Carol murmured to her vanity mirror as she prepared for bed. The reflection staring back seemed to bear the weight of her chaos, her eyes holding stories of silent battles. Carol looked at herself as she was brushing her teeth. Was it that she didn't love Ed? "No," she mumbled out of her frothing mouth.

She leaned closer to the mirror and stared harder at her reflection. "Well, kiddo, why don't you feel more? I'm in despair, sure, but what the hell am I feeling?" Pulling back from her reflection, she was now shouting, her voice rising in frustration at the stranger mirrored before her. "Oh, shut up," she said, continuing her schizophrenic conversation. "What was that?" she asked as a sound from downstairs caught her attention. Her heart thudded, a jolt of alarm sharpening her senses.

Ed? No, his ghost, you dummy. The wind, just the wind.

Her thoughts circled back; *the feeling you can't admit is a relief,* her ego mind revealed.

"Yes, relief," she agreed. It was a hard pill to swallow—the attention of the press invading their lives, Ed's financial issues, the innuendoes of corruption that trailed after him like a shadow, and the gambling. Good thing she had gotten a massive sum for her company, TeleTech, when she had sold the business.

"I guess The Experiment is over, girls," she said to her good friends, Lisa and Jan, as if they were sitting there on her plush bathroom stools. Her voice carried a mix of sarcasm and sorrow, filling the room with the ghost of conversations past. The walls, if they could talk, would echo with the laughter and plans they had once shared, now just whispers in the chaos of her unraveling life.

She lay down slowly on the bed, the soft sheets a small comfort against the whirl of her thoughts. Her mind drifted back to the day it started—Wow, it was eight years ago, 1992, before the turn of the century, before this twist in her life. It was innocent enough then– three solid girlfriends, a trio of kindred spirits, walking through the lush trails of Phillipe Park. It was their cherished haunt, it was the favorite meeting place for Jan, Lisa, and herself, a place where they shed their city selves for a touch of nature's calm. Smiling to herself, she recalled her knowledge of the park's namesake, Odet Phillipe— a man shrouded in the mystique of history. He was quite a character.

Rumors suggested he was friends with Napoleon and consorted with pirates. They barely mentioned that he was a free black man as well as an entrepreneur, who carved his own path. The park, a refuge for osprey eagles and a birthing place for a family of great horned owls, was also a refuge for the three friends.

Carol was now fully immersed in the memory of that defining day. The three women laughing hysterically didn't know how their laughter would echo through the universe and their lives. They were unaware of the effects to come, but oh, they were keenly aware of the cause—**lack of sex**. This was the unanimous conclusion. After all, they were attractive, feminine, sensual, and energetic women. You couldn't go for years and months without masculine encounters, without it having a strong presence in your life; the "it" was sex.

"Carol, Jan, look at the unusual formation in this ancient tree," Lisa said while they walked together on the pristine green carpet of grass that stretched invitingly before them.

"A vagina," Carol had commented as their laughter floated down the meadow to the turquoise bay. "Have you noticed all the phallic symbols in nature," she continued as they hiked up the sacred Tocobaga Indian mound, the highest location in the park, a place that whispered of ancient secrets and forgotten lives.

"I should re-name you, mono," spurted Jan through her laughter.

"Oh, I couldn't possibly have the kissing disease," quipped Carol.

"Not because of the disease," Jan retorted with a smirk, "It's your one-track mind."

"Well, isn't this a pot/kettle thing? Didn't you comment that the branch looked like an erection?" Carol defended.

A moment of reverence fell over them as they reached the top of the tribal mound. The landscape before them unfolded majestically; the peaceful bay rolled out to the south and east, its waters shimmering under the gentle sun, while lush grass and towering trees dominated the north and west. Standing together in loving comradery and understanding were three modern female warriors surveying the beauty of their conquered land. Each had fought different battles: Lisa with her escape from a violent and abusive marriage, Carol grappling with the scars of childhood rape and incest, and Jan overcoming the shadows of an incestuous childhood. Each had fought and won many battles. And now, standing atop this mound, they sensed they were on the cusp of winning the war against their past.

"Why don't we have a male relationship in our lives?" Carol asked.

"Maybe we don't really want one?" Lisa replied, matching Carol's tone and volume.

"Bullshit!" Jan snorted as their laughter swayed the cedar trees that stood with them.

"Whine, whine, whine. That is all we do about it. I say we make a pack that, in 30 days, each of us will get 'some.' A real, meaningful connection. No excuses," Carol challenged. "You're on," Lisa stated.

Now, **The Experiment** began.

Carol's plan was simple. Open your eyes and find a likely candidate. It was during an innocuous visit to Tampa City Hall where fate seemed to align with her intentions. She was looking for the water utilities office to deal with her water bill when he appeared. Like a scene from a romantic film, their eyes met across the crowded hallway of the water utilities office. His presence was unmissable, and he had an air of accessibility that instantly drew her in. As she stood there, paperwork forgotten in her hands, Carol realized this might just be the twist of fate she needed to kickstart her daring challenge.

"You're Ed Wallin, aren't you, the councilman?" Carol asked.

"Yes," he replied and started to walk away then turned toward her. "Can I help you with something?"

"Oh, I have this outrageous water bill. Calling on the phone hasn't gotten me anywhere, so I decided a person-to-person might be better," Carol explained.

"Let me show you," He took Carol's elbow the way her father always did.

Kinda cute and old-fashioned, she thought to herself. *Did I spark?*

"Here we are," said the Councilman.

With her best smile, she turned and seized the moment. "Thanks, you wouldn't be free for coffee, would you?"

He stared down at her, still smiling, and to both their surprise, he responded, "Yes, Yes, I would. Have you eaten breakfast? We could walk over to First Watch. They have great food and excellent coffee. The line is long in the Utilities office right now. It should settle down in an hour."

"Breakfast sounds perfect," her best sultry voice responded.

As they walked the three blocks to the café, her ego mind went crazy. *What the hell do you think you're doing? Now what? There's probably a law against this. OK, Miss Seductress, you are playing with a public figure? So what, he's handsome.*

Their conversation flowed easily and was fun. They teased and politely flirted. As they were finishing up, Carol, glancing at him as he checked his watch, decided to dive a bit deeper. "Listen, the Spring is having their fundraising breakfast next Wednesday. Will you be there?" she asked, trying to sound casual.

"I usually support them, but the event must have slipped by me this year," Ed confessed.

"Well, I bought a table for my company, TeleTech; care to join us? I have an extra seat. One of the VPs is on vacation," Carol proposed, already reaching for her leather card case as she saw him hesitate. "Just let me know. I enjoyed the coffee and conversation. Well, I better settle my water issue."

He took the card and saw her to the door. *Another gentlemanly act, she thought. Must be crazy trying to seduce a Councilman. It's an experiment. Take notes, report, and move on.*

"You didn't!" Lisa squealed into the phone later that day.

"Oh, yes! I asked him to the event for the Spring since the HR VP isn't going," Carol gushed. *That was a strange few days. Jan and Lisa hounded me day and night for every single detail.*

"Well, did he call?" asked Lisa on their morning friend check.

"Not yet, but I think he will. We clicked, ya know?" Carol responded.

"He's not married, right?" Lisa's question cut straight to the point.

"No, divorced," Carol replied.

"Aren't we all?" Lisa chuckled dryly. "Well, Jan and I went to this singles dance. I felt like prime meat. Jan danced with some guy but nothing of interest. Most guys were old enough to be our fathers. How old is the Councilman—we must have demographic data?"

"He's 59, divorced, one adult male child who's into finance or something," Carol disclosed.

"Good work, Ms. Scientist. Twelve-year spread isn't too bad," Lisa commented.

"Lisa, do you think I am crazy?" Carol's voice wavered slightly.

"Yes, but what does that have to do with anything?" Lisa retorted with a laugh. "Gotta love the madness, Carol."

"Gotta go; I've got a call coming in. Oh, did I tell you I got an offer from FrontMedia for TeleTech? I might sell," Carol quickly added.

"Wow, girl, that's great. We'll talk about that later," Carol switched to the other line. "Carol Reiner speaking."

"Hi, this is Ed Wallin." His voice came through, the kind of voice that could ease any tension.

His voice was right; voices are important. Her hands started to sweat. *Sound casual.* "Oh Hi, Councilman Wallin. What can I do for you?"

"So formal! Please, call me Ed," he chuckled softly. "I was wondering if your water issue was resolved."

"As a matter of fact, they came out yesterday and determined there was a leak on the city side of the water intake to my home. They are adjusting the bill. They were very efficient," Carol reported.

"Excellent. Is that Spring charity breakfast offer still open?" he asked.

"Yes, it is. I don't know our table number yet, but I'll be there by 6:45 am. Think you can find us in the crowd?" Carol's response was playful yet inviting.

"Sure, how about I return the favor with dinner at Burns on Saturday night?"

"Saturday? Um, sure." She hoped she didn't sound too eager. *Why, you sly ole' fox.*

"Got to run, Carol. See you Wednesday," he said.

"Great. Bye," Carol hung up, a grin spreading across her face. *Well, my dear, you stepped in it this time. Remember, it's an experiment. No need to overreact.*

Carol was practically buzzing with excitement as she almost flew down to Jan's office. Jan, her buddy, business associate, and fellow 'scientist' had an office close by. She had been consulting with TeleTech for about eight months.

"Well, you have a big grin," Jan said as she entered her office. "It's **The Experiment**-right? OK, spill it."

"He asked me out to Burns Steak House," Carol blurted out, her grin widening.

"Well, obviously not a vegetarian," Jan quipped. "Did you notice how the bar looks like a house of ill repute with the red flocked wallpaper? And, ooh, the oh-so-delectable desert room and 40-pound wine list. That private little dessert booth, hmm. Heard they must watch those, or people actually 'get it on' in them."

"Probably just rumors," Carol replied. "Hmm. Maybe I could order one of those $40.00-an-ounce Sherries. That would test his interest, don't you think? Anyway, gotta get back to work. Let's have lunch. You free?"

"Sure am - wouldn't miss it. We finished the installations and are starting the Florida Power contract. I appreciate the business, Carol. You've been a lifesaver."

"Hey, you pulled me out of a hole. I need to talk with you," Carol shifted gears.

"About the Councilman?" Jan guessed, her eyebrows raised inquisitively.

"No, well, yes, but this is business. Can you spare a couple of hours at lunch?" Carol asked.

"Sure, no problem. See you at noon," Jan responded.

"Make it 11:30," said Carol.

"Must be important. See ya," Jan acknowledged. Carol left Jan's office, her mind a mix of excitement and serious observation. She remembered how glad she was that Jan was there. Jan was competent, easy-going, and caring beyond belief. Her easy sense of humor and smile made coming to work even better. Jan's company outsourced the installation services. Carol's company, TeleTech, had grown so rapidly since the de-regulation of the telephone companies. Without the training and planning know-how that AT&T provided, the telephone industry was struggling. There was a desperate need for comprehensive training, strategic planning, and careful installation services. TeleTech could just about handle the sales and service. Meanwhile, Jan's company, DigIn, specialized in phone system installations for small businesses when the boom hit.

There were new telecommunications companies starting every day. At the same time, contractors had to figure out how to run lines to support businesses. Carol was laid off as Director of Planning for AT&T. She was definitely in the right place at the right time. The phone companies, big and small, were in a race to get the most lines and the most towers. It was on a project for GTE she had met Jan. It was a perfect fit right from the beginning. They seemed to pick up the friendship from the middle like old friends can. Their connection was instantaneous. When Carol introduced Jan to Lisa, the trio quickly merged into the three musketeers, their camaraderie punctuated by an endless stream of jokes, shared secrets, laughter, and the occasional tear.

Lying in her bed, Carol couldn't stop the tears from coming despite her best efforts. "I still have my friends, my beautiful daughters, and my health." Squeezing her eyes didn't prevent the tears. "I have so much." Yet, the space beside her felt achingly empty. "I miss Ed beside me," she admitted softly to the room. *It's important to remember the good as well as the bad.*

Rolling over in her bed, Carol let her mind journal their relationship. The scenes of their courtship, the strategic decisions surrounding the sale of her business, and their engagement—all came up on her mind's movie screen. Parts ran together now like some bizarre roller coaster ride. Six months of talks, walks, and dates. Private side trips to New Orleans. He was a public figure, so by all appearances, it was an old-fashioned courtship. When the ride stopped, she was in her wedding dress, in her house off Swann Avenue. Uncurling and pulling the covers up to her chin, Carol's mind wandered back to her wedding day.

"So, Ms. Nobel Prize Worthy Experimenter, you're gonna be Mrs. Councilman," Lisa said as she handed her the bouquet.

Jan, always the voice of reason with a twinkle in her eye, chimed in, "No, she can't win **The Experiment** prize. She stopped recording and 'telling' details," Smiling her most loving smile, she asked. "Tell us one thing. Should we buy a Kama Sutra Kit? Is that part of the charm?"

Their laughter echoed. She saw them now at a distance, waving and laughing and whispering to each other. Knowing that no matter how the paths of their lives twisted, their connection was a constant, unwavering force. *Where were they? Where am I?*

Suddenly, a dark shape appeared from the shadows of her room. It came closer; she could smell him, Ed, musky and slightly acrid. That unmistakable scent she would recognize anywhere, now mingling with the ominous presence of a rope in his hands.

"NOOOO!" Carol screamed at the top of her lungs.

Jolted awake, she sat up in her bed, drenched in sweat. Her heart hammered against her chest as she strained her eyes to make out any shapes in the enveloping darkness of her bedroom. "Great, nightmares; I've got to get back to sleep," she muttered, almost breathless.

She got up, went down the stairs to the kitchen, grabbed a favorite cup, and selected a 'SleepyTime' tea. *Harmony is the inner cadence of contentment we feel when the melody of life is in tune.* The Celestial Seasonings boxes were always worth reading. Carol decided to watch the TV as the tea was steeping.

"Harmony, Yeah, right," her mind still replaying the harrowing images of her dream. "Well, I bet the media has a variety of lies and innuendoes I can listen to. What happened to responsible journalism? The job of the town gossips, bigots, mean high school girls, and other self-absorbed, self-righteous individuals has been usurped by the media." She smiled as she talked aloud to herself and turned on the small TV in the kitchen.

The screen flickered to life: "Tampa City Councilman Ed Wallin's cremation and memorial service will be tomorrow. No questions have been answered on the ethical violations and corruption charges. On the international front, an airliner carrying 106 passengers has crashed in…" CLICK.

Back in her bed, wrapped in the cold sheets, Carol's mind raced. *What the hell did you do, Ed? I think those tapes might have an answer.* She was tempted right then to pull on a coat, dash to her car, and listen to every word recorded on those tapes. *"Drink your tea and lay back, young lady,"* she reprimanded herself. "One step at a time," she muttered as she drifted back to sleep.

Chapter 5

Muffled voices mixed with the intoxicating aroma of brewing coffee. Carol sat straight up.

"I'm in that damn movie where the day keeps repeating," she muttered, rubbing her temples. "Or maybe it is the X-Files episode where the poor girl had to repeat the day over and over. She tries to warn Fox and Scully so they don't get killed at the bank. Over and over, it goes until she finally is the one that gets killed." Her voice cracked as she drew a sharp breath. "Stop it, just stop," she shouted into the emptiness of her room.

"Mom?" Stevie's voice echoed as he entered her room, his brow furrowed in concern. "Who are you talking to?"

"Myself," Carol scoffed, managing a strained smile as she observed him. "And I can tell you I am not a very good conversationalist. You look great, honey. Navy blue suits you. Hmm, that's a pun - aren't I the witty one? Great, now I'm rhyming. Sorry, sweetie, my own mind is a dangerous place to be," she finished; her voice a mix of jest and weariness.

Stevie rushed to her and embraced her shaking form. As they held each other, tears poured out of both their eyes, mingling in their shared sorrow and exhaustion.

"Don't mind me, Stevie. You know how dumb I get when I'm tired and upset. I can't believe it took so long to release Ed. I just want this to be over so we can heal. Have you heard from Roger? I can't believe he hasn't called or followed up on my calls. It's not like him. He's always been precise…like an accountant should be, and nice and, oh god, I hate this. I just want it over," she rambled, her words tumbling out in a frantic rush.

"I know. I hate to bring this up…" Stevie hesitated.

"Don't get hung up on niceties, just talk - Guess I shouldn't say that either, hung up, ha!" Carol attempted a weak grin, trying to inject some levity into the heavy air.

"Mom!" Stevie exclaimed.

"Sorry, what were you saying?" Carol said as she brushed away a tear.

"A Special Agent, Jim Perez, called and said he has arranged to meet you in the office at the funeral home. I don't see why they have to do that today. They're as bad as that so-called reporter who hounded Ed." Stevie's voice was tinged with frustration.

"He has a job to do. What time?" Carol asked in exhaustion.

"Nine, just before the family viewing starts," replied Stevie

"That's fine. Let me get myself together. Do we have any cucumbers?" Carol asked her question seemingly out of nowhere.

"Cucumbers?" Stevie echoed, a puzzled look crossing his face.

"I am not horny, Stevie. I wanted to put some slices on my eyes to soothe the swelling," Carol explained, a tired smile playing at her lips.

"I'll get them. And Mom," said Stevie, hesitating to get Carol's full attention.

"Now, what?" Carol asked.

"Take a Valium. And one more thing. Have you called Grandma?"

"Oh, Stevie, the last time I called Grandma was when Kay and Tony had that car accident. She said, 'Can't you ever call me with good news?' That was three months ago."

"I don't know what it is with you two. Do you want me to call her?" Stevie offered, a note of concern in his voice.

"What it is IS," Carol began, her voice rising with each word, "Let's see, her addiction to alcohol, her constant chatter, her self-centered attitude." She paused, catching Stevie's look of mild reproach. "Okay, I know you love her. I do, too! I'll call later or tomorrow. Truly! Now, go make sure there is coffee left."

"There is coffee, and I'll bring your cucumber. You are in rare form today," Stevie said, her attempt at lightening the mood only half-successful.

As Stevie left, the room seemed to close in on Carol, and her thoughts drifted into thinking how nice it would be to have a supportive Mom. She always envied Joanne's close relationship with her Mom. Carol and her mother never seemed to fit. Especially after she exposed Uncle Fritz as the family pervert. The only person relieved about that was Fritz's daughter. Carol's mother, on the other hand, was livid and mortified.

"He is my brother. You broke up a marriage on some childhood memory you can't prove. Carol, that's a sin," her mother had hissed at her once, her words sharp as knives. "Now, Fritz's wife left him. His daughter is claiming abuse and is in therapy. You ought to be ashamed!"

Those words still burned and stung in Carol's memory. Shame plagued her until she fingered that SOB for years of inappropriate fondling. "Don't go there," she whispered to herself, pressing a hand against her forehead. "One grief at a time."

The morning rushed by until the family got into limousines and headed for the Funeral Home. Everything seemed surreal to Carol, blurring into a foggy haze and then snapping back into sharp focus—like she was living in two life dimensions at once, and none seemed to be her life.

In the funeral home office was a somber reflection of tradition and comfort. A dark wood desk dominated the space, flanked by antique side chairs and adorned with an arrangement of white and yellow silk flowers that added a formal but comfortable appearance. On a side cart was coffee and the required tissue box. *What lovely coffee cups,* Carol thought. *So delicate and tasteful, more for an English High Tea than coffee.* Detective Perez was sitting beside Carol. His form was almost too big for the decorative side chair. Carol's 5'4" form fit perfectly, though the cozy fit made her feel even more cornered. Detective Carducci stood by the door, his presence like a silent sentinel. The office felt less like a refuge and more like a beautifully adorned cage where Carol was trapped.

"Sorry to bother you at this time, Mrs. Wallin, but I need to clear some things up," Jimmy said.

"You do have copies of all the financial records now. I don't know what else I can tell you," Carol replied.

"I noticed there are some separate accounts?" Jimmy pressed, looking over his notes.

"Well, when I sold my business, it took a while for me to close accounts, invest my profits, and we were getting married…. We maintained separate accounts," Carol explained, her hands nervously playing with the hem of her dress.

"You had a household account?" Jimmy questioned.

"Yes, you have those records. The only thing we had jointly was that account. The house was mine. I bought it before we were married. Ed was supposed to deposit checks to help cover the expenses," Carol responded firmly.

"Did he?" Jimmy looked at her intently.

"No, I ended up covering them all and then some. It is what we fought about on Tuesday night," Carol confessed, the memories of the argument flashing vividly in her mind.

"You fought?" asked Jimmy

Carol's gaze drifted momentarily to the window as if the answer might be found in the gray skies outside. Then, gathering her resolve, she turned back to face Perez, ready to dive into the unpleasant details of that last argument.

"Yes, when the loan and gambling stuff came out in the news, I asked him what he did with the money. He didn't tell me. When I reviewed the accounts--there was nothing there.

I thought he slept in the guest room. I didn't check. I left early Wednesday. It was my volunteer day at Joshua House with the Aids children. I thought when I heard the messages from his office looking for him that he was still angry. I didn't know where he was Wednesday night, either. He often stayed late with his friend, Dick Dinsmore. Or he was with Charles. To tell you the truth, I wasn't looking for him. We said some mean things to each other. I turned off the phone because that reporter, Andy Stevens, kept calling and calling. I hate that our last words were unkind." Tears ran down her face as she accepted the tissue Jimmy offered, dabbing at her eyes gently.

"Listen, I have covered all the debt. I can't be implicated in anything he did because I knew nothing. We are clear on that, right? None of the insurance will pay anything because it was ugh, ugh, ya' know…" Carol said, her voice almost dropped to a whisper now.

Jimmy nodded, jotting down notes before looking up again. "Just a few more questions, Mrs. Wallin. Were there any papers or records that Mr. Wallin kept that were not in the office or the house? Say, in a safety deposit box? Did Mr. Wallin discuss anything with you regarding GatWin or HarborTech?

"I don't know, I wasn't involved," Carol replied.

"Your husband was part of their board. Did you say Charles Atoll was involved?" Jimmy probed, his brows knitting together.

"I don't know. He discussed everything with Charles. I thought he had some money in but I can't be sure. You need to ask Mr. Atoll, or would that be attorney/client privilege?" she asked exhaustedly.

"Mr. Atoll was on GatWin's corporate records that were filed in Delaware. At least his firm's address was listed as the address of record. You think Mr. Atoll invested money?" Jimmy asked.

"I don't know, Mr. Perez, sorry, Agent Perez," Carol corrected herself with a small, weary smile. "We fought about that too much. Ed thought I should be interested because it was technical, it had to do with telephones, and I had a technical and telephone background with my company. All the hype about the company's potential, some deals they were going to make with CISCO and Microsoft. 'Easy money,' he told me. It looked like 'vaporware' to me -- all talk and no substance. It almost broke us up back then."

"So, you were filing for Divorce?" Jimmy leaned forward.

"Not that. As I said, we fought. I was reluctant to commit my funds. I am naked here, Detective. That is all I know." Carol's weeping eyes stopped, and she stared at Jimmy, almost willing him to disappear.

"There is nothing more I can tell you, Agent Perez. We didn't share a lot of information on financial matters. We just fought about them. You probably know more than I do currently. Now, if you'll excuse me, it is time to cremate my husband," Carol said, her voice breaking with a mix of sorrow and anger.

***

Jimmy stared back. Jimmy's instincts were buzzing as he stood up, his gut telling him there was something else. She was explaining personal stuff but avoiding answering his questions. Her emotional revelations felt like a diversion, and there was something she was hiding in a smoke screen of relationship issues. He'd have to dig that up and find that out on his own. "Well, thank you, Mrs. Wallin," Jimmy said as he turned to her before he left.

"As I mentioned earlier, Roger Barnes. Roger dealt with my financial affairs. Charles also should know or be able to tell you something,"

"Of course, thank you for your cooperation," Jimmy replied. As he and his partner Sal moved toward the door, he paused. "Oh, one more thing. Is Roger Barnes here?" Carol just shook her head, signaling no. So Jimmy and Sal walked toward the exit, then Jimmy's heart skipped. *Hell, what is she doing here?* He almost said out loud.

He caught a glimpse of Joanne talking with Carol's two daughters. She glanced at him briefly and gave an almost imperceptible nod.

What the hell, damn, what the hell? Jimmy shouted in his head while banging his fist against the sink. Sal was eyeing him as he got to the SUV.

"Whatzup, partner? That pretty lady standing by Mrs. Wallin's girls gave you the eye."

"It's nothing, Sal," Jimmy said, his tone a mix of dismissal and distraction. *Damn, he is good.* Jimmy almost hit a car pulling in as he was leaving. *How well did Joanne know Carol Wallin? What the hell?*

***

Carol sat for a while in the office after Detective Perez left. The quiet of the room intensified her sadness. Her guilt was finally exposed. She was so sorry that her last words to Ed were unkind. As she replayed their conversation, she clung to the hope that Detective Perez bought her not knowing anything. Technically, she hadn't lied—she hadn't analyzed the papers from the box, so she didn't know what was in there.

"Mom?" Stevie said as she gently touched her shoulder.

"Oh, Stevie, will this ever end?" she murmured.

"Soon, Mom. Just get through today."

The rest of the funeral unfolded like a theater play composed of rehearsed lines and somber faces. It was a series of niceties and platitudes. The Mayor delivered a speech about his friendship with Ed, while his friend, Dick, did a nice job of talking about his long-time buddy. Throughout it all, Carol was numb; part grief, part guilt, part harboring the 'secret box.' She wasn't sure how many valiums she had taken. She didn't feel attached to her body in any way, floating through the proceedings as if in a dream. She somehow drifted back to her home. Who were all these people in her house? *Oh yes, Ed's supposed friends. What were they doing in her home?*

Lisa was searching her eyes and holding her hand. "You with us, kiddo? Jan and I can whisk you away. We have the getaway car all set," her half-smile tight across her concerned face.

"She's gone; she doesn't seem to know where she is," Jan said.

"C'mon, sweetheart, let's go to your room and lie down awhile." Lisa gently took Carol's arm under the pit, ready to lift.

"Room?" Carol said as if waking from a dream.

"Yes, come, you are home now. You are safe." Jan said as she lifted Carol from the other side. They both guided her up the stairs.

"You did great. Nobody except us would know you weren't even there." Lisa quipped as they guided her toward the bed. "Jan, get a cold cloth from the bathroom. You kick off those shoes. Good, now, just lie down."

"No, please," Carol said quietly. "I have to tend to things."

"Never mind. The girls have that handled and almost everyone left when the Mayor left. We couldn't believe he and all the Councilmen came to the house." Jan reported as she handed Lisa the wet washcloth.

"You want to talk? Cry? Yell?" Lisa asked as she gently laid the cloth on Carol's neck. The coolness was a brief relief for her. Jan and Lisa were sitting on each side of Carol on the king-size bed. The room's muted colors of grays and beiges didn't interfere with the vibrant hues of friendship and support.

"I feel like a salmon swimming furiously back to the spawning waters, only the current is too strong, and I can't move."

"Spawning grounds? This is no time for sex talk, young lady," Jan teased.

The room filled with their laughter, a momentary release that was easier than shedding more tears.

"I wondered where you went," said Joanne from the doorway. "So, what are you guys plotting?"

"Oh, Joanne, good. Have you met Lisa and Jan?" Carol asked, motioning toward her friends.

"Yes, briefly, Kay introduced us. I just wanted to say goodbye and return your key before I left. I see you are in good hands," Joanne replied.

"Come in and shut the door," Lisa invited with a mischievous grin. "We tend to giggle a lot, and most people wouldn't understand. So, you're Carol's high school buddy?" Lisa said as she patted the bed for Joanne to sit. "I bet she was a sex kitten even then."

"I could tell you stories," Joanne responded.

"Please don't," Carol said with a strained smile.

"Oh, tell us," Jan begged.

"Well, there was this guy who lived in the next town over, kind of the Grosse Point of New Jersey. A real WASP type but beautiful—blond hair, blue eyes, permanent tennis tan," Joanne began.

"Oh no, you don't. You will ruin my reputation," Carol exclaimed, half-laughing as she reached for Joanne.

"What reputation? Do tell!" Lisa and Jan said together.

As Carol pulled a pillow over her head, a muffled "Oh God" could just barely be heard from beneath it.

"Ohhhhhh," Carol's groan came from under the pillow.

"Anyway," Joanne continued. "Carol decided we needed to get him back for snubbing me and robbing this delicate creature of her virginity. I had this great old Hudson. It was a tank. We used to run it into snowbanks just for fun. Oh, what was I saying? Ah, yes. One Sunday morning, instead of going to church, we rode to his town. We kept cruising in front of his WASPY church until the service let out. Then we saw him, his parents, and his 'Barbie' girlfriend; we mooned them. Rather, Carol did. I was driving."

"Ohhhhh!!!! No, please, Joanne, stop!" Carol's groan now mixed with their laughter.

"What happened to Carol's Mike?" Jan asked.

"He fell madly in love with Carol, but she was busy with her other fifty boyfriends, including one of mine if I remember correctly," Joanne said sarcastically.

"Who?" Carol said, sitting up.

"Ted," Joanne replied nonchalantly.

"Ted? He wasn't your boyfriend," Carol retorted.

"C'mon now, girls, let's not fight. It was a long time ago," Jan interjected with a laugh.

Joanne's sharp look and changed tone swept over the room as she stood up. "Gotta go," she said. "Call me, Carol."

"Sure, hey, thanks for everything," responded Carol.

"No problem," Joanne said as she exited.

"Well, Miss Mooner, I'd say she's still jealous of you," Lisa teased, winking at Carol.

"Oh, God, Lisa, that was over thirty years ago," Carol exclaimed

"I agree with Lisa," Jan chimed in.

"Ridiculous! I'm bushed and hungry," said Carol.

"I'll get you a plate of goodies," Jan stated as she left.

"So, Lisa, what do we put in the follow-up notes to **The Experiment**?" asked Carol.

"Well, since all Jan and I ended up with were a couple of lousy lays, it may not be one that others would care to replicate," Lisa replied.

"Guess you're right there. We could serve as a warning to others." sighed Carol.

Lisa put her arms around Carol, pulling her close. "Don't cave now, my friend. You had some good years. He treated you well. The media will go away now. There isn't any more dirty laundry to air."

"I hope you're right," Carol murmured.

They sat in silence for a moment, holding hands and gazing at the nothingness of the room. The air was thick with the weight of exhaustion and unspoken fears. Carol was out of energy and words. So was Lisa.

"Food, look—fruit, three varieties of cheesecake, and four chocolate somethings. All the major food groups," Jan announced cheerfully as she breezed back through the bedroom's double doors with a tray in one hand and a napkin draped over her arm.

"Perfect!" Carol remarked as she retrieved a chocolate tidbit from the tray.

"My turn, I'll get coffee," Lisa offered, already heading toward the door.

"That would be great; I'm glad you guys are here," Carol said through her chocolate-covered lips. Now it was Jan's turn to sit, holding Carol by the shoulders.

Lisa returned moments later, "You guys look like zombies," she said as she entered with coffee.

Carol grabbed Lisa's hand. "To tell you the truth, I'm terrified about what I may discover. Was I in denial?"

"I know a formula to disintegrate bones. The skeletons in the closet don't have a chance," quipped Jan.

"Oh dear, speaking of closets... Did I mention I found a box of audio tapes in the closet?" Carol's voice dropped to a whisper. "It was like Ed was hiding them there on purpose."

"A box? You gave them to the police, right?" asked Lisa as she handed Carol a cup of coffee.

"No, I want to listen to them first. I think Ed wanted me to know what was on them. He left them next to my favorite shoes. He made fun of me because I have three pairs of the same style in different colors. He knew I would see them," Carol explained.

"You're a mess right now. Let's each chocolate," said Lisa looking over to Jan frowning.

Chapter 6

"What's with you? You've been stomping about ever since you left the funeral," Sal observed.

"It's a long story. I need to focus on the case," Jimmy responded as he sorted through the files in front of him.

"Since you're not going to share, focus away," Sal quipped.

"We have a complex fraud situation," said Jimmy.

"The Wallin stuff? Lay it out for me," Sal urged.

"Yeah, well looks like Ed was involved in fraud, insider trading, in a stock shell game with a pump and dump, misuse of public funds and influence, as well as other petty crimes. I can't find where he got the seed money to invest in GatWin, Inc. I find no specific accounting of who gave him money and for what. That information has to be somewhere. And what happened to the money once the initial stockholders pulled out?"

"So you got a giant web but can't find the sticky parts," Sal summarized.

"Exactly. GatWin was supposed to be a great company. HarborTech, already a publicly traded company, was 'lucky' to get them. Still awake?" asked Jimmy

"I got it; go on," said Sal as he leaned back in his chair and looked at the ceiling. He did this when he was thinking as if the ceiling was a large TV set, and he was watching the show intently.

"Wallin got the latest loans from his employees in April. It appears those loans were for taxes. The employee loan timing is the pattern that prompted the Governor to take an interest."

Sal knew the statute forbids loans from a public employee to an employer, so he just nodded as Jimmy continued. "Over the years, there seems to be a pattern before the holidays and at tax time in his records. That could be a result of his gambling."

Sal sat up straight, his curiosity piqued and looked at Jimmy with raised eyebrows, then said, "And?"

Sal just circled his hand, signaling Jimmy to keep the information coming as he looked back up at the ceiling, mentally processing the complexities.

"Well, there is not much information on HarborTech except the complaints that were filed with the Public Integrity Squad after the

GatWin purchase. HarborTech was a clean, somewhat successful company before it purchased GatWin," explained Jimmy.

"Sounds like a friggin' mess to me. From what I know the Mafia uses the stocks to launder money. You think that's what is going on here?" asked Sal, sitting up straight and looking expectantly at Jimmy.

"I'm going to head over to the Tampa FBI office and annoy your friend, Donnie, again. He's been helpful in the past in educating me on what's going on with the different indictments," said Jimmy.

"Have fun with that!" Sal chuckled dryly.

"I know we're stuck with the money stuff, and he's cremated, but could you talk with the coroner anyway? Oh yeah, I think we need to talk with Roger Barnes, their accountant. He may know more than we think. You talked with him before this got ugly, right?" asked Jimmy.

"Yup, on it," said Sal, straightening up as he reached for the phone, ready to dive back into the investigation.

Jimmy mused over all he knew. It had been over a year since the mafia guys Abramo and Consalvo were charged here in Tampa Federal Court. Something Donnie discussed as pump and dump frauds. He needed to revisit those discussions and wanted Donnie to go over all of it one more time. However, Jimmy was cautious, and he didn't want to give away too much and lose the case altogether.

After he and Donnie were settled in the office, Jimmy reviewed a few of his concerns. After a brief catch-up, he laid out what he knew about the fraud, and what he wanted to know.

"All right, you're aware that the mob was involved in stock manipulation and charged here in Tampa. That was one day after the US attorney in New York brought criminal charges against 55 defendants. All stock fraud," Jimmy briefed Donnie as he sought to draw parallels and possibly anticipate their adversary's next move.

Donnie began to explain, "Here's how it works. The mobsters pay, say, 50 cents a share to buy a stake in a company that's going public. Then they go to a brokerage firm they control and have its brokers cold-call unsuspecting clients and hype the stock, so they sell for, say, $5 a share."

Donnie laid out the mechanics of the fraud clearly for Jimmy, who was leaning back in his chair listening intently but now leaned forward as Donnie continued, elbows on his knees, "Once the shares are pumped and dumped on the market, the hype stops. The mob sells its shares and makes a huge profit. Now, you have a glut of worthless shares on the market. The stock plummets. Investors are screwed."

"So, they make money when it is going up and when it is going down. They borrow money to do the transactions. They pay that back. Mob ends up with clean money and has a nice little investment. Legit businessmen." summarized Jimmy.

"You got it," Donnie agreed with a sharp nod, then continued. "To me, GatWin and the buyout by HarborTech appears to be first a Shell Game because HarborTech is a legitimate company. Then it becomes a pump and dump scheme because of the hype around the purchase."

Jimmy leaned forward, his forehead creased with lines of concentration. "That's how I see it. I can't find any specific records relating to investors. Sure, I've got accounts, but who bought what and when, and with what money?"

"We may be able to help when you're ready. I'm not trying to step on your case. You must report to the Governor. To tell you the truth, we're swamped. Online trading has changed the game. Businessweek and US News are way ahead of us in exposing what's going on," quipped Donnie.

"What we do know is that companies need money, and the Mafia has it," said Jimmy.

"Exactly," said Donnie.

"Aren't investors smarter than that?" asked Jimmy.

"Everyone was looking for another Qualcomm," Donnie responded.

"Qualcomm. They weren't a pump and dump?" Jimmy probed, trying to differentiate between legitimate success stories and fraudulent setups.

"No, they are a legitimate company. They adapted a complicated military wireless application for commercial use and marketed it at the beginning of last year," Donnie explained.

"So, it wasn't real?" Jimmy pressed, seeking clarity.

"Oh, it was real. It traded at just $27.72 at the start of 1999. One day, it went to $640 a share. If you had invested in the Initial Public Offering (IPO) and had, say, 100 shares. With all the stock splits, you'd have over a 15000 percent increase. Wow, if only I was smart enough to buy them," Donnie mused, a wistful smile crossing his face.

"Me too!" said Jimmy.

As Jimmy walked back to the FDLE, he mulled over the buildup around GatWin's purchase. *The hype was about combining the know-how of' HarborTech's management with some wireless protocol that would double the speed of the wireless connections. Sounded like a Qualcomm wanna-be. Maybe there wasn't any real software. That is what Carol Wallin said, vaporware. If the mob was involved and they were original investors, there must be a trail. Something is missing*

Jimmy understood that with the Shell game, recognizing the similarities in these circumstances, only HarborTech would face any real scrutiny. Since they were already public when they decided to merge or acquire a private company and disclose, GatWin didn't have to reveal anything or go through a thorough SEC investigation. GatWin's purchase would not force a new prospectus. They also can hide the investors. By the time all the hype is done and a new filing is required, everyone has already lost their money or made the money and run.

Back at the office, Jimmy found Sal in the break room, a place he rarely frequented.

"You making coffee? Is the sky falling?" teased Jimmy.

"Yeah, well, you shoulda gone to the coroner. You like details. He loves to go over every single one. He said the direction of the threads is hard to determine on Nylon rope. I did remind him of the other hangings," said Sal.

"What did he say?" asked Jimmy.

"I've ruled it a suicide, and that's that! Unless something substantial comes from the lab work, I will make it final." imitated Sal.

"Such bullshit. Things don't add up. My gut tells me there is more, but without facts, we're screwed," Jimmy grumbled.

"So, is it time to hand it over? Do we notify the Chief?" asked Sal when Jimmy settled back at his desk.

"To do our job correctly, we need to know who was involved. Also, we need to look at all the purchases made by the city. Did you get all the papers on that?" asked Jimmy.

"I can review those and look at the Council minutes to look for recommendations by Wallin." offered Sal. "The few I reviewed may have issues 'cause of Wallin being a Councilman and recommending the purchase. May be kickbacks. You can focus on the loans and the corporate money."

"That works. Then there is the gambling. I haven't received information from the IT guys at City Hall. The little I know, I got from the corporate papers filed for GatWin. Some from papers turned over by the wife and the lawyer. I know information is missing. It smells bad. Not quite sure where the smell comes from. May be out of my league, though," Jimmy confessed.

"You're out of your league on other things, too, I'm guessing." pushed Sal.

"You are a psychic," Jimmy shot back with a wry smile.

"What happened, man?" asked Sal, his tone turning serious again as he stepped closer.

"The lady knows Mrs. Wallin. She was at the funeral," Jimmy revealed.

"Cut it NOW. You'll ruin your whole life -for what? - a piece? What's wrong with you?" Sal's voice was stern, his warning clear.

Jimmy was wondering the same thing when, as if on cue, his beeper vibrated on his hip. "Damn," he muttered under his breath, glancing at the familiar number flashing on the small screen.

"Don't do it, Jimmy, you don't owe her anything," Sal said

"I can't just…"Jimmy started, his voice trailing off.

"Detective James Perez, YES YOU CAN. You must, or I'll be investigating you next," Sal retorted.

Jimmy first stared down at the paperwork scattered before him to clear his head. Next, he tried to recall all he knew about investments. He had recently become an investor himself. About eight months ago, Dayna had convinced him they needed to make their money work for them. Jimmy knew her father was the one behind Dayna's suggestion. He had stocks and had done quite well over the years. To Jimmy, it always looked like a crap shoot to him, but the financial facts about stock investments were inviting. Not the big money or fast money but long-term investments did seem to pay off. So maybe I should blame Dayna, he thought ruefully, a faint smile curling his lips as he remembered how happy she was when he decided to go to the investment seminar, "Responsible Stock Investing." Indeed, the seminar had been a turning point. After all, that is where we met.

It was innocent, almost fate-driven. Joanne was the presenter: professional, bright, and logical, with an easy wit that made even the driest financial theories seem compelling. She possessed an extensive command of the subject. She was an excellent speaker and made all the stock mumbo-jumbo fascinating. As Jimmy remembered, he could picture Joanne's animated form moving easily in front of the audience, her hands painting pictures in the air as she explained market trends and investment opportunities.

"You're right. What is your name?" asked Joanne.

"John, John Campbell, "the man replied.

"You're right, John. A lot of people think they can fool the odds by picking winners and moving money around like card sharks at a poker table," Joanne explained and continued as she addressed the whole group.

"What I am talking about is being an educated long-term investor with stocks being a part of your total financial strategy, not a 'get rich quick scheme. Financial strategy is more like a good marriage. You spend time and energy, and you get to know the person and their family. You wait out the bad times; communicate with a knowledgeable person about them. Even ask a friend what they know about them. Even the bad."

Everyone in the room laughed as Joanne continued.

"It's a true commitment with responsibility. You can't just take the advice of even a knowledgeable broker. You have a plan, you learn, you read, and you adjust to changing times." She turned her attention back to John, who had been following the conversation with interest. "Is that your lovely wife, John?"

"Yes, Marion," John replied proudly gesturing toward the simply but elegantly dressed woman who must be at least 70 but looked much younger. Jimmy could tell she must have been much taller from her long fingers with their tasteful rings. She was one of those women who had that well-bred demeanor. Even in a simple ensemble of jeans, a white shirt, and a blazer, she exuded a sophistication that was effortless and authentic—a natural poise that drew the eye.

"How long have you been married, Marion?" asked Joanne, turning everyone's attention toward her.

"Thirty-five years next month," Marion replied clearly.

"Then you know what I am talking about," Joanne confirmed.

Jimmy wasn't sure when in the two-day seminar it happened. He was listening intently, taking notes in his small, neat handwriting, watching, listening, and trying to understand all the terminology. His gaze was fixed on Joanne as she went through complex financial jargon with ease, her voice a captivating blend of professionalism and allure. Suddenly, he realized he was watching her differently. Joanne's voice started sounding sultry and smooth. He was aware of her body movements under the soft, gray silk dress. He wrestled with his focus, but it kept drifting. He tried to bring it back and succeeded several times. Then he felt it, the familiar pumping and tingling in his groin.

As Joanne continued her presentation, her movements seemed to slow down and become more rhythmical with each word. Jimmy found himself increasingly unable to concentrate, his mind caught in the gravitational pull of her presence. He would welcome the breaks, trying to regain composure, but he couldn't seem to find his way back to the subject. Each interval only intensified his awareness of her.

Then, at lunch, the situation escalated when she sat next to him; he could even feel her heat; her smell was musky and inviting. He was aware of her every movement. Her left hand lightly touched him as she was making a point. A surge went through him, fiery, electric. Then her knee touched his and he was glad he was sitting down with a napkin in his lap. Grateful, his black skin didn't show his flush, but nothing could shield his racing heart from her intuitive gaze. That was when she turned her smiling face toward him, her eyes locking with his in a gaze that felt both challenging and inviting. He was sure she knew. She held his eyes in hers. The room seemed to tilt slightly as he fought to maintain his composure. He almost felt dizzy, but he didn't dare get up. Her knee seemed to press harder against his; her hand was resting on his shoulder.

"Well, we better get back," Joanne commanded the table. "Are you all right, Mr?

"Mr?" parroted Jimmy.

"Your name?" Joanne said with a smirk.

"Perez, Jimmy Perez," he managed to stammer out, his name feeling foreign on his tongue.

"Well, Jimmy Perez - are you all right?" she inquired.

"Yes, why? Of course!" Jimmy fumbled for words.

"You seem a bit distracted. Not the most fascinating of subjects, I agree," she remarked.

"No, the seminar is, uh, stimulating," Jimmy admitted, wanting a big hole to bury himself in.

"Stimulating? Well, I was going for informative. Didn't know I had exceeded my goals. Are you an investor now, Mr. Perez?"

"No, I wasn't, I mean, I am considering…" Jimmy's words trailed off.

"I see," she said, seeming to know what he was really considering. "I have to get back," she said unconvincingly as Jimmy realized their knees were still attached.

"Of course," Jimmy said reluctantly, bringing his legs together and trying to regain a manly, controlled demeanor.

"Will you be staying for the afternoon session?" she said, still holding his eyes as if trying to read his thoughts.

"Oh yes, I'm committed," he tried humor to distract, but he knew he was dying, something was dying.

"Well, I hope the afternoon provides you with as much 'stimulation' as the morning did, Mr. Perez," she said with a half-smile, suggesting she was all too aware of the effect she had on him.

If he had walked out, then he would not be in this situation. But no, he stayed and lingered that night at the hotel bar until most of the other attendees had gone. The atmosphere was quiet, the buzz of earlier conversations a distant memory. And there she was next to him again. Her searching, dancing eyes were directed at him.

"Well, Detective Perez, are you still 'stimulated' by the seminar?" she teased.

"How'd you know I was a detective?" Jimmy asked.

"The information sheet you completed," she replied with a casual shrug.

"Ah yes, doing a little detective work of your own." Jimmy quipped; his words were more relaxed with two malt scotches and a light dinner. The renovated Venoy's hotel bar was more elegant and quieter than a usual Florida Beach Bar, more like a place out of a Fitzgerald novel with wood, brass, and old money solitude.

"So, are stocks going up, Detective?" Joanne asked.

"You'd know more about that," Jimmy replied, knowing somewhere inside he should leave. Somehow, his feet didn't feel the urge to move. They were being directed by his 'low' brain, as Dayna called it. "Can you predict a rise?" he asked.

"Well, that can be arranged as they say, Detective," Joanne quipped as her knee fell against his.

Chapter 7

In Carol's opinion, the Tampa Airport was one of the best. The wagon wheel design made it convenient to go wherever you parked. Of course, this was great when walking in heels with her suitcase and attaché. As she walked towards the terminal, memories of her last business trip to Appleton, Wisconsin, floated through her mind. It was before she had sold her company, TeleTech, which had secured a significant contract to provide a comprehensive communications package to a prominent paper coating company there. *Appleton, the birthplace of Houdini.* She was so focused on reminiscing she realized she parked in long-term parking —a force of habit from her days of frequent travel. She made a mental note that she was parked in the Tony James section, a reminder that might help her locate her car more easily upon return. She hurried onto the tram, the familiar hum of its engine another subtle reminder of her previous life on the road.

"Hold it together, girl. You can handle seeing your mom. You are early anyway and can enjoy the people-watching as you always did on business trips." Carol whispered to herself as she walked around the center of the airport's hub, where each traveler was absorbed in their own journey.

Ah, yes, business trips. She spends more time in airports and hotel rooms than in any destination. She found a moment of amusement as she remembered the unique personality of each airport she had frequented during her business travels. New Orleans airport had the best coffee. She had seen someone almost blown over by the wind at Chicago's O'Hare. Atlanta's vast terminals required so much walking, turning each connection into a mini-marathon. Miami always seemed dirty and had the strangest smells. Fort Lauderdale smelled like coconut oil as tourists in Hawaiian shirts came and went. Carol checked the electronic TV board for arrivals.

Carol found a quiet spot by the D Tram area, the hum of the airport evening settling around her. As she sat, her gaze scanned the now-closed shops at the hub with their last-minute souvenirs. Comfortably seated, she leaned back to indulge in one of her favorite activities: people-watching. She focused on the people around her and took note of their body language. Across from her, a woman's posture spoke volumes. The lady with her head tilted downward, showing submission as she listened to the man next to her as he talked to her. A young girl defended herself against her mother's chatter with her arms tightly crossed over her chest. Her chin was slightly raised in defiance. Meanwhile, two guys nearby tapped their impatience.

Suddenly, Carol thought, *Did someone call her name?* No, not for her. She scanned the faces of those around her as she recalled being in the Atlanta airport. She had been struggling with her baggage. Her overstuffed carry all contained one of those old-fashioned carousels for a slide projector. Her suitcase had unstable wheels. And, of course, she managed to trip, spilling her carry-all, and the slides went flying. Two gentlemen hurried to her rescue.

"Southern hospitality," Carol mused as they had quickly come for the fleeing slides. Their efforts had turned into a small hunt, with slides hiding under seats and behind bins.

"That's a laugh, wait, aren't you Carol Reiner, Ramsey class of 1976? Remember us? Dan and Roger?" One of the men had exclaimed, recognition sparking in his eyes.

"Oh my, you two best buds are still hanging out? exclaimed Carol "Yup, in business together," they'd replied.

They reminisced and exchanged cards. But no one ever followed through. Joanne was the only one she maintained contact with. It was her call tonight to check on her before she went to the airport that prompted her to come early and relax. Carol, while organized, always left leaving the house until the last minute. Joanne was right, though. Taking a chance to be late for Mom would not be prudent.

Did I remember to put on the alarm? Joanne's call had spurred her into motion to leave. She was getting so forgetful lately.

Looking up, Carol saw the tram doors opening. She positioned herself where Mom could see her. *She will be the last person. Probably clean the plane before leaving. Be nice!* Her good self reprimanded as her mom bustled out of the tram.

"Carol, here dear, take this," her mom said, shoving a large Saks Fifth Avenue bag into Carol's reaching arms, "We must hurry. Louise will be waiting."

Carol hugged the bag instead of her mother and trailed after her like a sullen teenager. Of course, her mom recounted every horrible moment of her flight. She half-listened on the twenty-minute drive. Carol tuned in and out, nodding at the expected pauses while they navigated the familiar drive home. They pulled into the alleyway behind the house. Back here was closest to where the little 5-pound Maltese beast could take a bathroom break.

"While I take dear Louise for her nightly walk, you should prepare her meal. The little dear must be starved," her mother instructed as she prepared to disembark. "Put down only filtered water. You did get *Nature's Blend,* didn't you? Carol, Carol!"

"Yes, Mom. You can walk her next to the hedge over there." Carol handed her mother a plastic bag out of the glove compartment. "I'll get everything prepared for the little darling. You can come through the lanai. There's a garbage pail right by that door. I'll unlock the French doors; the screen door to the lanai is not locked. Her dishes will be in the laundry room next to the kitchen so no one will trip over them. Make sure she finishes her bathroom duties."

"Really, Carol, you know Louise is completely trained," her mother retorted with a hint of reproach as she clipped the leash onto Louise's collar. "All those accidents she had last time were all Tony's fault. He kept exciting her. She should be eating at the table like she does at home but I suppose with all the hubbub, the laundry room will do for now."

Margaret rushed to Louise in the back seat while Carol removed all the bags. Then she carried them one by one to the back door before hunting for her keys. Her mother was constantly chattering behind her, encouraging Louise. As she opened the door that went through the laundry room and pantry, she stopped. Something was wrong. "The alarm isn't on, what the?" she whispered to herself. *Something else…a recent lingering smell like a stale cigar.* Carol backed up, put the bag down, and grabbed the broom hanging in the laundry room.

She reached into her purse for her cell phone, then hesitated. *We don't need more publicity, that's for sure.* Broom in hand, she did a quick tour of the kitchen and then the living and dining rooms. Everything was in order. Carol could see a sliver of streetlights across the living room floor. It came from Ed's office. She edged toward the door. Exactly what was she going to do with a broom? The cigar smell was stronger. She flipped on the office's light as she opened the library door with her foot…what a mess. Papers were everywhere, drawers were open, and a waft of cigar smoke seemed to hang in the air. She backed out and closed the door with a soft click, her heart pounding. She ran up the stairs, checked each room, and then back down the stairs. Thankfully, nothing seemed disturbed upstairs. *What were they looking for? Ed's papers and tapes were already in her trunk, ready to take to Joanne. Was that it?* As she was thinking, her mother's knocking on the lanai door came through her thoughts and snapped her back to the present. Carol hurried to unlock the door, her nerves frayed, her thoughts still racing with the implications of the break-in and the potential dangers still lurking.

"Coming, Mom!" Carol called out, her voice straining to remain calm.

"I can't believe you would leave us in the dark. Don't you even have one of those sensor lights? Louise is hungry and thirsty. What on earth are you doing with that broom? Did you unpack Louise's bed and bowls?" her mother complained the moment the door swung open.

Carol clenched her jaw and took a deep breath in to temper her rising frustration. She was afraid she'd say something she shouldn't as her mom rambled on.

"She is allergic to plastic, so I brought her special bowls. I suppose I'll have to do everything. I'd love a drink; how about joining me? You look frightful. Seen a ghost, dear? You know, after your father died, I used to think I saw him in the house. I'd come in, even call to him," her mother mused, wandering towards the kitchen. "Now. Where's the good stuff? Ed kept the good scotch in his library. I'll get us some."

"No!" Carol's response came out sharper than intended.

"Oh, for heaven's sake, Carol, he's not around to mind," her mother retorted with a dismissive wave.

"I mean, I'll get it," Carol quickly interjected, noticing her abrupt tone. She softened her voice, trying to smooth over the moment of tension. "You get Louise settled. I'll put her things in the bags on top of the washer in the laundry room. I'll get the scotch for you, then bring your bags inside and upstairs while you fix us that drink. How does that sound?"

"I guess I better get used to being ignored. Come along, Louise," her mother said.

Her mom went through the kitchen into the laundry room. Then she stood there with her arms folded, awaiting Carol.

Carol squeezed around her mother and grabbed the bags. She hoisted the one covered in paw prints on top of the washing machine for her mother to sort. Without waiting for further instructions, Carol grabbed the remaining bags still outside the door, her movements brisk as she crossed through the kitchen and headed up the stairs. Mumbling to herself, she dropped them in the guest room and went down again. *Who could it have been? What did they want? No police, no police!*

"Carol, I can get the bottle if you are busy up there," her mother shouted while Carol rushed to the office to retrieve the good scotch.

"I'm here, Mom." Carol was standing with her back to the office door.

"Oh my, you gave me a fright. Turn on some lights around here. Let's have that nightcap, shall we?" said her mom as she turned the dining room lights to bright.

It didn't take long for her mother to polish off several drinks while Carol opened some wine for herself. The alcohol seemingly loosened her tongue even more as she rattled on about her flight, relatives who were sick or had died, and something about parrots. "Parrots?" asked Carol.

"No, Carol, not parrots. I said Louise likes carrots, and you don't have any," her mother corrected her with an annoyed sigh. "Well, we are ready for bed. See you in the morning, dear. Get some rest. You do look awful. Well, I suppose that's to be expected. It's time to pull yourself together. I'm here, and there is nothing to worry about. You do have enough money, don't you? Carol, Carol."

"What? Yes, I'm fine financially."

"Good, we're off," her mom said as she and Louise climbed the stairs.

Margaret's chatter to Louise faded as they headed to the guest room. Carol glanced at the almost empty scotch bottle and was relieved to note her mother would be out for the night. Alone now, the weight of the evening's events pressed heavily on Carol. She needed to talk to someone. Had she forgotten to turn on the alarm? "Maybe I should get a dog to talk to," she mumbled to herself as she took her wine out to the lanai. She grabbed her cell phone along the way.

"Joanne, it's Carol…sorry to call so late," she said after dialing.

"No problem. You haven't killed your mom, have you? Don't worry; I'll help you hide the body," Joanne joked, then quickly backtracked, "Sorry. Not funny. Whatz up?"

"Someone broke into the house. They went through Ed's office. Papers were strewn about. Drawers opened, but they didn't seem to go anywhere else," explained Carol.

"Oh God, I'm sorry. What did the police say?" Joanne asked.

"I didn't call them. I couldn't face more publicity right now," Carol admitted

"Did they take anything?" Joanne probed.

"Not that I can see. I had already put the box for our meeting on Tuesday in my trunk. You don't think they were looking for those papers and the recordings?"

"Of course not. What good would those papers do anyone? They wouldn't be worth anything. Probably some crackhead looking for some money or a safe," Joanne speculated, trying to offer a rational explanation. "You may have scared them off when you came home. It will be fine. Want me to come by?"

"No, I needed to tell someone. I've gone over and over things in my head. At first, I thought I forgot to turn on the alarm, but I retraced my steps in my mind and I am sure I put it on. They must have had a key, too, because the back door was unlocked, and there was this cigar smell in the room. Am I going nuts," said Carol.

"You're tired. Your mom could drive anyone nuts with her constant chatter and drinking. Speaking of drinking…have one and get some rest. It has only been a week, after all," Joanne comforted.

"You're right, but I keep thinking…" said Carol.

"That will keep you up all night. Got a sleeping pill?" asked Joanne.

"Yes, but I think this wine will do fine. Sorry to bother you," said Carol.

"Anytime, my friend. Bring your secret box over to my place first thing on Monday. Hmm, secret box; sounds dirty," teased, lightening the mood.

Carol chuckled, grateful for Joanne's ability to inject humor into the grimmest of conversations. "You always know how to make me smile."

"Get some sleep, now," Joanne said gently.

"Secret box," Carol repeated. "Maybe I should listen to those tapes? I don't have anything that plays cassettes except my old BMW. I could listen in the car."

"Don't you dare! I'll take care of the dirty work. You take care of you. I insist. Go to bed," Joanne said as they ended the call.

Carol hung up the phone and carefully locked each door, checked windows, and double-checked the alarm before going upstairs. As she got into bed, she wondered why those things were separated from the rest of Ed's papers in the first place. They had been tucked away in the back of the closet, right by her favorite shoes, almost as if he meant for her to find them—keep them separate. *Oh, Ed, do I want to know what you've done? Damn you, Damn you!*

Chapter 8

After her unsettling conversation with Carol, Joanne frantically dialed numbers on her phone. Once connected, she couldn't contain her anger and screamed. "Benny, what the hell! You tossed papers everywhere! And you smoked that damn cigar. The smell was everywhere. What were you doing? I told you I had everything covered."

From the other end of the line, Benny's voice came through, edged with a calm that only fueled her frustration. "Keep your panties on; if that's possible, everything is fine. I thought I should get ahold of the tapes just in case we have competition for them."

"I have that handled. I told you. Wait…your instincts are saying this in an inside job. Do you think her son-in-law, Tony? If anyone, I vote for helpful Charles. Besides, you left a mess? She said there were papers everywhere, and the alarm wasn't on," said Joanne.

"I didn't do that! It was that way when I went into the office. I parked down the street and walked then came in the back. Actually,

I thought I heard the front door close as I walked into the kitchen. The alarm wasn't even on when I opened the door. You have the tapes, right?" said Benny.

"Not in my possession yet, but I'll have them Tuesday. They are in the trunk of her car. Did you get anything from her accountant, Roger Barnes, when you talked with him? He could be worth looking at. He doesn't seem connected to the mob, but you never know," said Joanne as she relaxed her death grip on the steering wheel.

"The open door had to be Tony or someone Charles hired," suggested Benny.

"Charles would never leave a mess. He's much too clever for that. I'm sure they're both connected to the mafia, LoScalzo and Raffa. We just need to make sure everything we collect is clean, or we will never make our case. Benny. a B&E isn't clean. And you remember how slippery LoScalzo can be."

"I know all about him. He's head of the Tampa Trafficante crime family. Indicted on racketeering charges that included grand theft." stated Benny.

"Hold on a minute while I get out of the car and go inside," Joanne interjected as she maneuvered her car into the driveway. She knew he would be listening for any trouble as she got inside. After locking her car with a beep, she trudged into her living room, dropping everything on her couch. She headed to the kitchen and grabbed a wine glass, uncorked a bottle with a practiced twist, and poured herself a generous helping. The sound of the wine glugging into the glass seemed to echo in the stillness of her home. "Alright, I'm back," she announced, her voice steadier now.

"Listen. It's good I was at the house. I probably scared away someone dangerous to your friend; also, I did a bug sweep and found three in the office. There may be more people interested than you think, both good and bad," Benny explained.

"Yup, it is good you showed up. Tell me what you remember," Joanne urged, settling into her couch with the wine glass cradled in her hand.

"Alright, let's see," Benny started. "The tape recorder was on the floor, almost under the desk. No tape in it. All the papers on the floor were eight and a half by eleven, with no handwritten notes. A few of the papers on the desk were legal size and seemed to be in blue jackets. I didn't see anything of importance in the short time I was there."

Joanne nodded slowly to herself, listening intently; she knew Benny was picturing the scene. He was great at taking mental pictures quickly. He was a treasure in their surveillance work in business and brokerages. He could recall details Joanne wouldn't even notice.

"I'm thinking maybe I do need to check into Roger Barnes again. Remember, I met with him a month ago when he was in Ocala with his family. He was only Carol's accountant, but I bet she confided in him. He told me Detective Carduchi had contacted him. I told you I thought he knew something."

"Ok, review your notes; I'll do the same," said Joanne as she kicked off her shoes and to slumped into the couch. The cushions didn't quite swallow her stress as she had hoped.

"Did Carol say anything about him and the stock stuff? You need to get more information from her. You're protective of her, but it's not doing anyone any good." said Benny.

Joanne sighed, rubbing her temple. She knew she was being protective of Carol by not asking too many questions. She also knew she was not helping anyone by not knowing Carol's involvement or knowledge of Ed's stock deals. *Guilt for my stupidity in staying away from Carol and her family for so long,* she pondered.

"I know. You're right about Carol. We don't want to step on the FBI's toes for any reason. We need their cooperation. We just provide the leads. We can't even plant a bug. If you or we know anything, we need to disclose it before we end up in a turf war."

"I know we have to report everything. Our contract is focused on stock fraud," Benny responded.

Joanne paused, considering his words. She wasn't sure whether that was a statement or a question. Benny could overstep at times, sometimes, so did she, but in different ways. *I over-stepped more. The NASD was not interested in the suicide or her relationship with Carol.*

"Please remember neither the SEC nor the National Association of Security Dealers have any jurisdiction as far as I know," she reminded him gently but firmly.

"Got it. We stick to bank and stock issues unless the feds directly assign us more," Benny conceded, a trace of irritation in his tone.

Joanne heard the annoyance in Benny's voice but kept up the lecture. "Remember, being cleared and trained by Quantico was a gift as a request from the Attorney General. It is not a get out of jail free card."

"I understand!" Benny replied.

Joanne knew she was hammering the point home a bit too fervently, but she was on a roll. Mostly, she was badgering herself.

"Our contract is with the SEC and NASD; it doesn't cover investigation for drugs or murder unless we are specifically tasked," she reiterated, her voice echoing slightly in the quiet of her living room.

"Yeah, well, the feds always seem happy when we put ourselves in danger and give them prosecutable info," injected Benny.

"True but the brief information we provided that resulted in helping settle the case with Waste Management and Arthur Andersen last year won't protect us if we cross jurisdictions or break the law. We were lucky that the way you got the information for the Brooklyn Grand Jury indictment can't be traced," Joanne pointed out.

"Hey, we did back that up with solid evidence against Consalvo. The indictments in Tampa are coming down against Abramo for the stock pump and dump scheme soon. That is just chump change, even though it will be a real blow to the mob," Benny retorted.

"I'm tired, Benny. What am I thinking, going on and on about this on the phone? We've said too much over the phone already. Let's meet early and hash this out before we get in trouble. Since Roger Barnes is a CPA and, as I remember he has an SEC license, we can look at him. No B & Es," Joanne suggested, her voice weary.

"I got it. Our phones and homes are safe tonight; I did a check on yours this afternoon and mine when I got home. Just be careful. Those tapes might stir up more than a stock fraud, and your involvement with the FDLE isn't helping," said Benny, reversing the lecture.

"You're right," Joanne conceded, the weight of the situation pressing down on her. "I thought I could wrangle some inside information on the FDLE investigations into any business, stock, or bank fraud when it started."

Trying to feel less guilty, she added, "He wasn't even looking at any specific dishonesty or Ed Wallin when we met. Then came Wallin's loans, HarborTech, and gambling. It was simple when it began, but it is out of hand. It is totally my fault. I could blow our whole investigation."

"Don't play the blame and shame game. Just end it," replied Benny firmly, a note of finality in his voice that suggested no further discussion was necessary. With that, they ended the call.

Joanne paced her apartment for a while. She checked locks on doors and windows before climbing into her empty bed; the sheets cool against her skin, her mind racing. She had too much to lose if she continued with Jimmy, but she was just so lonely. *What is your problem? He's not a future. If this investigation brings indictments, your private investigation business will thrive. That is much more important than that hot man. I'll tell him tomorrow or soon,* she thought as she turned over and hugged her pillow.

Chapter 9

— • ● • —

Carol couldn't wait any longer. Questions gnawed at her, unyielding and urgent. She had to hear the tapes; the uncertainty was unbearable. She had to know what was going on. Grabbing the phone off the nightstand, she punched in Joanne's number.

"Sorry to call so early, but the girls will be here by nine, and Mom will be up by ten. I must know what's on the tapes. What if something on the tapes puts the girls in danger? Ed's suicide makes no sense. Was I just naive?" Her voice cracked, a mixture of fear and desperation leaking through.

"Well, good morning to you too. I hear you," Joanne replied. "Wow, girl, slow down. You knew Ed was in trouble. You were just coping the best you could. You are not to blame for any of this."

Carol felt the knot in her stomach tighten, and she felt desperate. The sense of guilt and relief was raging a battle inside her. "We were having trouble because of the money issues. Then there was the Governor's investigation we knew would be coming.

"I can only imagine the stress," said Joanne.

Carol took a deep breath, tried to compose herself, and then continued. "That stupid reporter wouldn't stop harassing him about the gambling. Not that the press was so wrong, just that they were so, so. Oh, I don't know. Ed was strong, even cocky sometimes, but with everything, he was NOT depressed."

"Come over whenever you're ready. I'm close by. I rented a wonderful house close to you… right off Morrison about six months ago. I even have bagels and lox," Joanne offered warmly.

Another stab of guilt punctured her. "Wow, you are close. I didn't know. What an awful friend I am. I didn't even ask where you were staying,"

"I'd say you've been a bit busy. Seriously, no problem. I was up anyway. I'll make another pot of coffee," Joanne reassured her.

Carol sat silently for a moment, trying to ease the pressure in her chest. Rising from her seat, she put Joanne's address in her pocket and checked in the mirror to ensure she was appropriately dressed. She didn't trust herself now; she needed that reassurance. Satisfied, she grabbed her large purse and checked its contents. She organized her little make-up bag, notebook, and wallet to help calm herself. Another deep breath, and she was ready.

As Carol came down the stairs, she realized that there was coffee brewing. "What the hell? Kay? Stevie?" she called out, puzzled. "It's not even 7 am. What are you doing?"

"Kay and I thought you'd want some support this morning," explained Stevie, emerging from the kitchen. "I already cleaned the pee that was in front of the back door. Fed devil dog. Kay and Tony are on their way."

"Well, this may work out beautifully. I am on my way over to Joanne's. She's helping me with some stock stuff."

"You should ask Tony. He would love to help. You know he's good with stocks. He sold a ton of stocks for Ed's company. He made quite a bit in commissions from that one. Bought their new house and all. Kay said Tony was anxious to ask you something anyway. It may have to do with Ed Jr. They've been consoling him. Tony's gotten close to him lately,"

"He'll have to wait. I need to get to Joanne's. I already woke her up. It would be impolite not to go right away," said Carol. She dashed into the laundry room, kicked the dog's water bowl, and let out a string of curses before rushing back to the kitchen. Stevie was pouring coffee into her favorite cup as she re-entered the kitchen.

"I'll let them know. Tony has work anyway. At least have a cup of coffee with me, sit!" said Stevie as she phoned her sister.

"Hey, talked to Mom. No, I'm sure she won't be here. Tell Tony and Eddy another time. How about tonight? We could have dinner with Grandma. She would like that."

Carol gave Stevie a thumbs-up in acknowledgment as she listened to the conversation unfold.

"Okay, I know Grandma would like to have dinner with us even if Tony is with you. What did he say? No, she can't wait. She's going to Joanne's place. Why does he need to know that? Hold on," Stevie turned to Carol. "Mom, where does Joanne live?"

"Off of Morrison. Why?" Carol responded.

"Did you get that? Got it. Okay. See you soon, love," said Stevie.

"What is that all about? You know what? I don't have time for this. Thanks for the coffee, sweetie. Tell Grandma I'll be back this afternoon. Would you mind taking her shopping for HER food? You know how she is. Love you." said Carol as she went out through the laundry room. She was about to go to the trunk when she realized she stepped in dog poop. She did a 'poop ballet hop' back to the house. As she flung open the door to the laundry room once more, she heard Stevie's voice again, now speaking to Tony, the concern in her tone unmistakable.

"Why do you want me to stall her Tony? Wait. There she is again. Mom?" shouted Stevie.

"Cleaning dog poop off my shoe. Is that Tony? Who wants to stall me?" Carol shouted back.

"Both Eddy and Tony," Stevie whispered into the phone, then turned to speak more openly. "They're worried you're rushing into things so early in the morning. They wanted to slow you down a bit," she said, her eyes darting between the phone and her mother. "Eddy? Since when does he care about me? Anyway, no time to slow down," said Carol as she fled out the laundry room door.

Before she got in, she went to the trunk, carefully avoiding any further encounters with 'dog gifts.' She removed the tapes and placed them in her purse, holding two in her hand while contemplating the other contents. She wondered about the papers. There was something else heavy at the bottom of the box. She didn't want to waste time searching for it now; even though it was a short ride from her home to Joanne's, she wanted to listen to one just to hear Ed's voice. She decided to ride up and down a few streets to give herself time to listen. *Foolish girl,* she said to herself as she grasped the tapes tighter. Settling into the driver's seat, she started the car and popped one of the tapes into the car's player.

"I need to know what you wanted to tell me, Ed. Why, Ed, why?" she murmured to him. She pressed play, bracing herself for the sound of his voice that might just unravel everything.

The tape player squeaked to life with a voice, "Turn on," said Ed in a whisper. The machine whirred, accompanied by the sound of papers shuffling in the background. "You're early. I don't understand why you think this buyout is such a great idea. We're not ready. As Carol said, it is not even a product yet. Roger Barnes looked at the numbers and said they don't add up."

"I'll take care of your wife's precious CPA, Roger. Bottom line. You need the money," a second, more forceful voice countered. "I can't believe you used money that Tony and Ed Jr. got from Tony's uncle **again**. You did this to yourself. Now I'm going to fix it **again**. Listen to me carefully, Ed."

Carol's heart pounded as she listened; she could hear the strain in Ed's voice, bringing tears to her eyes. She recognized Charles Atoll's voice.

"You are going to do exactly as I say," Charles Atoll's voice hissed through the tape. "You are going to recommend the contracts that are on the list I gave you. You are going to sell the company to HarborTech. You are going to pretend the software is great. You are going to keep your mouth shut. Remember, you are being watched. You owe them. You owe me. You said no before, but you are not saying no now. I intend to retire on this money. I've got a nice island home selected and almost paid for. You'll probably be ruined, but I don't care. Your wife can keep you in the lifestyle you want."

"You don't have to point a gun at me," Ed's voice broke in. "I'll do what you say. Just keep your mafia buddies away from my family. I can't believe Tony and Ed agreed to this."

"Your dear Eddy and Tony aren't smart enough to understand. You are. They do what I tell them. Your stupid son-in-law thinks everything is legal. The big man thinks he will be smart enough to make money from stocks. He thinks he's protecting his wife and mother-in-law from your gambling debts."

"Bastard," Carol shouted at the tape.

"Your son really doesn't like you anyway. His mother taught him well. If you value Carol and her girls, you will act quickly. I've set up all the paperwork. Sign," Charles insisted.

"You were my friend," said Ed.

"We weren't friends. You're a meal ticket. Mr. Popular. Mr. Councilmen. It was easy. Just play the mortgage game. Recommend contracts to the city. The housing development in Plant City and your council position gave me the perfect opportunity. But no…you gambled away the profits before…." Charles's voice was persistent.

Squeeking tape, garbled voices. Carol pressed, 'Stop,' frustration and despair gripped her. "Damn, the tape is stuck. Damn you, Charles," she cursed, her hands trembling as she hit 'Play' again. More squeaking and a high-pitched whining sound. She pressed 'Stop' once more. "Damn tape. Ed what did you get into," she mumbled as she tried to remove the tape without it unraveling. She ejected it as tears overflowed. Pressure filled her chest as her eyes blurred. She knew the other tape would be as painful, but she had to know the truth.

The tape was in her right pocket. The seatbelt was in her way of getting it. "Damn it," she shouted to the belt as she struggled to get the tape out of her pocket. Holding the wheel with her left hand, she tried to get her other fingers into her pant pocket. Absorbed in her struggle, she didn't notice the other car. She hardly registered the sound of the crash.

Chapter 10

oanne was standing at her kitchen window when she heard a squeal, crunch, and shattering of glass. She knew. Her gut notified her with absolute certainty. She knew the gut didn't lie. The dread was real and instant. She froze for one moment before going into rescue mode. She ripped out the phone from her pocket, almost tearing her shirt in the process, and punched the numbers frantically. Her dread almost made her forget the three simple digits. Dashing out, she didn't bother to shut her door. She saw Carol, and instinctively, as if on cue, her legs picked up the pace.

"911, what's the emergency."

"There's been a car accident. Oh God. Two cars. Carol, Carol!" Joanne's voice cracked.

"Give me the address, please," the dispatcher responded with practiced calm.

"What? Send an ambulance!" screamed Joanne as she headed out her front door.

"Is this on the corner of Morrison and Fremont?"

"Yes, yes, just hurry!" Joanne cried out.

"Ambulance is on its way. Are you hurt? Lady? Are you hurt?" said the 911 operator as Joanne hung up the phone and shoved it in her pocket. "Ambulance" was too far for Joanne to wait. Running to the passenger side of the car, she pulled the door open and leaned in.

"Carol, talk to me." Joanne noticed her purse was on the floor with all the items within spilled in disarray, mimicking the chaos. Tapes spread all around – wallet entangled in the wires below the dashboard. Leaning fully in, she touched Carol's pulse. It seemed steady. Carol was not conscious and Joanne knew that was not a good sign. *Please be alright!*

Her awkward position didn't give Joanne a view of the rest of the scene. The crash site. She didn't know much about what exactly was happening around her. Also, at the moment, she didn't care much either. All she cared about was Carol, still unconscious despite the clutter and garble of loud voices outside the car. She reluctantly pulled away from her. The driver of the other car had his back to her. Someone else was in that car, too. She could hear the police and an ambulance. She was wishing for the ambulance to arrive sooner when she, even with the cacophony around, heard a little movement.

Instantly, she turned back to Carol. She saw her raise her head slightly and whisper, "Tapes."

"Carol, please be okay!" Joanne pleaded as Carol's head rolled down again. She gathered up Carol's purse and the tapes on the floor and seat. She was reaching under the passenger seat and checking for more tapes when the police and ambulance pulled up.

Hurriedly, she got out of the way as she saw the ambulance nearing. The paramedics jumped out of the ambulance as it came to an almost-screeching halt. She pointed to Carol. One quickly assessed the scene, the other readied the equipment, while another took a gurney out. One of them checked for a pulse, announced it was there, and started putting a brace around Carol's neck. Joanne was frozen watching them work. "How is she?"

"Her breathing is shallow but steady. We'll take her to St. Joseph's Hospital. Let us check you. We have room in the ambulance for both of you."

As the one paramedic started toward her, Joanne backed away from the car, gripping Carol's purse like a shield. "I wasn't in the car. I'm her friend. I'll call her family. Please take good care of her."

The policeman had been talking with the other driver, who looked familiar. *Is that Eddy? Ed's son? Couldn't be. What do I tell the police? I'll leave her wallet on the seat. This way, I can keep the purse and tapes safe.*

Joanne watched them carry Carol to the ambulance. She willed her to be okay. She jumped when the policeman touched her arm. "Are you sure you're okay, ma'am?"

"Yes, I'm her friend. She was coming to visit me. I wasn't in the car. I live right there. The house with the open door," gushed Joanne, pointing to her house with a finger that was badly trembling.

"Good. Did you see the accident?" asked the policeman while jotting down notes.

"No, I heard it," Joanne answered more questions as calmly as possible. She reiterated that she only heard the crash and added the extra bit that she was in the kitchen. She remembered her cell phone in her pocket. "I'll call her daughter and have her meet me at the hospital," she said, waving her phone.

"You weren't in the car?" confirmed the policeman.

"No, as I said, she was coming over to see me and have breakfast. I see her wallet on the seat right there," said Joanne. When the officer turned toward the open passenger door of the vehicle, Joanne called her daughter.

"Kay? Yes...Well, sort of...She was almost here...There was a small accident. They're taking her to St. Joseph's. I'll meet you there. Don't worry. They're taking good care of her." Joanne gave all the details in pauses, ensuring not to overwhelm the voice on the other end. Raising one finger to signal the policeman to wait, she finished the explanation to Kay.

As Carol was rushed away in the ambulance, some relief settled. Now back in charge of things, she tightened her grip on Carol's purse. She took stock of her surroundings as she reached in and took out the small notebook and pen she had scooped up from the floor. "Where are you taking the car?" she asked the policeman.

After giving the girls' names and phones, her name and phone, and answering some of the rehearsed questions by the officer, she rushed back to her house. The aroma of the burnt coffee pot filled with the burnt aroma of the scalded coffee. The contents of the pot were long gone. She ensured the pot was off and gathered her things. She was tempted to drag out her tape recorder and listen to the tapes, but Carol came first. She needed to know she was okay.

What to do with the tapes? Take them with me? Hide them? Put them in my trunk? Should I let Donnie or Jimmy know I have them? She knew Carol wanted Joanne to guard them. Head swimming, she stuffed her own purse into Carol's and headed to St. Joe's. *Carol first.* She thought.

Chapter 11

"Where are you?" questioned Sal.

"I'm heading south on Dale Mabry toward the office. What's up? Did I miss a meeting? It's only 8," said Jimmy, glancing at the clock on the dashboard.

"It's a news flash I just got from Tampa Police about Roger Barnes, Carol Wallin's accountant."

"What did they want with him? Was he arrested? You said you couldn't reach him."

"He's dead. I'll meet you at the crime scene. He lives in Carrollwood, North Tampa, close to your place. Off of Fowler. Messy, real messy," stated Sal.

Jimmy pulled his SUV into a strip center parking lot and wrote down the address. "What the hell is going on? This has to be related to Wallin's death," he muttered to himself before speaking more loudly, "Ok, I'm not far. I'll be there in ten," he told Sal, turning his vehicle back north.

The cul-de-sac where Barnes lived looked like a police street pajama party. Vehicles with flashing lights, CSI, the coroner, uniformed officers, and neighbors in and out of PJs. Jimmy nearly hit a kid on a skateboard riding out of his driveway toward the police cars blocking the circle. Sal was waiting for him at the left perimeter. "Three ambulances. Damn! Must be quite a mess in there to attract all this attention," Jimmy said as he walked across the lawn to Sal.

"Mess means something was tidy. This place was so tossed it looks like the guy was a paper hoarder who liked to sprinkle blood on his accounts to get his rocks off," Sal growled.

"Wow, partner. You're usually not so graphic. You're angry? Why?"

"Well, for starters, I wanted our CSI team to process. Tampa guys and their CSI threw a fit, then threw me out. And, and… Shit, Damn, Fuck!"

"Okay, calm down. Sal, you couldn't have prevented this. He was probably dead already since you've been calling."

"I told you I talked to him. I gave you that note about it. I should have pressed him. I did think he knew something. I was being lazy. 'Let Jimmy handle him.' Shit! I should have pursued it. If whoever did this thought I might get the stuff, then this…" Sal trailed off, his fists clenching.

"What the hell! This is not your fault. You've seen worse, man."

"His kid, wife, and her mother found him. The old lady had a heart attack, I think. Anyway, she went down and the kid... Jimmy, the kid saw everything," Sal said slowly.

"Oh damn! Got it! I'll call our CSI unit. They're friends with the Tampa CSI. They know they can't do this alone. They're territorial right now, but they'll loosen up soon. Let's just sit down for a bit. Tell me what you do know," Jimmy suggested.

As if snapping to attention, Sal walked briskly to Jimmy's vehicle and waited for him to unlock the door. When he settled in the SUV, he was deep in thought, his head leaning back. Jimmy knew he was watching an internal movie of the scene. Jimmy turned on the AC, waited, and watched the bizarre scene playing out in front of him like something from a Slicer movie. When he sensed Sal was ready to talk, he grabbed a pen and paper.

"Okay, unpacked suitcases in the bedroom, papers everywhere, pinky finger seemed removed but bandaged, naked, bruises on the face and upper torso. And hung from a rafter in the garage," said Sal, pausing as Jimmy furiously scribbled notes.

"He wasn't at the funeral, or at least I didn't see him. What else?" asked Jimmy.

Sal paused, now looking at the dashboard as if it had writing on it. "Ok, let's see. I talked to him before Wallin's death to set up an appointment for you when the Governor's office said we needed to be prepared." Sal closed his eyes and tapped his temple.

"As I understand it, he wasn't Ed Wallin's accountant," Jimmy said.

"Right. He was Carol Wallin's accountant."

"Okay, so he could still know something," said Jimmy.

"Yes. Barnes said they were going on vacation and would be back in a month but gave me a number at his wife's mother's home. I called him in Ocala. He didn't have much to say about Wallin himself. He did say he met with Wallin a few times at Wallin's wife's request."

"I read your notes. You suspected he knew more but wasn't saying anything."

"He did say the numbers on HarborTech's buyout of Wallin's company didn't make sense and that he had told Carol Wallin."

"I talked briefly to Barnes's wife before they threw me out. Just came in early from Ocala because she and the kid wanted to surprise

Dad on his birthday. He had returned from their vacation early because someone called him," Sal paused.

Jimmy could see Sal clenching and unclenching his jaw, trying to pump his memory.

"His computer is missing. Judging by the looks of things, he could have been tortured for hours, then hanged. I think there was more than one person. The finger was wrapped like he took care of it, then something else happened. Neighbors called because the TV had been blaring day and night for a week. He knew something. Damn it!" said Sal, winding down.

Jimmy's mind was racing. He reviewed his notes again with Sal. When the FDLE CSI unit arrived, Jimmy and Sal filled them in on the type of papers that would be most important. "Our CSI team is sharp. If there's anything there, they'll find it. It's going to take time. I think we should spring this on Wallin's wife and see her reaction," said Jimmy as they got back in his SUV.

"Great idea! I'll see if she's home," said Sal. He grabbed Jimmy's clunky Nokia portable car phone, looked at his notes, and dialed Carol Wallin's house. "Good morning. This is Agent Carducci with the Florida Department of Law Enforcement. Who is this? Is… okay, Tony. What! Hold it!" He listened, smiling, then frowning. "Why are you mad at me? I am not a reporter. FDLE Agent... What accident? I see. What hospital? St. Joseph's. Got it."

"Accident?" asked Jimmy as Sal hung up, shaking his head.

"Seems Mrs. Wallin was just in a car accident. She's at St. Joseph's. That's where they are taking Barnes's people."

"Accident?" said Jimmy again. "This just gets messier and messier. Is she okay?"

"He didn't elaborate. He seems to like the word 'fuck' and dislikes reporters and cops. Go figure. I'll talk to Garten when the FDLE unit. You head to St. Joe's. I'll meet you back at the office. If she's not badly hurt, let's press the wife harder," reiterated Sal.

"I agree."

"She's hiding something. You know it, and I know it. Roger Barnes did hint there were some oddities and that Wallin left notes that he was going to review. He actually used the word spreadsheets. He seemed nervous about them and made a point to say they weren't accounting. Said it twice, as I remember."

"We do need to find that information," said Jimmy.

"Oh yes, be careful. In his tirade, Tony mentioned Carol Wallin's high school friend was with her, her daughters, and her mother. And we are not to talk to any of them, or he'll rip my face off," Sal quipped as he exited the car.

Chapter 12

Jimmy's stomach was churning. Joanne had been a selfish comfort, and he knew he'd acted like a child to get back at Dyna for cheating. Sure, she'd been wrong, but he had ignored her, too, trying to get ahead. The move from Tampa Police to FDLE was supposed to be a promotion. He was going to be a big man: Mr. Agent, who knew about stocks and was a savvy investigator. He didn't impress anyone, especially not himself.

Think, man. He could feel everything was connected: Wallin's supposed suicide, the gambling, the alleged kickbacks with the city contracts, the GatWin-HarborTech stock fraud, Barnes's death, and now this accident. Joanne's friendship with Carol Wallin was complicating things, a mess he had caused. *Was she involved? Did she know about the stock issues? She was a stock expert, after all. Which side was she on? She was from New Jersey. Were his instincts wrong?* He was still hitting the steering wheel and cursing as he pulled up to St. Joseph's Hospital.

Jimmy was just about to use his credentials to get into the ICU when he overheard an argument coming from a private waiting room near the ICU's sliding glass doors.

"What do you mean you're putting her in a coma? The Mercedes has those airbags—aren't they supposed to prevent head injuries? We'll sue everyone—Mercedes, the guy who hit her, the hospital!" Carol's mother yelled.

"Grandma, please! Let the doctor talk, or I swear I'll throw you out myself," Kay said, pulling her grandmother back from the Doctor.

"Why don't you all just sit and catch your breath for the moment?" the doctor suggested. "I'll explain everything the best that I can at this time," said the doctor while Kay and Joanne helped the grandmother sit. "It appears your mother. Eh, your daughter has a trauma to her skull, which has caused swelling. We'll try steroids, but the pressure can be dangerous. We're closely monitoring the situation."

"And if that doesn't work?" Stevie asked.

"If there's no improvement, we may need your permission to induce a coma. The other option is surgery, but let's just give her a chance to improve first." said the Doctor. Carol's mother struggled to get up while Kay and Joanne yelled at her to stay put.

Jimmy used this opportunity to enter the room through the half-open door. Chaos continued as Joanne fought with Carol's mom, Tony started to attack Jimmy with Kay holding him back, and the doctor flattened himself against the wall. Stevie dragged the doctor out of the room and slammed the door behind her.

"Let me make myself perfectly clear. I am my mother's healthcare surrogate. I make the decisions. That group of ingrates has no say. Now, please explain everything as best as you can in terms I can understand," Stevie demanded, holding the door shut.

The Doctor barely had time to exchange a few words before a deep voice boomed from inside the room, followed by silence and a soft knock at the door. Stevie let go of the knob slowly, finger by finger. The knob was twisted, and Jimmy emerged. She pulled him toward her while shutting the door behind him. Shouting ensued inside; he opened the door and said, "SHUT UP, NOW!" Jimmy turned and straightened his suit jacket, still holding the door handle. "You were saying, Doctor?"

Stevie exchanged a look with Jimmy, then nodded slowly to the Doctor. In a quiet voice, the Doctor explained the process and treatment options. Stevie and Jimmy both listened without questions. Finally, Stevie said, "What happens now?"

"We wait," the Doctor replied, turning to head back into the ICU.

Stevie's eyes locked on Jimmy. "Not to be impolite, but what the hell are you doing here? How dare you implant yourself into this situation? Haven't you caused enough grief around our family? Wasn't it enough that you invaded the funeral? Can't you just leave us alone?"

I wasn't here for this, exactly," Jimmy replied. "I was investigating another matter... but it *is* connected to your family. Maybe you should sit down. Can I let go of the door now?"

"Probably not," Stevie said coolly. "Why don't you tell me what's going on first?"

"Have you or your family heard from Roger Barnes?"

Mom's accountant? Eh, no, I don't think so. He wasn't at the funeral. He was Mom's comptroller in her company and friend, and…well, he went into private practice. He's a CPA. What the hell difference does he have to do with this?"

Jimmy reached out, thinking she was going to pass out. Then the door to the side room burst open, and chaos resumed just as Stevie fainted. Jimmy caught her and picked her up. Kay grabbed her grandmother and slapped her, then slapped Tony as he struggled to wrench Stevie from Jimmy's arms. Suddenly, Joanne started to laugh.

Everyone stopped and glared at her. "What the fuck is so funny?" Tony demanded.

"All of you," Joanne replied through fits of laughter, walking out of the room still giggling.

Stevie awoke and struggled out of Jimmy's arms. When she straightened, she said, "We're in a hospital. Everyone, stay quiet. Now."

Obediently, the family crew did as Stevie asked like sullen children. She stopped Joanne before she entered again, walked out, and then closed the door behind her. "You were saying, Detective? About Roger Barnes?"

"Yes," Jimmy said, avoiding Joanne's gaze. "He's been injured. One of his family members is in the ICU. I was checking on them."

Joanne wasn't even looking at Jimmy. She was drawing Stevie to her side by the far shoulder and trying to see her eyes like they were a screen into Stevie's present state.

Stevie turned to her, saying, "I'm fine. I haven't eaten since yesterday. I was about to eat breakfast when Mom ran out. Kay and Tony constantly called about where Mom was going, and, of course, Grandma and that evil dog who pops and pees everywhere, and then Mom's accident."

Seemingly calmer she turned to Jimmy, "So what did happen to Roger? He's a super guy. Kind. Had his kid late, you know. Oh God, I'm rambling. I think I need to sit."

Jimmy pointed to another small family waiting area across from the room where Carol's family was. Stevie slowly let go of the knob, then walked across to the smaller room and sat.

"I'll get you a snack," said Joanne as she rushed down the hall to fetch a snack, leaving Jimmy standing awkwardly in the doorway.

"So," Stevie prompted, "what happened?"

"How well did you know Mr. Barnes?"

"Longtime friend of the family. Kind of an uncle. When I was younger…before Ed…I thought Mom and he might get together. Then he found Donna. She is a treasure. Quiet, yet so full of life. Perfect for Roger, who was so conservative. Oh, God. I didn't ask…was she hurt? I remember they were going on vacation. Oh, what about his son?"

"I think they are fine. The grandmother was upset, so they took her here. When did your mom last speak with him?"

"After Ed died, but before the funeral I think. No, wait, she said he didn't return her calls. Why? What has this got to do with Mom? She said she was worried about him. What happened?"

"Why was she worried? Did he mention not coming to the funeral?"

Stevie's expression shifted from curiosity to suspicion. "Detective, tell me what this is about."

Joanne returned, handing Stevie a breakfast bar and soda. "Jimmy, for heaven's sake, just tell her."

Stevie stared at Jimmy and then said. "Yes, Jimmy, do tell."

"He was murdered," Jimmy blurted. "That's all I can say right now. Please let me know when I can speak with your mother." He turned and hurried down the hall to the nurse's station. He heard Joanne shout, "Coward!" as he flashed his badge and entered the ICU.

Chapter 13

"That cop's a real shit. You seem to know him. Want to elaborate?" said Stevie as she stood and straightened her clothes. Joanne could tell she was preparing for another battle with her family.

Joanne raised her hands slightly, trying to calm the brewing storm. "We can talk at another time, my War Wu," she said, hoping to cool Stevie back down.

"Hmm, War Wu…Warrior Women…you called me that when I was a kid. Well, I'm not a kid anymore. "Mom missed you, you know. We all did. Are you here for good?"

"I've been busy trying to pull my life back together," said Joanne as guilt rose into her throat like bile. She reached out, wanting to touch Stevie's arm, but stopped herself, sensing that Stevie wasn't ready for that kind of comfort yet.

"You disappeared for some years," Stevie continued. "Mom said it was hard for you when your husband died. She said his children screwed you out of everything, and you just... shut down. She wanted to help, but you didn't respond. She could use your support now... if you're on our side."

Stevie's words hit their mark. Joanne felt as though her insides were twisting. She pressed a hand to her stomach, trying to keep her composure. "Of course, I'm on your side. I was shaken by my husband's death and the losses. I had to start from scratch. I started my own business. You know I teach and do some investigations, right?"

"Mom mentioned something about your stock expertise," Stevie replied more curiously. "I think she told Ed to contact you."

Joanne blinked, surprised. *Ed hadn't contacted me. Maybe I could have helped him.* "I met the agent at a seminar I gave. Please believe that I am on your side. I love you guys. You're family to me."

"I hope that's the case. My mom looked so helpless. I want to trust you. She trusts you. There's so much to deal with right now," said Stevie, finally lowering her shoulders. Joanne could finally breathe as she reached out and lightly rubbed Stevie's arm.

"You ready?" asked Joanne as they walked across the hall. Listening, she noticed it was eerily quiet. They looked at each other quizzically before opening the door. Only Tony was in the room.

"Where is Kay? Is Gram okay?" asked Stevie.

"They went to take care of the dog. She must be terrified," said Tony.

"Gram will be fine," said Stevie.

"Not Gram, the dog. What did the cop have to say? He had no right to barge in here," said Tony.

"Really, Tony? The dog? The detective was here because of Roger Barnes. He's been murdered. Roger was such a lovely man. I wondered why he hadn't been around," said Stevie as she sank into the two-seater couch, letting out the breath she'd been holding in a whoosh.

"What? No, no, no! I gotta go. Please. Gimme the keys to your car. Now, Stevie," Tony said, grabbing Stevie's purse that was next to her.

"Hold on, Tony. What's going on? Do you know something?" asked Joanne as she grabbed at him.

"Ms. Reiner?" said a nurse from the doorway.

"Yes, can I see my mom?" said Stevie, getting up and turning her attention from Tony to the nurse.

"Come this way. Only one, please," said the nurse as Tony reached the door at the same time as Stevie. He had Stevie's keys in his hand. He tossed her purse to Joanne and squeezed past Stevie and the nurse.

Joanne went to grab him, but he was gone. "I'll be here. Go see your mom. Maybe she's awake," said Joanne, scrambling to hold onto the purse. *Better face the music with Jimmy,* she thought, looking down the hall. She spotted Jimmy and motioned to him. He walked slowly toward her. *He's really pissed. Shit.*

"I'm sorry I called you by your first name. I was upset."

"Upset? You were laughing like a hyena," said Jimmy.

"I know. I can't help it; I laugh when I'm upset, even though I know it's inappropriate. What's going on, Jimmy? What can you tell me? Is the family in danger? I know more than you think."

"Really? And what is it you think you know?" Jimmy questioned.

"Okay, this is no longer confidential. I'm doing an investigation into stock fraud, funded by the SEC and NASD. I'm tasked to assist the FBI's investigation of the fraud."

"What's NASD? FBI?" asked Jimmy.

"National Association of Security Dealers," explained Joanne.

"And Wallin is part of this investigation? And you didn't bother to mention this?" said Jimmy.

"It wasn't an investigation when we first started talking. It sort of happened after. Remember I told you I was working on a big job that was good for my career and business? I did tell you I went for some special training. Listen to me, please. Jimmy, we didn't talk much about our work."

"You didn't. You should have told me. You could get me fired or at least demoted. You've put me in a bad position. Now I get all those questions you asked about the type of investigations I did. Damn you, Joanne," said Jimmy as he shook his head.

"It could ruin my investigation as well. Listen, we can stop our...uh, personal association. Then we could work together. Strictly business. Anything you find on Barnes might be useful. He might have had information on the people attached to the stock deal," said Joanne, trying to calm down Jimmy, but instead, just fueled his anger. She waited a beat, paced to the window, and back. "You must know the stock deal with Wallin was dirty by now. I could be helpful. Carol trusts me. His gambling and money must be attached to this. Jimmy, I can help you."

"Detective Perez to you. And stop paging me. You're going to ruin my life."

"Wow, such a drama king. We are adults, Detective Perez—consenting adults. If you don't want my help, fine. I am attached to the FBI in this investigation anyway, so I don't need you," she said, turning and walking back to the windows. *Come on, be reasonable.* Her mind begged.

"And?" asked Jimmy.

Turning back, she said, "I suggest you talk to them about Barnes. They already had some information on him and Wallin which I gather they didn't share with you. And some guy has been hanging around both my place and Carol's. Plus, as I said, there are some things I know that might be helpful. So, don't cooperate…"

Joanne stopped as Stevie came toward them.

"Any news?" asked Joanne.

"I've agreed to let them put her in a coma. I hope I did the right thing. Oh, Aunt Jo Jo. Her face and arms are a mess. She has a splint on her wrist. Something about her spleen. I can't lose her. I can't."

Joanne could tell Stevie was crashing. Her voice was tight and high-pitched. Her face was stripped with shed tears. "Listen, my War Wu, it will be fine. The doctors are taking good care of her. The swelling will go down. She'll be ordering all of you around in no time," said Joanne as she guided Stevie to a chair.

Focusing on Jimmy, Stevie straightened up. "And what are you doing here, Jimmy Boy?"

"I…" mumbled Jimmy.

"He is part of an investigation my company is doing. Please call him Agent Perez. My slip."

"Fine. Get out, Agent Perez," shouted Stevie.

"I'm going," said Jimmy as he went to the door.

***

Jimmy was sick to his stomach. *I'm such a fool. Sal was right. I could jeopardize everything important to me: my wife my life. For what! Stupid fool. Does Dayna even care anymore? I'm still neglecting her. That's partly what drove her to HIM. Perez, you are a fool.* He kept abusing himself from the hospital to the office. Sal was talking with two guys. They looked FBI.

"Hey, Sal. Anything new?" asked Jimmy.

"We'll talk later. I left some notes on your desk for you to review. I need to check something with my CI, Toco. You remember him?" said Sal as he got up and turned to walk out.

"Sal, wait. You said you can't understand him. Now, you don't want my help?"

Blowing out a big breath, Sal said, "Listen. Something big is going down; the fewer people that know, the better. You need to be careful, real careful."

"You seem angry," said Jimmy.

"Did you take care of your personal business? She's hot in more ways than you know. Everyone involved knows her. She's a damn investigator working with the FBI."

"I'm just finding these things out myself. Your wife's nephew works for her."

"Yeah, I thought he was a nice Jersey Italian guy. But nooo. Former NYPD. A PI. Go figure. We're related. We're both being watched. You understand that," blurted Sal in a firm whisper.

"I do now. My head's exploding. Got any aspirin? You've known more about who's involved than I have from the start. It has to do with Miami and New Jersey. Right? Talk to me, Sal."

"Let's go to your car and have a talk. We'll head over to see Toco. He's around where Wallin's wife's accident happened," Sal said softly as he guided Jimmy to the office door.

Seeing Donnie on their way out, Jimmy whispered, "What the hell is he doing there? I still don't trust him."

"Be cool, man. Let's go talk."

They walked briskly to Jimmy's SUV. Jimmy filled him in on what Joanne had revealed about the SEC and NASD. Jimmy asked, "It's the mob, isn't it?"

"Now we both know a lot is going on here. Stock fraud, payoffs, bribes, and a dangerous killer. I'm sure he's a contract killer that may have gotten out of control," explained Sal as they got in the SUV. Sal went over the mob connection as Jimmy drove. He explained how the FBI had been tracking new companies along with the SEC and NASD. He also explained how the mob could violently pressure brokers.

"So, they tasked Joanne to find the fraud," said Jimmy.

"It's highly volatile; many moving parts. No one person seems to have the full picture yet. There are connections we can't see," said Sal.

"It's like you said before about the nylon cord. Other crimes are out there, but no solid connections. We're in the middle of things, aren't we?" asked Jimmy.

"We need to protect ourselves in several ways. First, follow the governor's orders. Find the money trail. Second, be very careful about what you say and to whom. You put others in danger if you give out the wrong information. It may be hard to know what info is hot right now."

"I told Jersey Girl it was over. We both agreed. She told me about her investigation and her connection to the FBI. She wanted a partnership to share info. I see that as one-sided—her benefit only," said Jimmy.

"Don't rule her out. From what I gather, she's well-respected and very knowledgeable about the stock business. Found out that both she and my nephew were trained at Quantico. Keep it strictly business and share cautiously. The guys that were in the office also cautioned that she might be in danger."

"Joanne told me she knew things that could be helpful. I guess that could place her in danger."

"That is why we need to speak to Toco. He's been seen hanging around her place. I think he is keeping an eye on her. Toco seems attracted to Jersey Girl."

"Okay, let's start with him. Jersey Girl—I mean Joanne—said someone was hanging around her place and Carol Wallin's," said Jimmy.

"Right, head over to the overpass to the Crosstown Expressway on Euclid...a step up from the overpasses in Ybor," said Sal.

"Yeah, better neighborhood, better trash. He doesn't add up. Maybe we should press him," said Jimmy.

Jimmy saw that Sal was lost in thought. As they went from downtown through the nicer neighborhoods, Jimmy tried to stay calm by appreciating the history around him. The older mansions of Hyde Park were well-preserved, and the surrounding neighborhoods were getting their facelifts. There were still cobblestone streets that added to the charm.

"How do you want to play this?" asked Jimmy.

"I don't want to spook him. Let him ramble. If he knows something or needs to warn us, the clues will be in the details he decides to share," answered Sal.

As the SUV pulled under the overpass, Jimmy noticed a figure hiding around the west side of the concrete support. The person almost looked like a large bush. An arm moved out from the support and motioned them over. Both Jimmy and Sal inspected their surroundings as they exited and locked the vehicle.

"Man, man, man, this is big, this is big. Got any food? Money? Jersey girl got something—oh yeah, she's somethin'. Bonita. Curvilinea. Jersey's hombre barriendo, barriendo en la casa…oh yeah. Mira, mira me. Jersey girl takes somethin' from Tech lady's car. The guy who hit also know a Jersey. Oh yeah. Grande, accidente no accidente. El hijo del esposo no me gusta lady," said Toco, jumping around.

"Stand still, man. I can't understand you when…" said Sal.

"Algo grande sucederá pronto. Peligro! Peligro! Tengo comida? Dinero?" Toco was now dancing in a circle.

"Stand still!" shouted Sal, handing Toco a twenty.

"Gotta go, gotta go. Mira, mira me," Toco shouted before running off.

"Stop, asshole!" yelled Jimmy, but it was too late.

"No sense in chasing him right now. Toco can sure squeeze a lot of info in a few crazy sentences," said Sal as they settled back in the SUV.

"Ok, sucederá...happen. I think he means something big will happen. Let's see what else?" said Jimmy.

Sal cranked up the car's AC while Jimmy made notes.

Squeezing his eyes shut in forced concentration Jimmy asked, "What else? Someone other than Toco is watching both women and Toco. Joanne, aka Jersey Girl, took something from Carol Wallin's car. I think your wife's nephew is Jersey's hombre.

"That could be right. There's more than one Jersey. Maybe Joanne...or even the killer. Why do you think it's Benny, Joanne's partner?" asked Sal.

"Barriendo means sweeping. Bet he means removing bugs from the house. Makes sense that Benny would do that, which means someone is bugging the house. Probably Carol Wallin's as well. Anything I missed?" asked Jimmy.

"He also said the accident was not an accident. We need to check to see who else was involved," said Sal.

"Loosely translated from his Spanglish, he said the son of the husband doesn't like the lady. And maybe was involved in the accident. That's Eddy, Carol's husband's son. I'm sure of it. But the accident seems to be the least of our worries unless she's hurt worse than we think. I need to check in with Donnie and Jersey Girl."

"Remember to be careful about what you say to whom and what you do if you get my drift. Loose lips sink ships, and open flies attract crying eyes."

"Aren't you a fucking poet," said Jimmy as Sal got out of the SUV and headed for his car.

Chapter 14

Joanne sniffed the empty, burnt coffee pot and groaned. The ringing phone distracted her. "Jimmy, I'm surprised you called. Carol is holding her own, but there's been no change yet. You sound stressed." *Little boy is still pissed because I didn't tell him everything.*

"If you need to talk, you can come by later this evening. I want to spend as much time as I can with the girls. Yes, I can be available this afternoon. Fine, I'll come by the FDLE office if we must be formal. Men!" shouted Joanne as she hung up on Jimmy.

She walked over to the kitchen window. *Who the hell is that?* she thought, turning back toward the phone to dial Benny.

"It's me. I think that same bum is hanging around my yard again. Yeah, the one I saw outside of Carol's. Good. Check him out more carefully. Should I unlock my gun? Sal knows him? Really?" As she continued listening, she took ice from the fridge, dropped it into the pot, and swirled it around. Joanne kept swirling the ice to loosen the burnt coffee stuck to the bottom. She listened as Benny explained as much as he knew about the connection between Sal and the bum hanging around her house.

"Oh, she's still in a coma. I'm worried about her. No, I won't carry the gun to the hospital," Joanne said as she stretched the phone's long spiral cord to place the coffee pot in the sink. She knew she shouldn't have mentioned the gun. *He hates that I bought one. Seems to think I need a gun safety lesson each time I mention it.*

"Benny, I'm not a child. Stop telling me what to do. See if you can check this guy out. Use your connections." *Should I tell him how pissed Jimmy is? He'll give me another lecture.*

"What? Oh, you got a call from your uncle, Sal?" Joanne's mind raced. Guess the meeting at the FDLE is important. "I got a call from Jimmy, who is still angry with me." *Hope I haven't ruined everything.*

"Maybe we should meet and decide what to say right now. Okay! You can meet me at the hospital around 2:00."

Seeing the black residue still clinging to the bottom of the pot, Joanne added more ice and kept swirling, hoping to get the burnt coffee to release. *It's like trying to let go of my stained past,* she thought. She was finally starting to feel at home in Tampa. *Carol and the girls are here. I need a family. Without Mom and all my aunts and uncles, I'm adrift.* Benny had even found a condo he liked.

Maybe she could find something in Hyde Park. Maybe the guy who owns this place will sell it to me. I mustn't screw up this contract.

Her business is doing well. She could finally afford her own place. No more pretending. Her father's suicide when she was a child left deep scars, always trying to be someone she wasn't. Her tragedies, however, could help Carol and the girls now. She had experienced pain. They could lean on her if necessary. Carol was strong, and so was Stevie. Kay, though younger, was so kind that the cruelty around her would be tough to bear. Yes, it was time to start again.

Joanne loved being an investigator. It fit her nosy, Italian upbringing. In her family, everyone knew everything about everyone. She smiled, thinking of her mother and her aunts gossiping about family members. It wasn't ever mean. It was their way of knowing how to help—giving clothes, money, and most of all, food. She loved how they would slip a ten, twenty, or even a hundred-dollar bill into someone's purse or jacket and share that knowing look. Her mother had done it for her the last time she saw her. Oh, how she missed her. *What had Mom said when they* spoke *after Big Wasp's death?* "Per nozze e lutto—si lascia tutto. *For weddings and mourning, one leaves everyone behind.*"

Now, her mom was gone, too. Losing her was so hard.

Letting go—that's always the hard part. She ached for Carol and the girls. Losing her mom and seeing Carol's struggles reminded her of how stupid it had been to let jealousy keep her away from them. How stupid. Carol was her best friend. She stuck by her at the worst of times. She loved the girls. It wasn't Carol's fault that she signed a prenup to catch her Big Wasp. All his money went to his kids from his first marriage. They didn't/wouldn't give her a dime. She thought she loved him, but JoJo was a poor Italian Jersey girl. *Silly girl, this pity party is over. Time to heal and move on. Take a shower*, JoJo. She mumbled, "*Tesoro*, mi *stelino. I'm always my mom's treasure and a little star.*"

"Good grief, poor Carol, she was no one's treasure. Certainly not her mother's, " Joanne mumbled as she stepped into the shower.

After rummaging through her closet and selecting an outfit, Joanne gave herself a knowing look in the mirror. She wasn't dressing for Carol or the girls. She couldn't help wanting to look good for Detective Perez. *Stupid ego.* She felt embarrassed that she had seduced him. She had played a role, knowing he was vulnerable. He had mentioned how his wife's family had money and invested in stocks. He felt like the poor black/Cuban kid who wasn't good enough. She had played on that. He was guilty, too.

She was vulnerable as well. Her marriage had been so cold for years before Big Wasp died. Her longing was palatable. *Time for me to grow up and for him to grow a pair.* Joanne grabbed her purse but then decided to stash Carol's big bag in her trunk to give it to Benny before talking to Jimmy about it. She didn't trust leaving it in her house, not with that bum hanging around. *Who knows who he is?*

The hospital wasn't far, but it gave her time to mentally organize a task list. She was good at keeping things organized without leaving a paper trail, a skill that came in handy for tricky investigations. The ICU area was quiet. Joanne had stopped at Subway, picking up sandwiches and drinks for everyone. Stevie, Jan, and Kay were in the waiting room outside the ICU. The space felt *sterile and cold.*

"Hey, guys, any news?"

"The doctor says she's improving. Glad you're here. Lisa will be by around 3 or 4. I'm going to run to my office for a bit to put out a minor fire," said Jan as she stood.

"Thanks for coming. You don't have to sit around with us," said Kay.

"Don't be silly. I want to be here," said Joanne.

"We all do," she added, laying out the sandwiches on the small round table in the room. "Common War Wo and Kickum Kay, try to get some food down. I got Dr. Pepper for you, Kay. Still your favorite?"

Stevie and Kay surrounded Joanne, their arms tight around her as their tears soaked into her shoulders. They stood holding each other for a time.

"Big breaths now, you guys. Good news any minute," Joanne whispered.

"Are you Mrs. Wallin's family?" the nurse asked as she entered the room. "She's awake, asking to see her daughters. The doctor is with her."

"Yes, yes. Wonderful news!" the girls cheered.

"Go on, bring back all the facts. I'm right here," said Joanne.

"With that good news, I'm going to shower and rest," said Jan.

"Sounds like a plan. You're a great friend to Carol. I know she appreciates you. I'll be here until Lisa comes," said Joanne as she sifted through her purse. Benny entered the room, scanning the space.

"Where's everyone?" he asked.

"Carol's awake. The girls are with her and the doctor. Do you have any information for me?" asked Joanne.

"Lots. Let's start slow with the FBI. Your buddy Jimmy has been busy asking questions about Wallin's stock deals. We need to close the loop around the lawyer, Charles Atoll before his other dealings take precedence and get buried by the State of Florida's investigation."

Benny examined the sandwiches before picking one.

"The lawyer's a piece of work. Talked to my uncle, Sal. He hinted we might want to tell him about you, Carol, and the accident."

"That's starting slow?" Joanne raised her eyebrows. "I have all the tapes in the trunk of my car. Didn't want to risk leaving them at the house. Time to give them up," she said, handing Benny her car keys.

"We need to be careful here. I think he was warning me," said Benny.

"You're right. Getting caught up in obstruction by the FBI, FDLE, or the locals would not be prudent. We need to give the tapes to the FBI and let them deal with the FDLE. What else do I need to know now? I want to be ready for the FDLE interview. We're both there at 4, right?"

"Yep. I brought that summary report we made on Barnes. I collated all the FBI reports into a neat summary for the FDLE. Cleaned up some details like a post-mortem. I'm getting good at this computer stuff—it'll look like you prepared it just for the FDLE, not just the FBI."

"We did. I did. Well…never gave it to the FDLE. We did warn the FBI about Barnes knowing too much about the SEC case, and I was preparing a more thorough report. He is such a tragedy. I told them what you said about the New Jersey boys being in town and that Barnes could be in danger," said Joanne.

Benny's face darkened. "Listen, they didn't just murder him, Jo. They tortured him. The FDLE and FBI know by now I talked with him. I even went to Ocala."

Joanne shivered at the thought as she reviewed the report Benny handed her.

"Everyone knows we're working with the SEC, NASD, and the FBI now. We'll need to bring the FDLE up to date. Our involvement might work in our favor to keep us safe. I'm telling you. A couple of nasty dudes are out there. Be careful, okay?" warned Benny.

Joanne nodded. "Anything else in this report I need to be aware of?"

"I included everything I know about the Jersey connection. I think I saw them in a car the night of the break-in, but it was dark, and there were a lot of big cars in that neighborhood. We should both mention them again."

Benny's eyes met Joanne's. "Also, no one wants Carol to know about Barnes. Not yet."

"Damn. More secrets," Joanne muttered. "We need to be careful about the break-in. Technically, we should've said something sooner, but those tapes would get Carol in trouble, too."

"What trouble?" Kay asked as she entered the room.

Benny and Joanne quickly turned, trying to look casual.

"Aunt JoJo, what do you know?" Kay pressed. "Tony's been asking about papers and tapes, but Mom's been evasive. He was only trying to help. He's smart and knows about Ed's gambling issues. He even helped Ed get some loans."

Joanne stood and put her arms around Kay, trying to soothe her. She led her to a seat and handed her a soda as Kay continued to ramble.

"Tony's the only one Ed Jr. talks to. He's been trying to protect the family. He told me Ed owed some bad people money."

"I know, sweetie," Joanne whispered, tightening her arm around Kay's shoulder.

Kay's voice trembled. "I'm so worried. Did they hurt Mom? Uncle Roger? Or Ed? Tony ran out of here, according to Stevie, and he hasn't been back. I'm scared, too."

Joanne guided her to a small sofa. "Kicky, no. My Kickum Kay, don't worry about anything. My friend and co-worker, Benny here will find Tony, won't you?" Joanne said, glancing at Benny. "He used to be a policeman. Look at him—big, tough, right? He'll take care of this. Won't you, Benny."

"On it! Are these your extra set of car keys?" Benny said as he walked to the door.

"Yes, I brought them with me. You can keep those. Do a thorough sweep. I'll see you at 4:00." said Joanne as she turned back to Kay. "Now, how's your mom?"

"She's got cuts and bruises all over her face and arms. Her one arm, well wrist, is in a cast. Some loss of hearing in her left ear. But she's fully out of the coma, and the doctor said the swelling is gone. I thought airbags were supposed to help."

"They do, but not completely, sweetie. She's strong, and she'll heal."

"Oh, she wants to talk with you. She said it's important. Stevie told them you're her stepsister, so you can visit. Do you think Tony's okay?"

"I'm sure he's fine. I'll talk with your mom. Then I have to head over to the FDLE. They need a statement from me for a case I'm investigating."

"Is this about the stocks? Tony knows a lot about stocks," Kay added, her concern evident.

Joanne's thoughts raced. *Poor thing is so in love with that guy. I'm going to break her heart. Damn.*

"Your mom's friend Lisa will be here around 4. I'll be back after my meeting. Can I bring you anything special? We still have sandwiches and drinks. Oh, what's happening with your grandmother?"

Joanne got up, fixed a plate with a sandwich, and grabbed a drink, handing them to Kay.

"She's fine. Tony bought her some excellent single malt scotch. We'd gone to four stores and brought almost 300 dollars' worth of her kind of food.

Joanne laughed. "I'm sure she's cooking up a storm and drinking away."

"Yeah, she was cleaning out the fridge when I left. She and Louise should be set," mumbled Kay with a mouthful of sandwich. "Tell Stevie to come back here and eat something. I think all she had was vending food."

"Your Gram is certainly a piece of work. I'm off to see your Mom. Did you see your Black and White cookies? Be sure to save one for your sister," Joanne said as she gathered her things. *Such good kids. I hope I can protect them. It feels so right to be with them and Carol. Damn, why did I wait so long to be with my other family?*

"I hear you're looking for attention," Joanne teased as she entered Carol's hospital room.

Stevie rose and hugged her tightly. "Go grab a sandwich before you pass out again. That's an order," Joanne said to Stevie as they ended their embrace.

"You better listen," Carol croaked from the bed.

"You know she'll get out of that bed to feed you if you don't," Joanne joked, squeezing Stevie's shoulder.

"Going, going. I'll eat; I promise," said Stevie and blew a kiss to her mom.

"Hey there, girl. Don't strain yourself. Let me talk. I've got your purse and all the tapes from the accident. I know where your car is and can get into the trunk. You relax and focus on getting better. I'll take care of this."

For a moment, the room was silent. Joanne gathered her thoughts knowing Carol would wait patiently.

"I do have to speak with the FDLE and the FBI eventually, especially if there's anything stock-related. You know that, right? I'd never betray you, but if I don't reveal certain things, it could get messier. It's my business. You and the girls are my family. I love you all."

Carol seemed to hold her breath as Joanne talked. With a labored burst of air, she said, "Do it, do whatever it takes to protect the girls. But don't—don't talk to Charles Atoll. Don't let him near the girls. On the tape, Ed said Charles had a gun. Oh god, the tape in the player," she said hoarsely.

"Easy, easy. Okay. Charles Atoll. He had a gun?"

"On the tape, he was pointing it at Ed."

"Good to know. I know all about his stock manipulations—now this. Got it. Listen, I'll do everything in my power to help. You can rest easy. I will find the damn tape. Nothing, I repeat, nothing will happen to the girls. But is it okay if I let the authorities have your mom?"

Carol snorted, almost managing a smile. She squeezed Joanne's hand and mouthed, "Thank you."

"Your job is to get better. Between Jan, Lisa, and me, the girls are covered. There's so much I want to talk with you about. I know you have questions. *I hate that I'm hurting this family.*"

Carol nodded weakly, her eyes still filled with pain and uncertainty.

"We haven't really discussed my business," Joanne continued, her voice soft but firm. "I want to be clear with you. You already know I'm an instructor for stocks and finance, but there's more to it. The consulting side of my business involves working with the SEC and other agencies. And to be completely honest, I had a... dalliance with Agent Perez before all this mess. He attended one of my seminars when I first arrived about six months ago. But it's over now. I swear!"

Joanne paused, watching Carol carefully. Carol nodded again, so she continued.

"We never really talked about that, and I don't want you to worry. My investigations include Ed and all his business dealings. I'm coordinating with the FBI and, in this case, the FDLE."

"Go on," Carol said, her voice barely above a whisper, but her tone urged Joanne to continue.

"No, no, don't stress," Joanne replied quickly, noticing Carol's heart monitor beeping faster. "I can see the monitor spiking. I know you had no part in any of the stock issues. We'll nail Mr. Big Shot— Charles Atoll. Okay? Got it. I'm sorry for bringing all of this up now, but I need to be open with you."

"Tony? Eddy?" Carol said, her voice cracking as she struggled to speak.

Joanne hesitated, then sighed. "I may not be able to protect them. I'll do my best, but Tony... I know he's important to the family. Please, rest now."

Before Carol could respond, the nurse entered the room, her face tight with concern. "Rest indeed. I don't like this elevated blood pressure and heartbeat. You need to go," the nurse said firmly.

"You're right," Joanne replied, glancing one last time at Carol. "I'm going for now. The girls are here. Lisa is with them. I brought them food, and Kay told me your mother also made a lot of food. Look on the bright side—your house will be spotless."

Carol gave a weak smile. "Keep me informed," she whispered.

"I will. I'm going," Joanne said, letting the nurse direct her out of the room. As Joanne walked down the hallway, she felt a wave of relief wash over her. "This is better. So much better," she murmured to herself, stepping into the empty elevator.

When she reached her car, she realized she had been holding back tears. Now, in the quiet space of her car, she let them fall, finally releasing the tension that had built up over the past few hours. Relief surged through her—relief that Carol was going to be okay, that she had finally been open about her investigation into Ed, and that things seemed to be moving forward.

But now, she had to face Jimmy again. *Benny warned that things were dangerous*, she reminded herself, as she wiped her eyes. *So many kinds of danger swirl around me.*

Her mind raced, considering her next steps. *I wonder if I'll have time to get into Carol's car.* Then, a new thought hit her. *Maybe Jimmy can facilitate it.*

Chapter 15

s Joanne walked up to the reception area of the FDLE, her stomach lurched. Donnie Castillo was heading toward her. *Shit, what did he tell Jimmy? Does he know about me and Jimmy? My damn horny self could ruin everything.*

"Hey, Donnie, doing your best FBI co-op thing? What's going on?" she asked.

"Well, the investigation is heating up. Thanks for the report. You warned me about Barnes. I should have listened. I told the FDLE Agent that."

"Oh, good. What did they say?" Joanne asked, holding her breath.

"Not much. They seemed annoyed with you—at least, Jimmy Perez did for some reason."

"Really? Can't imagine why," Joanne said in a rush, her voice almost betraying her. *Stay calm, girl. He's just testing the waters.*

"You can trust the FDLE agents. They're good, and they're smart. Just tell them whatever you know."

"Can I assume they are fully briefed on my involvement and assignment? Have they been tasked as well?" Joanne asked, trying to maintain control of the conversation.

"I told Sal Carducci some of it. He then briefed Jimmy Perez. I know you know them, so let's not play games. Sal will finish tasking you when you meet with him."

"Benny and I report to Sal?"

"No, everyone reports to me. Sal will give directions based on my orders. I told the SEC that their investigation is not our priority. Since you and Benny have been fully vetted through the FBI, everyone has agreed I can assign you tasks that are necessary to our priorities."

"No problem, but if I might ask—who signs the checks?" Joanne asked with a slight smirk.

"The same process. All expenses get approved by me. For the next ten days, we'll pay your daily rate. We'll see after that."

"Benny and I have worked this routine before," Joanne assured him.

"We've got to get the guys behind all this nastiness. We will find Barnes's killer. If our SEC deal gets blown, so be it. Don't be late for the Task Force meeting. Sal has the details."

Joanne's stomach churned with anxiety, but she forced herself to maintain eye contact as she fumbled in her purse for some antacids. "I hope our information will be useful."

"I'll be sharing your insights with the group. Remember, the murders take precedence."

"Murders? More than Barnes?" Joanne asked, her heart racing.

"There seems to be a pattern forming from some previous mob-related incidents. We'll talk," Donnie said as he turned and walked away.

Joanne's mouth was still agape when Jimmy came up to her. "Mrs. Douglas? Please put on this badge and come this way. Mrs. Douglas? This way, please."

"What? So formal, Agent Perez," said Joanne. They remained silent during the elevator ride and the walk to the FDLE offices. Once inside a small interrogation room, Jimmy broke the silence.

"So, you know Agent Castillo," Jimmy said, settling into a chair.

"Donnie Castillo? Yes," Joanne replied.

"You were seen taking something from Carol Wallin's car. Care to explain?"

"About what?" Joanne asked, playing innocent.

"Are you going to make this difficult, one-word answers and all? I do know about your relationship with the FBI," Jimmy said, his voice tightening.

"Jimmy—or should I say Detective Perez—am I a suspect? Should you and I even be talking?" Joanne shot back.

"Sal will be here in a moment. I just wanted to make it clear-"

"Trust me, I'm clear," Joanne said as the door opened. Sal stood in the doorway with Benny behind him.

"This room is too small for this conversation," said Sal.

"It's time we talk you through what we know as professional investigators for the SEC, assigned to the FBI for an investigation of Wallin and Atoll," said Benny as Joanne stood.

Jimmy looked at Sal, who was motioning toward the door with a nod of his head. "Let's go, Jimbo. Just as you suspected, this is bigger—and even more dangerous—than we thought," Sal said.

Once they settled into the large conference room, Joanne took the lead, doing most of the talking. She laid out the SEC issues, the case they had, the hard and soft evidence they'd gathered, and the people they'd been watching. She hardly took a breath until she was finished. "There, that covers most of the background."

"So, you knew all of this for months?" Jimmy asked.

"Before you start asking questions, read our reports to the FBI," Joanne responded, pulling copies from her briefcase. *Guess my instinct to bring those copies may pay off.*

For the next twenty minutes, the only noise in the room came from the pages turning and Jimmy scribbling notes. Joanne cleared her throat and hesitated before speaking again.

"Oh yes, there is a cassette tape in the car Carol was driving. I'm not sure what it says, but Carol Wallin said it may implicate Charles Atoll in something. Please don't read anything into her not giving it to you. She found it after the fact and just wanted to listen to it before she gave it to you. We were going to listen to it together, but she put it in her car's tape player on her way to my place."

"So, you withheld evidence from me?" Jimmy's tone was sharp.

"Oh, for heaven's sake, Detective, don't pout. It's unbecoming. We didn't even know what was on the tape," Joanne snapped back. "Ed left some tapes in an upstairs closet on the floor. She didn't even know it was there," retorted Joanne.

"Like how you didn't tell me you were working with the FBI?" Jimmy asked pointedly.

"Enough! This is not productive," Sal interrupted. "Benny, do you have anything constructive to add?"

"Yes," Benny began. "I've been trying to keep tabs on many of the key players involved in all this chaos—Carol Wallin, Ed Wallin Jr., Tony LaNina, Roger Barnes, Charles Atoll, and, of course, your, as I found out, informant, Toco…is that his name?"

"That's what he prefers," Sal confirmed.

"As our report states, we've already handed all the information to the FBI. We've been working with them for months, even before Ed died," repeated Joanne.

Jimmy's demeanor had now seemed changed from annoyed to intrigued by all the information. His head was slightly cocked to the left as he looked from Joanne to Benny, then turning and moving his head to the right, he looked at Sal and said very quietly. "You knew most of this, didn't you?"

Sal nodded. "Some of it, yes. Some I only suspected. As far as anything that Benny was doing, I just found out specifics today. From my wife and a few friends, I knew Benny was a detective with NYPD on the streets and undercover. Left when one of his own blew his cover on purpose."

"Not part of the case," Benny said, throwing Sal a hard look.

"Neither is the fact that I went through special training at Quantico along with Benny because of the type of characters we encounter," Joanne added.

"Our role has changed, and I suspect yours has as well," said Jimmy as he straightened all the papers and tapes.

"We are all on special assignment with the FBI task force," Sal explained. "There's a meeting at 7 tonight. As I understand it from Donnie, there are three areas of investigation. The primary is this: the killer and their associates. Next is stock fraud and public corruption, as well as any involvement by the Mafia. Third is tying in Wallin's involvement, including his son, son-in-law, and other family connections."

Jimmy nodded and then glanced at Joanne, who returned the look before shifting her eyes to Benny.

"Can we all work together?" Sal asked.

Everyone glanced at each other before breaking into smiles. "Of course," Joanne said to the group. The oxygen levels in the room shrank as everyone took a deep breath. You could almost feel the temperature shift, along with their attitudes.

"We have got a few hours before the task force meeting," said Sal. "Let's not give the FBI any reason to doubt our competence.

Too much is at stake—for all of us and the people involved. Joanne, you seem to have an overview of this; where should we start?"

"I'd suggest you and Benny get the tape out of Carol's car, and we listen to it. Did Donnie leave any information? If so, I think Jimmy and I should review that," Joanne said, then paused. "Is Jimmy ok, or do you prefer Detective Perez?"

"Donnie left a box on my desk. It's full of papers, some spreadsheets, and those tapes you mentioned. We can split up the contents. Jimmy is fine."

"I usually go by Carducci or Carduch, but Sal works too. Joanne? Benny? Everybody good? Let's stop fucking around and get to work. Come on, Benny," Sal said with a nod toward the door.

"BTW, this conference room is ours until the task force disbands," Sal continued. "Joanne, you can set up here. Does that work for you?"

"Yeah, I can live with that. Why don't we bring the box in here?" Joanne replied. "Oh yeah, Benny, explain to Sal and Jimmy about the type of bugs you found. And it's time to get clarification on Toco. When we talk to Donnie, you take the lead," Joanne instructed Sal.

The tension in the room began to dissipate as Jimmy and Joanne got into an easy working mode. Their previous attraction and intimacy seemed to add value to their interactions. They understood each other's movements and flow. Joanne made notes while Jimmy moved between his computer and the conference room, cross-checking details. They were both engrossed in reviewing typed notes when Sal and Benny returned more than an hour later, tape machine in hand.

Benny entered first, holding the machine, and Sal followed with an extension cord.

"What took so long? The impound lot is not that far," Jimmy asked.

"Had to stop by technical," Sal replied. "The tape in the deck was unraveled. They are working on it now, but we found another one wedged under the seat in the back of the car. I asked one of the guys to catalog all the tapes when they get the chance. In the meantime, we can start with this one." He looked toward Joanne.

"Oh good, the tapes may give us some insight into who this killer might be," Joanne said. "Carol was just looking for answers about her husband's suicide."

Sal gave her a knowing look. "No worries, Joanne, I understand what you were trying to do. You were wrong, but I get it. You get a pass for now. I'm not going to mention anything specific to Donnie. Found them on the floor on the passenger side of the car. You intended to hand them over today. Gave them to the FBI because of your relationship. That's the story, okay? All good?"

"Yes. Thanks, Sal. I just—" Joanne started, but Sal cut her off by raising his hand.

"Let's listen to this tape first and see where we go from there. Agreed?"

Everyone moved their heads like bobblehead dolls as Benny inserted the tape into the machine and pressed play. The room fell silent, with all eyes on the recorder.

Clearing of a throat, scratching sounds, papers moving, soft curses, squeaking of the recorder. A crack of thunder, distant rain

"What's that sound?" asked a voice on the tape.

"Rain, lightning. Thunder?" another voice replied.

"No, the squeak."

"It's just my chair. Just be quiet and let me read these corporate papers. Are you sure this is the best course of action? *I don't* get *why Eddy and Tony have to be involved."*

"You don't get it, do you? Eddy and Tony want money. Eddy because he's greedy, and Tony wants to prove something to his wife and your precious Carol."

"Carol is the most understanding woman you'll ever meet. You don't like her because she sees right through you. I should have listened to her about you."

Sal paused the tape. "Looks like Wallin was taping his meetings with Atoll, at least at the beginning, without his knowledge." He pressed play again.

"Well, it would have been better if you just stopped gambling. Just read and sign those papers. The stock hype is all set. The boiler room is set up a little north of Tampa in a new office park. Everything looks nice and legitimate. We'll move everything to Ybor once the crash comes."

"I don't like this."

"Too bad. You straight on which buildings that you and the City Council condemned that need to be purchased. We'll use the cash the New Jersey guys gave us. And don't be stupid. The cash is just for the purchase of the buildings. If you gamble any of that money, you die. You understand that, right?"

The tape went on about the stock deal and corporate business for another fifteen minutes. The group was transfixed, hanging on every word between the two men. Jimmy reached over and stopped the player, causing the others to jolt as if they'd been startled by the rain on the tape.

"Sorry. I thought we should jot down some notes before continuing. The tape doesn't sound like it's in good shape," Jimmy explained. "Joanne, you know the players best. Would you confirm the voices as Atoll and Ed?"

"Yup, bossy asshole is Charles Atoll, and the other one is Ed Wallin. My experience tells me that would be clear to a judge. They're just backing up what I already have on the pump-and-dump scheme. I'm determined to nail Mr. Charles Asstole."

The tape continued with more scratching sounds, Ed humming, and papers being shuffled. After about ten more minutes, Sal stopped the recorder and closed his notebook.

"Remember, we have a murderer to catch. That's the priority right now. This murderer is here in our town wreaking havoc. I know we want to nail Atoll for the stock stuff and any involvement in public fraud. But now it's better to catch him hiring the mob monster."

"How did Atoll get so deep with the Mafia?" Jimmy asked as he stretched.

"As I understand it, it dates to a bank scandal here in Tampa back in '92. I was undercover at the time in Jersey and Miami. Of course, that investigation was so messed up that the prosecution couldn't make their case stick," Sal explained.

"I heard about that mess from my husband," Joanne added as she stood and rubbed her lower back.

"Atoll was one of the guys arrested along with the mayor's husband. But when the wiretaps got tossed out by the judge, the case fell apart," Sal continued.

"Were you involved in that?" Jimmy asked, still stretching.

"I heard some of the conversations from the tapes," Sal replied. "I think the bank was laundering money for the Trafficantes, but nothing was ever proven."

"We're definitely on the right track," Joanne said. "Jimmy and I have almost finished reviewing the other tapes. They are just as damning, covering stock fraud and bribes. The spreadsheets are a bit confusing, though."

"I think Jimmy and I should decide what to say to the FBI. Why don't you and Benny check on the Wallins? I'm concerned about them, but we don't want to alarm them," Sal suggested. "You want answers. You do, too. Right? Don't let your relationship get in the way, or you might end up with a warrant in your name."

"No worries, I want what we all want. First to catch the killer…I got it," said Joanne as they all stood up, gathering their belongings. She tossed her keys to Benny. "You drive."

"We'll meet back here at 6:15," Sal said. "We'll go over everything and then head over to the Feds."

At street level, Joanne and Benny headed in one direction while Jimmy and Sal went the other.

Chapter 16

———— • ● • ————

"**Please** leave me at the entrance to the hospital. You should check Wallin's house before parking the car," said Joanne.

"I'll take a quick sniff around the outside, but the old lady is a problem if I try to do more," replied Benny.

"You could tell her that Carol sent you to pick up some food. It would be easier if everyone was in one place, but I seriously doubt she'd get in a car with you or let you in. Don't be offended if she slams the door in your face, goombah," Joanne yelled over her shoulder as she walked to the hospital door.

Joanne smiled, but her insides churned as she entered the ICU's private waiting room.

"How's your mom? Is Kay with her?" Joanne asked Stevie. She nodded at Lisa, who was holding Stevie's hand. *Carol had loving friends in Jan and Lisa. They were* always *there for her. I need to step up,* Joanne thought.

"Kay went to the gift shop to buy Mom some flowers. She needs to do something besides just sitting around. Did you find Tony? We're worried about him," Stevie said, standing to hug Joanne.

"Everyone's working on this, Stevie. Focus on your mom," Joanne whispered into her ear.

"There's food left. I put it in the kitchen area across the hall. Want something?" asked Lisa.

"That would be great. How about you, Stevie? What have you eaten?" Joanne asked.

"I had a sandwich and my black & white cookie. That was so nice of you, JoJo. Please, tell me what's going on. Where could Tony be? Why isn't he here?"

"Detective Perez is working on that. We all are. For now, tell me about your mom."

"She got better, then had trouble breathing again. She seems better now, but they're keeping a close watch. Someone important-looking in a suit came by and said they were keeping her in the ICU, and no one was allowed except family. Mr. Atoll came by with some guy before that, but they wouldn't let him in. He was pissed."

"Who was the guy with Mr. Atoll? Did you recognize him? What did he look like?"

"Why? Is he important? I don't know, I didn't look at him. Umm, he was white, small like Mr. Atoll. He wasn't husky, thin. It was a quick look, but something about his eyes."

"What color hair? Any facial hair?" asked Joanne.

"No facial hair. Blond. You're scaring me, Aunt JoJo. Is this guy dangerous?"

Joanne gently smiled and said, "Sorry, my warrior women. Breathe. Hands on your hips, chin up. Remember your strength. Anything else you remember?"

"He wore white sneakers. Weird?"

"Sneakers, okay. Good. Now gather everything up, say goodbye to your mom, and take charge of the home front. Your mom is well cared for and fully protected. There'll be security outside the house as a precaution, but you keep everyone calm and focused. Got it?"

"I'm good. I'm my mother's daughter. We're strong and capable."

"You're right. By the way, do you know the man's name—the one with the ID who spoke with your mom?" Joanne asked.

"Donnie Castle—no, Castillo, I think. He did show an ID, but I didn't look at it. He started to give me his card but got distracted. Kay said he was talking with Mom when she started having trouble breathing. Anyway, he's gone now. He had another person with him, and he was sitting in a waiting area around here. What's going on? Do you know?"

"Not fully, sweetie. I'm sure everyone is doing everything they can to keep things under control. Lisa, you're good staying with the girls, right?"

"Absolutely. Stevie, why don't you clean up here," Lisa suggested.

"I'll take care of the food in the fridge with Lisa," said Joanne as she and Lisa walked across the hall to the kitchen.

"What's up?" asked Lisa when they were alone in the kitchen.

"Things are somewhat dangerous right now. I can't explain fully, but it would be helpful if everyone was in one place so we could keep track of them," Joanne said.

"You mean protect them, don't you?" Lisa pressed.

"Yes, I do," Joanne admitted.

"Not a problem. I'll take Stevie and Kay home. Tell me, Joanne, what's your role here?" asked Lisa.

"I'm a friend. I love Carol and the girls. I also work with the FBI and the SEC," Joanne stated.

"Is Carol in trouble with the SEC? She was never involved in Ed's mess. Kay's husband was, and so was his son. They're the ones in trouble, aren't they?" asked Lisa.

"I can't get into all the details. I know you and Jan always support them. I've been a lousy friend to Carol these last few years. Please, sit a moment."

Joanne hesitated. *How much should I tell her?* she wondered. *Carol trusts her, so I will. Girl to Girl.* "I was too stuck in my misery, trying to start my business and make a living, dealing with my own husband's death and all the garbage that came with it."

Lisa listened and placed a hand over Joanne's.

"You do know I have their best interests at heart. I'll keep them informed as best as I can. Okay?" said Joanne.

"Okay, first things first. Do you know anything about Tony or Eddy?" Lisa asked.

"Kay is strong, but Tony and Eddy are going to face some troubles. Just be there for them as best you can. Don't tell the guys or any of the family anything if you talk to or see them," Joanne warned.

"Don't worry about that. I'll stay close. So will Jan," said Lisa.

"If you do see Tony or Eddy, call me immediately. Here's my card. It has my number and the big guy's, Benny's. Carol knows Tony and Eddy are in trouble."

"Got it."

They stood and hugged. *Should have known Carol's friends would be understanding and loyal like she is.* Grabbing Lisa's arm, she warned, "Under no circumstances should Mr. Atoll be anywhere near them or talk with them. Best if you control the home phone if you can. Contributing to their worries won't help anyone. You know this, I'm sorry. Giving orders is a weakness. Do what you can, and I'll do what I can. There will be police and FBI around."

After Lisa left, Joanne opened a sandwich and took a small bite, thinking about her life. She was grateful for Benny. *He's a big guy but surprisingly fast. What was he? Six two, three? Light on his feet and, like a boxer, always ready for the next punch.*

She sat down for a while, nibbling on the sandwich, and closed her eyes, trying to chase away the worries. When she got up and approached the drink machine, she saw Benny passing by.

"You're back from Carol's already? Stevie asked about Tony. She said Atoll was here with someone. Also, Donnie was here and left someone. Did you find anything out?" Joanne asked.

Benny grabbed her sandwich, took a bite, and then, after finishing chewing, said, "There's trouble coming. I got a bad feeling on my way to Wallin's place, so I came back."

"What is it? You've always had a sixth sense for trouble," said Joanne, searching his eyes and looking around.

"Just a bad feeling. I can almost smell the killer. Did you get a description of the guy with Atoll? We need to get it to Donnie and Sal," Benny said, taking another bite of the sandwich.

"Did you talk with Donnie? Stevie said he spoke to Carol before he stopped and talked with her."

"I saw Donnie leaving when I dropped you off. I talked with him briefly. He mentioned he spoke with Carol. Not sure how much he told her. I don't think he mentioned Barnes. He did leave one of his team members, Al Fernandez, to watch the area. Still no news on Tony, though. I asked."

They both munched on the cookies Joanne had stashed in her purse as they sat down in the kitchen.

"Anything else I should know?" Joanne asked as they left the kitchen area.

"Donnie mentioned he might ask Tampa police to post some guys around, but I get the feeling he doesn't trust the local cops," said Benny.

"Yeah, Tampa police have cleaned up their act, but the stain from years ago still shows on attitudes. Son of a bitch! Isn't that Toco or whoever he is? Sal's informant?" Joanne pointed to a man passing by the doorway.

"I'll call Sal and let him know Toco is here. You stay with the girls. Call me immediately if you see that joker again. I'm going after him," Benny said, standing up.

"No need for that right now. Lisa is taking the girls home. Also, we need to call your contacts and see if we can figure out what happened to Tony," said Joanne.

"Okay. Donnie's guy is over in the general ICU waiting area. I'll let him know the girls are heading home. Write down the description of the guy with Atoll. I'll give it to Al," Benny said.

Joanne took out a small notebook and jotted down: slight build, around 5'9", no facial hair, blond, white sneakers.

"What about that crazy bum?" Joanne asked.

"I asked Sal about him before. Sal worked with him in the early '90s. So did Donnie. As I understand it, the guy was an undercover agent who went off the rails. He was a deep cover for the FBI and Interpol."

"I remember how crazy I felt working undercover for that brokerage," said Joanne.

"You know how it goes when someone stays undercover for too long. I think this Toco had issues all along, and no one noticed," explained Benny.

"You don't think he's dangerous? We all get a little crazy when we're playing a role," said Joanne.

"Yeah, I know. But don't let your guard down now. I can tell you're focused, and that's good. No one's better when they're locked in like you. You finish what you're doing here, and I'll inform Donnie's guy," said Benny.

Too much going on. No way to protect everyone. Someone's gonna get hurt. I feel it. But Who? Where? When? Joanne's thoughts raced as she cleaned up the kitchen area like it was her home. She wiped down the tables, chairs, and even the front of the refrigerator.

"Any food for me?" Benny asked when he returned. "The FBI guy is on alert."

Handing Benny a cookie, Joanne said, "How about we head to my place so you can make the calls and try to track down Tony? We'll pick up your car and regroup before our meeting at FDLE. We need to be fully prepared for the FBI. I sense they're not happy with us or the FDLE."

"Solid plan," mumbled Benny through a mouthful of cookie.

"Things aren't going to be good for the next few days," Joanne said, shoving a bag of food at him before turning and heading back into the private waiting room for a final check.

"Everything set?" Benny asked when she returned.

"Carol's girls have headed home with Lisa. She's going to stay with them. Wish we could do more to protect them."

Chapter 17

Carol focused on the ceiling of the ICU room. She felt trapped, almost paralyzed with fear. Every breath felt fragile as if any movement might unravel everything. If she stayed still, maybe—just maybe—nothing horrible would happen. *That FBI agent was so intense, his eyes sharp, calculating. He was definitely hiding something.*

Lying on her back, she started counting the acoustic tiles to calm her racing mind. *I wonder if there are cameras in the ceiling. Tiny, invisible cameras,* "Stop," she muttered under her breath. *All will be fine. I'm surrounded by doctors and nurses. Safe. How did things get this bad? Is this my fault? Charles was so much worse than I thought.*

She took deep breaths, drawing the oxygen from the tubes. It felt good. She needed to send the girls home.

Is sending them home the right thing? I want them with me. Am I putting them in danger? I should have told the agent about the break-in. The agent said someone would watch the house.

Carol shifted slightly in bed, almost choking herself on the oxygen tube. She didn't want to think about the tapes, Charles holding a gun to Ed's head or his death. Her whole life felt like it was spinning out of control. For years, she had prided herself on managing ambiguity—that's what made her a successful entrepreneur. All those years after her first husband died, so young…things happen…you adjust…one foot after another. She blinked back tears.

Vulnerability and loss of control. I strike out at them; they counter-attack. The overwhelming sense of how exposed she was right now threatened to take all the oxygen she breathed. She could feel herself hyperventilating. Carol pulled the oxygen tubes out of her nose, sitting up sharply. She knew she had to regain control. The negative thoughts weren't helping—they were feeding the panic. *Go with the flow, they say. This river has rapids and big rocks. Everyone is going to be bruised.*

"Damn it, Carol. You can do this. Stand up slowly," she said to herself as she let the slight woozy feeling pass.

Then, she felt it—an urgent need. She had to pee.

"The tubes are out, so… come on, girl. Do it before you pee yourself." She chuckled dryly at her predicament. Slowly, carefully, she shuffled toward the bathroom. Her thigh muscles were shaking. After she closed the bathroom door, she said, "Breathe!"

Once inside, she stared at the contraption in front of her. "Stupid toilet," she muttered under her breath. Frustration bubbled up, but she sighed, giving in. "Damn it. I'll just fill it up, I guess." Feeling like a naughty child, she took care of business, grateful she was tall enough to maneuver on top of it.

Carol continued her self-guided instructions in her head to calm herself. *It helps to plan. What's first after getting out of the hospital? It's time I fully involved the police. God, I hate to do that. Maybe just talk with the FBI only. Yes, that's better. I will talk with them. Joanne can help. She's working with the FBI and FDLE.*

Just as she reached for toilet paper, she froze. Sounds—muffled but unmistakable—came from her room. *Is that the nurse? Is someone cleaning the room? One of the girls? What were they doing?*

"Mrs. Wallin?" A husky male voice cut through her thoughts like a knife.

Carol's blood ran cold. She didn't want to talk to anyone. Not now. Not when she was still trying to pull herself together. They knew about the tapes, according to the FBI agent. She needed to regain control. *Maybe it's just the doctor.*

"Be right there," Carol called to the bathroom door.

"Excuse me, doctor. Can I help you? I don't think we've met. I'll get Mrs. Wallin's chart. Ow! Wait, who are you?" The sudden voice of a woman, sharp and alarmed, broke through the quiet.

Hearing a scuffle, Carol held her breath. Her hand stilled on the door handle.

"Jerry, get the officer outside! Tell him someone was in Mrs. Wallin's room!" The voice again—this time urgent.

"Mrs. Wallin?" The female voice was closer now.

Carol exhaled slowly, her hand trembling as she opened the door.

"Are you okay?" asked the nurse.

"Who was that? I'm sorry, but I filled the toilet pot," said Carol.

"Don't you worry? We'll take care of that. Let's get you back in bed. We'll take care of the toilet," said the nurse, soothed, her tone professional yet gentle.

"But who was that guy?" asked Carol again.

"There's a police officer right outside, Mrs. Wallin, so he'll take care of everything. Now, let's get you back in bed."

The nurse guided her back toward the bed. Carol wanted to resist—her mind screamed to get dressed, find her girls. Then, it hit a dizzy spell. Good thing the nurse was holding her arm. Carol obediently climbed back into bed.

"I'm going to call security as well," said the nurse.

Carol watched as the nurse went over to the central ICU nursing station and picked up the phone. The world was still spinning a little. Her head was throbbing. "I need to see my girls," she said to the empty room. Then Carol's attention was on the nurse's station outside her room. The nurse's voice rose.

"He headed toward the stairway, not the elevator. Yes, I saw the FBI guy follow him. Toward the stairs. Should I call anyone else?"

Carol sat up, her breath quickening again. *Be strong. It's okay not to be in charge. Just listen and control yourself.* The door was left open, and Carol could see the nurse's station in full view. The usually calm nurse was almost shouting on the phone.

"Send someone up here. And another thing. There's another guy, kinda like a bum, hanging around just outside of here. I saw him when I went to get supplies. Okay, I'll look. Hold on the phone," said the nurse. Carol strained to listen. She couldn't see the nurse, but she knew she had just left the ICU doors. Moments later, the nurse returned to the phone.

"Yes, I see the bum. No sign of the FBI guy or police. The bum's in the waiting area, on the phone. Send help now!"

Carol watched this scene play out as she calmed herself. Tapping into her deep well of inner strength, she drank from it. Her body had been weakened but not her determination or her instincts. She knew the next few months were going to test her family's resilience even more than the past few years had.

What was it Abraham Lincoln said? Be sure you put your feet in the right place, then stand firm.

Yup, standing firm. Or, in my case, lying down firm.

Chapter 18

Jimmy was busy typing up reports when Sal put his phone on speaker, signaling Jimmy by pointing to his ear.

"Okay, okay, she saw me," Toco mumbled into the phone. "You there, Sal? Sally, yeah, it's me, it's me—you know me, right? Monster's here, bad smell in the fix-it place; don't like antiseptic; saw the monster, gotta go, Jersey Girl saw me."

"Toco. What the... Don't hang up! Damn, he's gone," said Sal. "We need to get to the hospital."

The look on Sal's face told Jimmy not to question him, so they headed out of the FDLE building in a hurry. They drove in silence for a while, the tension thick in the air. The way Jimmy was driving, the usual fifteen-minute trip would only take five.

"What's the story?" asked Jimmy, breaking the silence.

"I was trying to get ahold of Donnie at the FBI to ask a question when Toco called. You heard him. The 'monster' must be our Mr. K., and the Jersey Girl is Joanne. It doesn't make total sense, but I'm not taking any chances," Sal explained, reaching for the car phone again.

Jimmy started to respond but paused when Sal raised a finger, signaling him to hold off.

"Damn, Donnie's still not answering. Anyway, Toco said he saw the monster and Jersey Girl at the hospital. What was he doing there? That son-of-a-bitch got some 'splainin' to do."

"Can you call Benny?" asked Jimmy.

"I'm trying now. When we get there, I'll check on Carol Wallin in ICU, and you find Donnie's guy—Al. You know him, right? Big guy. Doesn't look FBI."

"Will do," Jimmy replied, scanning for a parking spot. "Wallin's family was in a room near the ICU. I'll check them first. You think Wallin's wife is in danger?"

"Someone's cleaning house. I don't know who's on the list, but I'm sure they suspected Barnes knew something. Whoever that is might also suspect Carol knows something. You better get ahold of Joanne if you can. Benny's phone didn't answer."

As soon as Sal put the phone down, it rang again. "Hello?" He straightened almost to attention as he listened. "Damn, yes, sir, got it. We're on our way there now."

He maintained his formal posture, listening intently, then shook his head. "No sir, not psychic. My informant called and gave information that directed us to the hospital. Okay, we'll talk later."

"Who was that?" Jimmy asked, speeding up, sensing the urgency had increased.

"The Captain. Donnie's guy is dead. Security found him in the stairwell. They've also sent guards to Carol's room."

When they arrived at the hospital and parked, two FBI vans pulled up beside them. Jimmy and Sal approached Donnie. "Sorry, man. What can we do?" Sal asked.

"How the hell did you know?" Donnie demanded.

"First, I heard from Toco, then my captain called and told us about Al," Sal explained.

"Toco's got some…." Squawking came over Donnie's earcom.

Jimmy could tell everyone was on high alert. *I need to alert Joanne. She'd try to catch the guy herself.*

"I'm heading inside," said Jimmy.

"We'll look for any of the Wallins still in the hospital," Sal told Donnie.

"Wait. We're not sure he's still here. We sent two guys over to Wallin's house and alerted the Tampa Police. We don't know where

Tony or Eddy are. Shit... why was Toco even here? I'm starting to suspect he's not as innocent as he seems. His ex-FBI creds can only go so far. Same goes for yours, Sal," Donnie said, his tone sharp.

"I did ask him to keep an eye on the Wallins," Sal said. "He mentioned seeing the 'monster' when he called. He might be heading to the Wallin's house now. That means he knows who the 'monster' is. I'll track him down and try to get a description."

Sal's cell phone rang again.

"Hey, Captain. We're at the hospital now. Tampa Police called? What did they want? Are you telling me he just walked into their station and turned himself in?" Sal questioned, his brow furrowing in confusion.

"Let me talk to him," Donnie said, grabbing Sal's phone and walking away to continue the conversation.

"What's going on? Who turned himself in? Is it Tony?" asked Jimmy as Sal raised his index finger to hold more questions, and both strained to hear Donnie's conversation with their Captain. From what Jimmy could catch, Donnie wasn't just listening—he was giving orders.

"You belong to me now. Completely. We need information. Get it. Whether it's from the Wallins, Toco, or any of the players in this mess. Get me a description of this killer. You understand, Sal?

Toco's not one of us. Your Captain will fill you in on the rest," Donnie said, handing the phone back to Sal before walking into the hospital.

"What are our orders?" Jimmy asked.

"We need information. We should head to the Wallin's place," Sal replied.

"Talk to me. What's going on?" Jimmy pressed.

"You won't believe it. We need to find Toco. He may be at the Wallins'," Sal said as his phone rang again.

They both turned and headed back to Jimmy's car as Sal continued talking to the Captain.

"Sorry, sir. Donnie hung up the phone. Yes, sir, we were here to look for my informant, who was at the hospital. Then we were going to head to the Wallin's place. Okay, head to the Tampa Police Department. Got it. Information is key. We're on it," Sal said, his mouth twisting slightly into an Elvis-like smirk as he held the phone close to his ear.

His index finger was still raised, keeping Jimmy silent. Jimmy pulled the SUV into traffic as Sal kept listening. "What the fuck? Atoll wants us to protect him?"

Jimmy kept driving, following Sal's wild gestures that directed him downtown instead of to the Wallin's place.

"Shit! Sorry, sir, you're right. We'll go by the Tampa Police Offices and pick him up. Yes, sir, we'll take him to the FBI. I understand we're to report to Donnie Castillo," Sal said.

Jimmy pulled into a gas station and parked near the store. He waited silently while Sal finished the conversation.

"Yes, sir. Donnie's losing it over at the hospital. We've got to catch this bastard. Talk later," Sal said, turning to Jimmy. "I've got some direction from the Captain. I'll clarify with Donnie in a minute."

"Sure. I'm grabbing a drink. Want anything?" Jimmy asked.

"Maybe a coffee. No, a Coke would be great."

Jimmy's instincts told him things were falling apart quickly. Nobody was going to come out of this situation clean. As he paid for the drinks, he watched Sal from the corner of his eye. Sal wasn't his usual calm self. Something was really bothering him. Was it the murder? The assignment? Or maybe it was Toco?

"Here's your Big Gulp. Now talk," Jimmy said, handing Sal his drink.

"Okay, you heard the madness. Atoll walks into the Tampa police station downtown, gives the desk sergeant some bullshit story, and somehow gets sent up to the chief. Can't believe he made it past Shirley... Anyway, he tells them that the Tampa police Force needs to protect him because there's a serial killer on the loose, and the guy's crazy."

Jimmy shook his head in disbelief. "How does he know? He's a piece of work. I bet he hired this guy and now can't control him."

"Who knows? We've got to make him talk. We need a description of the killer. Listen, take me to my car. I need to find Toco. You handle the handover from the Tampa Police. Sound good?" Sal asked.

"Let's do this," Jimmy replied.

Chapter 19

It's time to bring Toco in. I'll see what I can get out of Atoll. He might have a description. You sure you can bring Toco in by yourself? He might take a runner," said Jimmy as he pulled the SUV back into traffic.

"I don't know why, but I think he needs me right now," said Sal.

"I'm picking up Atoll, but what about the Wallins? Should we send some Tampa Police over there to cover? I sense you're not confident about their loyalties," Jimmy said, pulling up behind Sal's car.

"Donnie said he sent two of his guys over. Tampa cops are good. Most of the bad ones are gone. Every force has some idiots. You good with Atoll? I don't think we should question him without Donnie's crew involved. What d'you think?" asked Sal.

"I'll get in touch with Donnie as well. I'm qualified to question him, but I don't want to miss an opportunity while he still needs us to protect him. Are you concerned about Donnie?"

Jimmy could tell Sal was anxious. He pulled into a strip center lot and waited for Sal to talk. "Sal, you okay? Are you worried about something else? What's going on?"

"What, nothing. Give Donnie another call before you pick up Atoll."

Jimmy waited. He knew Sal was distracted, just like himself. "This Toco thing is a barrier between us. It's screwing with your thinking. I'm distracted enough for both of us. Give me the short version. Spill," Jimmy said.

"It was Miami, the mid-80s. I had just started working undercover on a special assignment with the FBI. Young, fearless. Another crazy was my FBI contact, Sullivan. Oh boy, Sullivan, that was a major screw-up. Sullivan and Breen."

Jimmy pushed his seat back and gave Sal his full attention.

"They were a pair. Sullivan, the FBI's supposed undercover Italian language specialist, even worked on the big 'Pizza Connection' case that made the prosecutor in NY famous. What was his name... Giuliani."

Jimmy kept the engine running but shifted into park. Facing Sal, he knew he had to hear him out. Sal's undercover days had always been a blind spot in their relationship. More importantly, Sal's relationship with Toco was getting in their way just like Jimmy's tangled feelings for Joanne.

"Sullivan and Breen were supposed to have my back. They didn't. Toco did."

"What happened?"

"It was Toco who told me Sullivan was on the take. He kept warning me not to get too close to those two. He saved my butt. He saved my life."

Jimmy could see Sal shiver as he remembered. "That was the night you were shot. Weren't you wearing a vest?"

"Toco was wearing a vest. I couldn't; it would have tipped them off. Not that it mattered. I got shot in the head and arm. My pregnant wife went into labor wondering if I'd live."

"She lost the baby, didn't she?"

"Toco was with her, held her hand. Pretty sure it was Toco who called the ambulance for me. But am I wrong about Toco? Is he the devil too? No, he couldn't be," said Sal as Jimmy readjusted his seat and began maneuvering back downtown.

"You go find him. Get him to give you a description if you can. I'll deal with Asstole," Jimmy said as he dropped Sal off at his car. He was worried about Sal, but he knew their jobs were on the line if they didn't perform.

A few minutes later, Jimmy pulled into the parking lot of Tampa Police's main offices. Rushing out of the car, he muttered, "What a shitshow. *What's the best approach with Atoll? The tapes reveal he's in this. We have him. But the tapes might not get to court. First, we need to catch this monster. I need to focus.* When he reached the door, he paused to gather his thoughts.

The FBI is using Sal and me as gophers. We haven't shared much, either. Tampa's Chief Holder's a good guy. Hell, he's one of the reasons I'm where I'm at. First black Chief. He's made a difference. I need to make a difference.

"You need something, Jimbo?" said the desk Sergeant. "Hopefully, you're here to get the fancy lawyer. I'm catching heat for letting him past me. What's his deal?"

"He's a piece of work, Sarg. I'll take him off your hands. Where's Carmen babysitting him?" asked Jimmy.

"They've got him in the Chief's conference room. I'll let them know you're coming up."

The Tampa Police's offices were large but had just undergone renovation as the force completed its decentralization. *Getting closer to the people* was the theme of the three districts. *Holder's doing a good job of reducing crime,* thought Jimmy as the elevator opened. He could see Atoll impatiently pacing the glassed room. Carmen was looking at her nails with a slight smirk on her face. She was probably teasing him as they waited, trying to enjoy herself as she babysat the self-imposed 'big shot'. Jimmy slowed his pace, watching them through the glass. He pushed open the door, "Mr. Atoll, I'm James Perez. I—"

"Finally! I don't understand why I have to be transported to another facility. You could've just put me in a nice hotel with guards. And another thing, I don't appreciate this girl…eeaa …officer's insinuations that I'm some kind of criminal. Actually, if I were a criminal, I'd be treated better!"

"I'll grab the paperwork and let the Chief know you're here," Carmen mumbled as she left, still smirking.

"Mr. Atoll, why don't we sit while the paperwork is processed? I'm interested in your concerns. Why don't you tell me why you believe you're in danger?"

"I am not sure I should say anything, given how I'm being treated. What exactly is your position? Why should I talk to you?"

"Ahh, of course, you have every right to be cautious. You met my associate, Agent Carducci, a few weeks ago. I'm Agent Perez with the Florida Department of Law Enforcement. I have been assigned to ensure your safety during the transfer from this facility to the.."

"The Governor assigned you?"

"The Governor is kept informed of all our activities. I'm assigned to look at the circumstances surrounding Ed Wallin's death, so I am familiar with you and your role as his corporate advisor."

"I had nothing to do with poor Ed's death…"

"So, do you believe it was a suicide? I heard you told Chief Holder about some 'monster' hanging people."

"I'm not here to discuss hanging or strangling, whatever! The point is, I'm in danger."

"Of course, Mr. Atoll. Please, sit. Would you like a coffee? Or some water? I'm sure it's been a stressful day. I'll step out and check on the paperwork."

Jimmy walked around the corner to Shirley's desk in front of the Chief's office.

"He's not in. He had a meeting at City Hall. He wants you to keep him informed. Anything I need to know?" asked Shirley.

Sharp one she was. She had more years on the force than he did but liked it if you just called her Shirley. It worked for her. People opened up to her easy demeanor. Most never noticed she was in a wheelchair. Shot in the back in a drug raid. She had read his face more than once during the two years he was on the Tampa force before he'd gone over to the FDLE. She was reading him now.

"Spit it out, detective—oh wait, they call you Agents now, don't they? No matter. What's on your mind? Carmen's done with the paperwork, but she's giving you a chance to bond with Mr. Important. You're puzzled. I can tell. What's eating at you?" said Shirley.

"I liked being one of you. I'm tasked to the FBI today."

"You were one of us. He doesn't forget. He'll support you if you're on the right side of the law. You know that. What's your face telling me?" said Shirley as she smiled at him.

Jimmy's shoulders relaxed some as he smiled back at Shirley. "You should be the one questioning him. You've got an uncanny ability to read people. Well, what you're reading is confusion. We've got an informant who's not telling us everything."

"And?"

"Atoll's got the info we need. But he's a lawyer. I'm turning him over to the FBI. They're running the Task Force on Wallin,

Barnes, and the FBI agent who was murdered. Chief's been told about them."

"Quite the shitshow."

"You got that right. We're running in circles—Carol Wallin is in the hospital, and now, the FBI agent is dead. Any suggestions?"

Jimmy knew Shirley had been one of the best detectives on the squad. She had gone back to college and gotten her master's in criminology when she ended up in a wheelchair. Now, she was the Chief's right hand. She was smart and clear-thinking. He also knew she had an educated grasp of everything going down because of her position and her connections around town.

Jimmy started pacing back and forth in front of Shirley's desk. She frowned at him.

"You seem to be stuck in what's happened and happening, the drama. Go back to the basics. You already know someone is cleaning the house. But why? You might already have the facts you need," said Shirley.

"Money," Jimmy said.

"I'm sure the money tells you that Atoll is not big enough to pull all the strings. Don't let the FBI 'one-side' their information. They are used to sharing what makes them look good. What do you see?"

"A rogue killer."

"What does he need? C'mon, detective. Something's throwing you off your game. Whatever it is, you better drop it now. Is Sal in a bad spot, too? Are you two out of sync? What's Sal's emotional attachment, and to whom? Why? You're both going to get hurt if you continue on this path."

Jimmy sat down hard in a side chair. *Damn, Sal too. I'm so wrapped up in my pity party with Dayna and Joanne that I missed the true importance of Sal's Miami connection when he was shot. Toco saved him. That's when he transferred full-time to the FDLE.*

"Thanks, Shirley, I needed the pep talk. You're right. We need to get back to basics," Jimmy said, getting up.

"Now, back to the Asstole—oops, I mean Mr. Atoll," Shirley said with a sly smile.

Jimmy was signing the paperwork when Shirley grabbed his wrist.

"You were told to follow the money. Money can get you killed or give you power. People always want power," she said, winking as she let go of his wrist.

She's so right. All those indictments of the mob guys are telling me someone needs to protect assets, right? Where's the money? I'd kill to get that, or maybe I'd trade it for other information to keep myself safe. Okay, Asstole, here I come.

Chapter 20

* ● *

"Lisa, we appreciate that you're here," said Stevie as Kay blew her a kiss. "I know how special you are to my mom. You're special to us as well." Lisa put an arm around her sister's shoulder.

"Kay. Kay!" called their grandmother, Margaret, as she walked into the kitchen. "Make sure you use the nice china. Can't we set up a place for Louise? She always eats with me at home. I mean, she's more like family, don't you think? Your mom's not here."

Kay smirked at Lisa as she headed to the dining room buffet to get the good dishes.

"You don't mind, do you, Lisa? Well, you're not family, so I guess you don't get a vote."

"Grandma, that's not nice," called Kay from the dining room.

"Grandma, please," said Stevie. She knew her pleas wouldn't help. *You can't argue with a drunk.*

"Well, it's true. Oh, yes, my bottle's almost empty. Lisa, can you grab the spare from the laundry room? Why are the two of you just standing there smirking at each other? I know a smirk when I see one. Did I miss a joke? So rude. Lisa, did you not hear me? Get the bottle," Margaret snapped.

Lisa did as she was told. As she entered the laundry room, she closed the door, lifted the phone receiver, and dialed Jan. "It's me. What are you doing? Can you come over? I don't think I can handle Carol's mother without another non-family buffer. She's worse than last time. Bring some good scotch, so she'll let you in without argument. Okay, thanks. See you in a few."

"Louise, Louise, come here, darling. Why are you sitting at the lanai door? Kay, where's Stevie? She needs to tell that policeman to get off the property. He's upsetting Louise. Stevie? Stevie!"

"I'm here, Gram, right behind you."

"Oh my, don't sneak up on people like that. Go tell that policeman to get off the property. You're all forceful and manly, so you can chase him away."

"He's here to keep an eye on us, Gram."

"We can handle ourselves. I took a self-defense course at the community center. I can throw a grown man, you know. It's all leverage. I can show you! Well, maybe not—you're big and bony and wear boy clothes anyway. Go on, tell him to leave."

"Gram, what's wrong with you?" Kay asked, exasperated.

"Let her ramble, Kay," said Stevie. "Gram, the police are necessary. I don't have any leverage with them." She knew her grandmother had finished almost half a bottle already.

"It's all Ed's fault. My poor Carol" said Margaret, her voice suddenly trembling.

"Gram, please. Let's just finish cooking and eat," Stevie said, hoping to placate her.

"Come, Louise. Oh, Kay, your mafia thug husband called earlier. I didn't think you should talk to him, so I told him not to call here. He's probably one of the reasons the police are around. I told you not to marry him."

"Oh my God, Gram. I need to talk to him. What time did he call?" asked Kay, her voice rising in concern.

"I'm not in charge of keeping track of him. Just after 3, I think. I told him to buy me some more scotch. He's good at that, at least. He did say he wouldn't be coming by today, or at least, that's what I think he said."

"Are you sure he said he wasn't coming? Should I set a place for him?"

"Or maybe he did say he would be coming? No matter. He was insisting on talking with you. No one wants to talk with me. They call for your mom or Stevie. Do they ever say anything nice to me? No. That's why I chose Louise. Louise. Where did you go now?" rambled Margaret as she headed toward the lanai, scooping up Louise along the way.

Kay just stood there, tears streaming down her cheeks. Lisa and Stevie each put an arm around her, guiding her toward the stairs.

"Why don't you take a rest? There's a phone in the second guest room, so you can lie down and still hear any calls. Lisa and I will monitor the calls, too. Want me to come up with you?" asked Stevie.

"I'm fine. I never understood why Mom didn't want her around. I used to think she was just silly, but she's mean, Stevie. Really mean."

"I know. She can be. I don't think she means everything she says. It's the booze talking. Please, go rest."

"Go on. We'll take care of everything down here. Jan's coming by in a few minutes; she'll keep her busy. Go rest," added Lisa.

Stevie took Kay gently by the elbow and led her up a few stairs. She watched as Kay slowly ascended, glancing back repeatedly. Stevie waved her forward until she finally disappeared up the stairs. Satisfied Kay would rest, Stevie walked back to the kitchen.

"Where's dear Margaret?" she asked as she returned.

"I'm on salad duty. She took Louise for a walk. I think she's giving that policeman out there a hard time. Oh well, they're trained for that. I'm not. Good Lord, she's a handful. How are you holding up?" asked Lisa.

"I wish Mom was here with us. I miss Ed. Grams was always nicer when he was around. He'd flatter her," said Stevie, her voice softer now.

Lisa stopped chopping and gave Stevie her full attention. "She was nicer when we were young. But her drinking has gotten out of control. I can't believe all that's happened these last weeks. I should be exhausted. Yet, I'm mildly exhilarated. It's so weird."

"Your Mom mentioned you and Karen broke up. That got lost in all the chaos. How are you with that?" Lisa asked.

"She wasn't ready for the hassle our lifestyle brings. The millennium might've changed, but people's attitudes haven't. I understand. I'm thinking about moving to San Francisco, New York—maybe even Miami would be better. Tampa's still a small Southern town with plenty of small minds," said Stevie.

"You know you're supported no matter where you go, right?" Lisa reassured her.

"You guys are great. Aunt JoJo always knew. Ed was wonderful. Even Tony lovingly accepted Karen and me."

"So much chaos. Poor Kay's worried sick about Tony. I think he's in real trouble," said Stevie.

"I think you're right." Lisa continued to chop vegetables as Stevie reflected on the family. So much has happened. Everyone's got their grief. Kay's sensitive, but she's strong.

"Oww!" Stevie yelped as her hand grazed the oven rack.

"What's Grams doing with that policeman?" asked Lisa.

"Probably reducing him to tears," Stevie quipped as they heard Margaret, Jan, and Louise return from the lanai.

"Look who's here! And she brought Louise some gourmet dog treats. This is a really good scotch, Jan. So kind of you to think of us. Unlike some others around here," Margaret rambled, waving the bottle. "You may need to help Lisa with that salad. She seems to be struggling. I think I'll try just a bit of this lovely scotch. A treat for you, dear girl, as well. Yum, Louise."

Margaret continued her babbling, fixing herself a large glass and feeding more treats to Louise.

"Oh, that policeman is very polite. An English background, I'd say. Probably good stock. Maybe you should talk to him, Stevie. He's quite handsome, with a nice smile and all. Now, listen for the timer. Baste the turkey every half-hour," she added while feeding Louise more and pouring herself another glass.

Margaret kept talking, wiping the counter Stevie had just cleaned. "We'll have a lovely dinner and enough leftovers for me to make Louise some special meals. Stevie, dear, can you handle the mashed potatoes? You've got strong hands for that. Oh, and someone's got to string the beans. We'll just have a little lie down before dinner."

Stevie, Lisa, and Jan quickly turned their heads away. They made faces and suppressed their laughter while Margaret chatted on.

"Where did Kay go? No mind, Jan, you do the beans. We're off," said Margaret.

The group in the kitchen just stood still and watched as she swooped up Louise and left the kitchen scotch glass in hand. They peeked around the corner, watched her climb the stairs, and giggled quietly.

"She's a whirlwind," said Jan, pulling a bottle of wine from her bag. "Shall we join Gran ma ma in her stupor?" she suggested. "Where's Kay?"

"She's upstairs, resting," Stevie said, then sighed.

"You okay, Stevie? Grams has been unusually nasty. We've got so many people to worry about—Kay, Mom, Tony, and Eddy. What do you think is going on…really?" asked Lisa.

Stevie glanced at the turkey and the half-prepared salad. "I think we better check the turkey and finish the salad so we can relax a little. Jan, let's open that bottle. We might as well enjoy this," she said, forcing a smile.

Jan got out the glasses and poured them as they all scurried around the kitchen. They fell into a kitchen dance as women do, moving around each other, fixing this, cutting that, putting things away, taking things out. A half-hour passed when Jan finally caught Stevie by the arm and pointed toward the lanai. Lisa didn't seem to notice.

"What's up?" asked Stevie, settling into one of the armchairs.

"You're avoiding something," Jan said bluntly. "You know more than you're saying about Tony, your mom, and your breakup with Karen. And Joanne—she's noticeably absent from all this. Where do you want to start?"

Stevie shook her head and smirked. "You're too smart for your own good. Well, you know Roger was murdered, right?"

"Oh damn. I knew something happened, but I didn't realize he'd been murdered," said Jan as she put her hand over her heart. "How awful," she whispered. "What else?"

"Well, that's when Tony freaked and hasn't been seen since. I think he's up the proverbial creek without a boat or a paddle. I was never comfortable with all the money Tony and Eddy made from stocks. Something felt off. So did Mom. But I've been so wrapped up in my mess with Karen that I didn't pay attention."

They both settled deeper into their chairs, sipping their wine.

"I knew things weren't good between Mom and Ed. They were civil at family gatherings, but they were cold. You know, you can tell. Hell, I was suffering from the same condition with Karen— arguing, then making up, then arguing again," Stevie admitted.

"I know, your Mom told me. She was worried about you two," Jan said, touching Stevie's hand.

"Ed always seemed so controlled. Distracted is how I would have described him lately," said Stevie.

"Good word for what your Mom thought as well. She wasn't worried about depression, just that he was hiding something. Then came the investigation and the damn reporters..." Jan trailed off.

"I wasn't really there for her. Not really. I showed up, but I wasn't there. Maybe I could've helped, ya' know, talked to Ed, supported Mom more. Damn."

"Your mom knows what you've been going through. Ed was fighting his own battle. Your Mom is strong. She needs you kids to be okay," Jan reassured her.

Stevie poured herself a refill, trying to relax.

"Your Mom knows how much you love her. Now, what else do you know?" asked Jan

"Well, let's see. Aunt JoJo's been investigating Ed, Tony, and Eddy. That's what she does for a living. The thought crossed my mind about why she's here but not here, ya' know? She and Mom used to be close."

"And?"

"She also knows Agent Perez with the FDLE. She says it's business, but I think there's more."

"Does your mom know what Joanne's doing?"

"I'm not sure how much Mom knows about her investigations. I know they've talked. But what else? This is such a fucking mess," said Stevie, reaching for the wine bottle.

"Joanne's investigation makes sense. I thought she was hiding something. She told me about all the drama surrounding her husband's death. She also mentioned her involvement with the FBI," said Jan.

"She's on our side. I'm sure of it. It's just her job. I think she's been protecting Mom from something, but I don't know the details. Mom trusts her, so I trust her. I think Tony and Eddy will get arrested, but I'm not sure what for," Stevie replied.

Silence fell between them again. The warm, breezy night seemed to envelop Stevie as she let herself drift for a moment, carried by the soft wind. Jan watched her quietly, deep in thought.

"Kay's going to need your support," Jan said, breaking the silence.

"I know, but…" Stevie trailed off as they both stood up, startled by a sudden thump.

"What was that? Where's that policeman who was out back? Do they take breaks?" Stevie asked, her eyes darting toward the sound.

"There was one out front and another in the back when I passed by. I spoke to him. Maybe he took a bathroom break," suggested Jan, trying to stay calm.

"I'll check the front of the house. You check the laundry room and make sure the door's locked. I've got the emergency code for the pad in there. Just touch 2-5-8, then #. The center numbers. Wait there until I knock. Shit, shit! That stupid mutt is barking upstairs," said Stevie, frustration creeping into her voice.

They both entered the house at the same time, freezing for a moment, listening as Louise barked relentlessly from upstairs. Stevie quickly locked the lanai door and pointed toward the front of the house, signaling Jan to stay quiet. She moved slowly toward the front door while Jan headed for the kitchen.

Stevie could faintly hear Jan and Lisa exchanging small talk in the kitchen as Jan made her way to the laundry room.

As quietly as she could, Stevie opened the front door and peered outside. No one in sight. *Where the fuck are the cops?* she shouted in her head. Closing and locking the front door again before heading toward Ed's office. She flipped on the light—empty. Moving through the living room, then the dining room, she finally reached the kitchen. Lisa was checking the turkey in the oven.

"This is a damn big turkey. We could feed the whole neighborhood," Lisa joked as Stevie walked in.

"You got that right," said Stevie, knocking lightly on the laundry room door. It was slightly ajar, but the light was off. She slipped in, but as she reached to flip the light switch, a hand caught hers. She froze, recognizing the scent of expensive cologne—Tony.

She opened her mouth to speak but stopped herself. The faint light from the backyard filtered through the door's thin curtains. Her eyes darted to Jan, who was backed against the dryer, shaking her head frantically. Stevie looked down at the hand gripping her arm. Tony was holding a gun.

Chapter 21

J**immy** helped Atoll into his SUV. As much as he wanted to punch the guy, he did his duty and drove to the FBI building. He had considered putting him in the back but decided that treating him like a non-criminal might work better. Before leaving the Tampa Police, he had managed to speak with Donnie and get his orders. Donnie had emphasized the importance of getting a full description of the killer.

"Where are you taking me?" asked Atoll.

"As I said, the FDLE is coordinating with Donnie Castillo from the FBI. We're headed there."

"Why not just take me to a hotel? This is very uncomfortable. You don't seem to know anything, and I'm in danger. I didn't even have time to pack," Atoll complained, shifting in his seat.

"Really? No packing at all? Was someone at your home?" asked Jimmy.

"That's not what I said. Are you sure you're a policeman?" retorted Atoll, clearly irritated.

Jimmy clenched his jaw. He wanted to pull over and throw Atoll out of his car. Instead, he kept his cool, finding a parking space close to the FBI headquarters. As he parked, he thought he saw Sal's car pass along Kennedy Blvd. Concern flickered—he hadn't spoken to Sal in a while, but now wasn't the time to dwell on it.

"We're here," Jimmy said. *Asstole was even waiting for me to open the door for him.*

"Now what?" asked Atoll.

"We're meeting with the FBI for coordination of your protection," explained Jimmy.

"I hope they are ready to place me somewhere comfortable. This in-and-out of cars in July heat is not appropriate. What are the arrangements for me?" Atoll pressed.

"Let's just get inside, out of the heat first," Jimmy muttered, walking ahead.

Exiting the elevator, Jimmy looked around him as they passed inspection and went into the plusher interrogation room Donnie had arranged. He had told Jimmy on the phone that it was fully equipped with recording devices and two-way mirrors but comfortably furnished. Donny said they used it to lure more elite criminals into comfort. *This bastard didn't deserve comfort,* thought Jimmy as he settled Atoll in the room. "I'll be right back. There's water in the little refrigerator if you're thirsty," Jimmy said, locking the door behind him. He heard Atoll grumbling something about the water as he headed over to Martin, one of Donnie's men.

"I put Mr. Atoll in the interrogation room. You up on Donnie's orders?" Jimmy asked.

"Yup. Donnie said to let him stew but to make sure we get the info we need. I'll be in and out of the watch room just in case. Florida law prohibits recording him without his consent. See if you can get under his skin and make him talk anyway," said Martin, grinning slightly.

"I'll do my best," Jimmy replied, already formulating a plan. He headed back to the interview room.

"Did you lock that door?" Atoll asked, clearly annoyed.

"Force of habit," Jimmy replied coolly.

"I demand to know when the FBI will get me settled," Atoll snapped.

"They didn't say. They're kind of busy right now, especially since one of their guys at the hospital was murdered—strangled, actually. As I understand it, you were there just before that," said Jimmy, watching Atoll closely for a reaction.

"What are you implying?" Atoll shot back as he began pacing the room.

"I was stating a known fact, Mr. Atoll," said Jimmy.

You should…" Atoll started, but Jimmy cut him off.

"Another fact is that you were with someone. Do you want to tell me about that person?" asked Jimmy.

"Now you listen, Detective…"

"Agent Perez," Jimmy corrected him, his voice hard. "You seem to be avoiding simple questions. Why is that? Are you hiding something, or maybe someone?"

"I.."

"And another thing—you keep asking for protection, but you haven't told me from whom or why. Is that another secret, Mr. Atoll?"

"I insist on talking with the FBI in charge, not some underling," said Atoll as he paced the end of the room.

"Hmm, is that so," Jimmy said quietly, opening his bottle of water and taking a slow sip. "He might be a while. As I mentioned, his agent was killed at the hospital. Maybe by the man you were with… But don't say anything to me. Feel free to wait."

Jimmy gestured to a chair and waited. He could see Atoll's agitation growing. Atoll paced, fidgeting, until Jimmy said casually, "Maybe I'll just head back to the FDLE and keep investigating. I've got all the corporate records. Oh yes, and there were some other things Mrs. Wallin had in her car…"

Atoll stopped pacing, his eyes narrowing. "What things?"

"Let's see, there were… memos, notes, some accounting stuff. You don't know this, but I'm a forensic accountant. Funny, huh? How does an underling like me get so smart? Been reading up a lot on stocks lately."

Atoll was looking at Jimmy with slit eyes and a tight mouth. *It's like he's trying not to talk. Need to push some more buttons.*

"Stocks are fascinating, don't you think? What do they call it? Oh yeah, Pump and Dump.' You wouldn't know anything about that, though. But if the FBI got a whiff of stock fraud, they'd be very interested. Maybe they'd even catch someone laundering money. Don't you think?"

Jimmy finished his water and tossed the plastic into a can next to Atoll, just like a pro basketball player.

"You're bluffing. You've got nothing," Atoll said, his voice shaky.

"Nothing, hmm, why do you say that? Do you know something I should know?" Jimmy asked, leaning forward slightly. "Oh, sorry. You don't know anything, right?"

"I know plenty," Atoll spat back, trying to regain control.

"That's good. Is that why someone's trying to kill you? Because you know something? Of course, you're a lawyer—you know better than to obstruct justice. You know not to withhold information that is pertinent to our investigation. That could make you guilty…are you guilty of that, Mr. Atoll? Information can be an asset, of course." said Jimmy.

"You keep accusing me of things! I need protection," stated Atoll.

"Protection from whom, Mr. Atoll? That information is crucial, don't you think? I want to help you. You give, we give. You're a smart man—you know how leverage works. You're holding all the cards here."

Atoll stopped pacing again, staring at Jimmy but saying nothing. Jimmy watched his eyes shift, calculating.

"Think about it, Mr. Atoll. Now's the time to use your leverage," Jimmy said as Martin entered and signaled that Jimmy had a phone call.

"If you'll excuse me for a moment while you're thinking. Agent Martin Floyd will be right outside if you need anything."

"Do not lock—" Atoll started, but Jimmy closed and locked the door, smiling as he heard Atoll pounding on it from the other side. The muffled yelling faded as Jimmy reached Martin's desk. He slipped into Martin's chair and picked up the phone, pressing the blinking light.

"Perez here," he said, listening to the voice on the other end.

"Damn, Sal, you sure you're okay? I'm stuck with Asstole right now. Let me get this straight—the Sheriff's guys took you to the hospital?"

Jimmy listened while nodding his head. "You were knocked out? An ambulance took you? Donnie's still there? Make sure you're fully checked out—why? Because you were knocked out, you fool."

Jimmy was fidgeting with a pen, then stopped and barked into the phone, "I've had it with Toco. We need to put a bolo out on him. No, no—bullshit. You wouldn't be in this shape if it weren't for him. You're not thinking straight. Don't make me call Marie. Fine. Go talk to Donnie. Did the Sheriff put a bolo on your car? Good. Just… think about what I said, Sal."

As Jimmy hung up, Martin approached with a coffee.

"What happened to Sal?" asked Martin.

"Everyone heard that, huh? Sorry. His stupid informant tackled him and knocked him out. An ambulance took him to St. Joe's, and someone stole his car. Toco's a problem. I don't care what Sal says. We need to find him and bring him in. Can you help with that?" Jimmy asked.

"We already have a BOLO out on him. Donnie knew him back in the day, but the guy's lost it. According to Donnie, Toco was deep undercover in New Jersey and Miami. Sometimes, those deep-cover guys can flip—lying all the time, developing split personalities. Donnie thinks the FBI owes him. I think he's dangerous."

Both men just stood in silence for a moment, letting the tension settle. Jimmy got up from the chair and walked to the kitchen for a cup of coffee. *Gonna be a long night.* He smirked as the distant banging of Atoll pounding on the door echoed down the hall.

Chapter 22

· ● ·

Seeing Tony's gun, Stevie gasped. As her eyes adjusted, she saw Jan still against the dryer and the gun pointed at her. "Tony, Jesus, what are you doing?" Stevie whispered.

"I have to protect Kay and you guys," said Tony.

"By pointing a gun? There are police outside, you idiot," said Stevie.

"He knocked one out," Jan muttered.

"Please listen. Kay is in danger. I have to get her to safety," Tony said, his voice tinged with urgency.

"By knocking out a policeman and pointing a gun at us?" Stevie shot back, disbelief evident in her tone.

"Be quiet! I had to. They would arrest me. They don't understand, and neither do any of you. You have to be quiet now, please. I need to talk to Kay," Tony said, the desperation in his voice more pronounced now.

Stevie could hear how scared he was. "Okay, I'll take her to Ed's office. You go out this door and come in through the front with your key. I know it's locked. Please put the gun away. I'm not sure Kay will want to go anywhere with you if she sees it."

"She knows me. I have to protect her. She can't be hurt. He'll hurt her," Tony said in a whiny whisper.

"Who? Atoll? Eddy? Who, Tony? You have to tell us," Jan urged.

"Shhhsh!" Stevie hissed. "That's Kay coming into the kitchen," she whispered. With a nod from Tony, she cracked the door slightly to listen. They heard Kay and Lisa talking about the size of the turkey and when to start the beans. Knowing they weren't paying attention, Stevie nodded to Tony and entered the kitchen.

"Did those two sneak away to drink and leave you with all the work?" Kay asked, smiling.

"I have no idea. They were out on the patio. Who knows what they're up to?" Lisa said as she rinsed dishes in the sink.

"There you are," Kay said to Stevie as she entered the kitchen.

"Did you get a nice nap? I heard Louise barking. Did she wake you? I've got something I need to discuss with you. Let's go to Ed's office. Lisa, you holding everything down here?" Stevie asked as she began to guide Kay out of the kitchen.

"What? I can't hear you with the water running," Lisa called out.

"Nothing important, just keep working," Stevie shouted back as she and Kay left the kitchen.

***

Lisa flicked some soap suds at them as they left, then continued washing the knives. After finishing, she wiped her hands on her apron and walked toward the laundry room door, hearing muffled sounds.

"Who's in there? Hello? Jan?" Lisa asked through the laundry room door. As she opened it, the lights suddenly went out.

Tony grabbed Lisa around the neck and pointed the gun at Jan again.

"What the hell?" gasped Lisa, fear flashing in her eyes.

"I have to talk to Kay," Tony insisted.

"Fine, you don't need to hurt us. Go, talk to Kay. We'll stay in here. But I can't promise what Margaret will do if she sees you. Just don't shoot anyone, please," Lisa whispered as Tony went out the back door.

"Stay in here while I talk with Kay," Tony said as he left, placing the gun at the small of his back.

"But the turkey. Shit, God, he handles that like a professional. You okay? He didn't hurt you, did he?" Lisa asked Jan, who was still sitting on the washer.

Jan shook her head. "I'm fine," she said, her voice shaky. Lisa turned on the outside light and glanced at the laundry room door leading outside.

Lisa gave Jan a questioning shrug and pointed to the door. Jan shook her head firmly and pulled herself up on the washer. Lisa, ever practical, opened a pantry cabinet and pulled out a bag of chips.

"We have enough food to feed a battalion," Lisa whispered, tearing open the bag. "We need to baste the turkey again. What do you think Tony will do if we come out? I think they went into Ed's office."

"He won't shoot us in front of Kay," Jan replied, trying to reassure herself. "But he did knock out a policeman. I don't know what'll happen when they wake up."

"Knocked out a cop? Oh great. That's comforting," Lisa said with a sarcastic edge, grabbing a handful of chips. "Hey, don't hog the chips," she added as they waited, listening intently to the sounds around them.

"You're quite chipper for someone facing death," Jan muttered under her breath, trying to steady her nerves.

"As you said, he won't shoot us," Lisa shrugged. "He's just scared. But did he really knock out a cop? That's serious. Any wine in here?" she asked, casually rummaging through the pantry.

"Will you be quiet, please?" Jan whispered Jan.

"Why?"

"In case Margaret or devil dog is out there," said Jan

"Oh, please. Margaret would just smack him with a frying pan, and devil dog loves him," Lisa replied dismissively but then paused. "Wait. Did you hear that? Someone's out back. Maybe the cop's awake. I could sneak out and check."

"What if it's that someone that Tony's afraid of? I think there is someone bad out there. That's the impression I got from the FDLE guy earlier. Stevie said they put an FBI agent around the ICU to protect Carol. And they had police posted outside here. We need to take this seriously, Lisa."

"You're right," Lisa admitted. "I'm just scared. I don't want to think about more bad stuff happening. Carol's been through enough. So have the girls. And now Tony, with a gun, no less. Shit!" She trailed off, nervously rummaging through the cabinets.

"Aha!" Jan suddenly said, pulling out a bottle of pineapple gin. She unscrewed the cap, took a quick swig, and held it out to Lisa.

They passed the bottle back and forth in silence, munching on potato chips as they sat in the dimly lit room. After a few moments, Jan put a finger to her lips and turned off the light. Together, they leaned toward the laundry room door, peeking into the darkness beyond.

"You see anything?" Lisa whispered.

"I thought I heard something, and I swear I saw someone moving around, but now I don't see anything," Jan said, squinting into the night.

"This is fucking ridiculous," said Lisa as she opened the laundry room door and went into the kitchen. "I have to baste the turkey. It's almost done."

Jan followed walking over to the dining room entrance, tilting her ear toward Ed's office. They both stood a moment and listened. They heard Tony mostly. His baritone vibrated the door to the study. He was pleading. Kay's voice could be heard, too, but they didn't catch any sign of Stevie.

"Do you think she'll go with him? Isn't she safer here?" asked Jan.

"I thought so, but we don't have any protection now, thanks to Tony. If the cops wake up and rush in, that's not going to end well. The real danger right now is if Margaret and Devil Dog get up. What do we do? What do we do?" Lisa muttered to herself, pacing back and forth.

"Eat lots and lots of food," Jan said, grinning drunkenly.

"You're drunk, aren't you?" Lisa said, raising an eyebrow. "Damn it! What are we supposed to do?" She continued basting the turkey, the tension starting to weigh down on her. Tony seemed completely out of control, and she didn't know if they could trust him.

"We could hit the bad guy with the turkey or shoot him with the hot juice from the baster," Jan suggested, giggling as she took another swig of gin from the bottle.

"Gimme that bottle, you idiot. It's not good for us both to get drunk. We need to be on our toes," said Lisa as she snatched the bottle from Jan.

"I know you're right. what's the plan?" Jan asked, her nerves showing. "Do you think we can talk any sense into Tony? I think he's gone over the edge. Maybe we should call Joanne. She knows all the players—the police, FBI as far as I can piece together. Stevie said she's been in on some kind of investigation ."

"She did mention that. We can't forget Roger was murdered. Joanne could be our best bet," Lisa said as she picked up the phone to dial Joanne's number. Just then, Tony reappeared.

Lisa quickly hung up the phone but held onto it.

"I'm not going to hurt anyone," said Tony.

"You're holding us at gunpoint, and you expect us to believe that?" Lisa said, moving slightly toward Kay when they all entered the room behind Tony.

"Just put the gun away, please, Tony, please!" said Kay.

"What do you think, Stevie?" asked Lisa when she saw her behind Kay.

"Tell them what's going on. You know you can trust them. Don't be more of a fool," said Stevie. Lisa quickly positioned herself in front of Tony.

"That's not fair, Stevie. Tony's trying to help us. Do the right thing. It's not his fault," said Kay.

"Put the gun down, Tony. We're listening," Jan added softly.

Tony hesitated for a moment. "Okay, everyone, just be quiet. I can't be sure the police are on our side," he said, the gun still in his hand.

"And with a gun pointed at us, we're not sure you're on ours," Jan replied.

"Right," Tony sighed. "Here's what I can tell you. No one is safe. The police think I'm involved with a killer," said Tony, still gesturing with the gun in his hand.

"Are you?" Stevie asked sharply.

"No! Not really. I was involved in Ed's company, but Charles said I was helping Ed. You know Ed was a gambler. Hell, the whole world knows that now. But it was worse than you think."

"He was always good to us," Kay said quietly.

"Honey, you need to understand. He was taking kickbacks on city contracts. Plus, I was all wrong about the new company. I thought what I was doing was great. —making money, ya' know. Sellin' like crazy. Come to find out, it was all a setup."

It wasn't your fault," Kay said.

"I don't know. I just don't know who to believe anymore. I'm sure Charles was lying, Eddy, Jr was lying, and Ed, well, I just don't know what he knew or didn't know, but he was in big trouble. According to Charles, it was all Ed's fault...ya' know, his gambling. Then, he borrowed money from the wrong people. Jeez, this is bad. The more I tried to fix things, the worse it got," said Tony.

"Why didn't you talk to my Mom," said Kay.

"You're right. I should have talked to her. She's smart. She and Ed were already fighting, quietly but fighting. You said so, Kay," said Tony.

"I know, still," said Kay.

"To be honest, I didn't want to give up the money. It felt good, for once, to have something... to give you the new car, the house," Tony added, looking at Kay.

"Don't you dare blame this on Kay," Stevie snapped, stepping forward.

"Tony, Kay, Stevie... just stop. Give me the gun, and we can talk about why we're in danger and from whom," said Lisa as she stood firmly in front of Tony and the gun with her hand out, asking for the gun.

"That would be helpful," Jan said quietly from behind them.

"While we're all so friendly, let's remember that Tony knocked out a cop. Unless you killed them, they will be awake soon, if not already, and think we're in a hostage situation," said Lisa.

"That puts everyone in danger. We should call the police or FBI or even Joanne. We must protect everyone literally and legally," said Stevie.

"No cops," Tony said, his voice rising as he waved the gun.

Everyone jumped when the phone rang. Then came the barking of the dog, Margaret's voice shouting from the stairs, and suddenly the lanai door burst open. Shots rang out.

Chapter 23

Donnie arrived at the offices as Jimmy was headed to the interrogation room to work on Atoll some more. With a nod from Donnie, Jimmy moved to the other side of the building and followed him into a large room set up with long tables and chairs arranged like a training room. As Jimmy approached, he heard Donnie instruct another agent to take Atoll to Plaid Way. *Must be a safe house.*

"So sorry about Al," said Jimmy. Donnie gave him a hard look, then lightly punched his arm. Jimmy felt the grief and anger in that punch, in the expressionless eyes. He had felt that before, as many cops had. Lightly shaking his head, Jimmy surveyed the room as agents filled the rows of tables and chairs. Donnie quickly moved to one of the three whiteboards across the front. Joanne and her business partner, Benny, were already seated.

Jimmy took a seat next to Sal.

"We must catch this bastard. Donnie and his guys are pretty sure he's behind at least three murders. I am not so sure Ed Wallin wasn't also one of his victims. From everything the agents told me, this guy is clever," said Sal.

"He got you. Did they find your car?" asked Jimmy.

"At the University of Tampa," Sal replied.

"Did anybody see him?"

"A couple of students but Donnie's guys who interviewed people at the hospital and the students all had conflicting images—except for his shoes. White sneakers, small feet, ball cap. Stupid but interesting," Sal said thoughtfully.

Jimmy nodded as he watched Donnie draw a rough map of Tampa Bay, marking key areas: the airport to the west, Ybor City to the east, MacDill Air Force Base to the south, and the suburb of Carrollwood, Jimmy's home area, to the north. Donnie added red and blue marks on the map—red marked with a "K" and blue with a "T".

"What do you think this is about?" whispered Jimmy.

"I think we're about to find out, and I don't like the way Donnie's looking at me," said Sal, clenching his fists on the table.

This doesn't look good, thought Jimmy. "Sal, it's okay. Let's just listen to what he has to say."

"I know Sal wouldn't agree, and yesterday, neither would I," Donnie continued. "Yet everywhere there was a killing, Toco was also there. Please wait until I'm done," he added, raising a hand stop sign.

"Sal. Just listen," said Jimmy out of the side of his mouth.

"Toco's real name is Giannetto Costa. He was FBI deep cover in New Jersey, Italy, Miami, and God knows where else. I worked with him; Sal worked with him. We left him undercover for too long. Still, if he's a killer now, he's a killer," said Donnie as the room grew tens.

A 'but' died slowly on Sal's lips.

"Hold it together. We'll figure this out," said Jimmy, giving Donnie a pleading look.

Donnie raised his stop sign again. "Sal, I know he saved your life in the past. You think he protects you and others now. I don't want to discuss your feelings about him. I have them too. We all understand," Donnie said, and the room seemed to relax as everyone took a deep breath.

Jimmy poked Sal's thigh with his knee. "Keep your cool." Jimmy's mind was racing a mile a minute as the room erupted into a dozen private conversations.

"Listen up!" shouted Donnie. He paused to let the room settle. "What I want is to catch a killer. I believe this person is responsible for at least three murders in Tampa. Our BOLO and MO have caught domestic and international attention. Right now, Toco is a witness or a person of interest. We will keep an open mind. Is that understood?" Donnie said.

Jimmy looked around. Everyone was nodding and looking from Donnie to Sal, waiting as Donnie reviewed his notes. Jimmy knew whoever this guy was; he was smart and dangerous. He could see it in the hardened faces around him; they knew it, too. Jimmy jumped when his mantra of *stay calm, stay focused* was broken by Donnie slamming his hand on the podium.

"To bring everyone up to date, we have prepared background files for review. We also have a problem with Ed Wallin's son, Edward T. Wallin, Jr., known as Eddy. You will find information on Wallin's son-in-law, Tony LaNina, in the files being passed around. Both Eddy and Tony are connected to known crime families. Eddy is up to his hairline in stock fraud, bribery, and extortion, connected through Wallin's first wife's family. Tony is directly tied to Tampa Mafia boss Alonso on his mother's side."

Jimmy's heart raced. *This is part of what's got Sal spooked.*

"We don't know the extent of Tony's involvement or knowledge. We do know he is guilty of stock fraud. Joanne or Benny can clarify any stock issues. In case you didn't know, they are on our stock fraud task force courtesy of the SEC and are fully vetted and Quantico trained."

Joanne and Benny raised their hands in acknowledgment, looking around the room as Donnie continued.

"We have BOLOs out on both Ed Wallin, Jr. and Tony LaNina, who's Wallin's son-in-law through his marriage to Carol Wallin's daughter, Kay." Agents started talking again. Until Donnie rapped the podium.

"Listen up! Eddy or Tony may have seen this guy, so we need their cooperation. Keep that in mind if you find them. We can leverage their stock fraud charges to help catch this killer," said Donnie.

As the agents sifted through the files, Jimmy saw sketches, photos, and reports. "This is bigger than the governor, bigger than Wallin. Shit, this is an international hurricane," said Jimmy to Sal as he sat back down.

"Toco didn't do it," said Sal.

"Sal, he's a person of interest. If anything, your crazy man has seen him and can describe him," said Jimmy, hoping to calm Sal.

"If nothing else, we think Toco—Mr. Costa—can describe him," echoed Donnie.

Everyone was shuffling the paperwork. Jimmy was glad he could read quickly. Meanwhile, Sal sat stiffly with his hand resting on the file cover.

"We've compiled everything we know about Mr. K in this file, both local and international. There are sketches from witnesses. However, all are different except for his height and shoes. No one's certain about his eyes since he was wearing sunglasses. Benny and Joanne have contributed to the description from Carol Wallin, her nurse, and her daughter's perspectives. He was last seen in Carol Wallin's room, so Al went after him into the stairwell."

That's our clue. Atoll was there at the same time. I can leverage that with him if Donnie gives me the go-ahead. Asstol does know what the killer looks like and probably who he is. Jimmy signaled to Donnie, who came over to his table.

"Is the FBI keeping control of Atoll? I have been priming him as you requested," said Jimmy.

"I talked with the governor. I am willing to make a deal with him but I'm not giving away the store. He's in this way past his ass in trouble. You're in charge. I'll make sure he knows you can make a deal. If you need more leverage, I'll let him know you have the Federal as well as State prosecutor's attention," said Donnie.

Finally, Jimmy thought.

"I'm just letting you know I back you 100 percent. Get that description. Don't wander. You understand the importance. Right? No excuses. Results and quickly."

Jimmy nodded enthusiastically.

"Remember, he's a lawyer, so watch yourself. Agent Talbot is also a lawyer, and I told her you might need to consult her. She's on the second floor if you need her. Martin will provide all the contact information you need, day or night. He also has the safe house coverage schedule," said Donnie.

Jimmy kept nodding. He turned to Sal at the same time as Donnie. *Stay calm,* he said to himself, willing Sal to just listen.

"Sal, you'll work with Martin, organizing and passing along information to the field as we follow leads. Sal, close your mouth. I'm not letting you in the field, and the FDLE agrees. No discussion," Donnie said, returning to the front of the room.

"Come on, Sal, Donnie's right. You were knocked out, and you're too close to Toco. I'm sure Donnie will let you help talk to him if he comes in. Keep cool, okay?" said Jimmy, squeezing Sal's shoulder. Jimmy wasn't worried that Sal would do something stupid. He was worried that Toco might.

"Everyone, please read the material before you head into the field with your assignments. Martin has outlined everything, including your area of responsibility and the reporting structure."

Jimmy turned to that page along with the other agents. He noticed that both he and Sal were reporting directly to Donnie.

"I know it seems a bit political. Well, it is. We're being watched by everyone. And…" Donnie paused as the door opened, and an agent signaled him.

"What do you think is up? It looks serious," Jimmy wondered out loud, noticing Donnie's expression change.

"What the fuck?" shouted Donnie, turning back to the room.

"Okay, folks, we have another situation. Agent Thompson stopped by the Wallins and found our agent, Alfonso, knocked out. He took him to the hospital and called local authorities."

Jimmy saw Donnie's eyes scan the room before landing back on Sal.

"Shit! Sal, please coordinate with Tampa police and the sheriff's office. Carson and Rodriquez, you're in charge in the field."

"On it," said Sal as he stood.

"Sal, Carson, Rodriquez—make sure the locals know they are to do nothing, absolutely nothing until our guys arrive. Joanne,

Benny, freeze. You are not getting in the middle of this. You stay put until I direct you somewhere. Sit, Stay, that's an order," said Donnie, pressing his fingers to his temples.

Jimmy watched as Donnie issued new orders. After clapping Sal on the back in encouragement, he stood to go to the safe house. His mind raced with strategy. He had to get a description of Mr. K from Atoll. He could do this. He heard Donnie direct Joanne and Benny to stay with Carol at the hospital and bring her here if possible. *Good thinking. She must be frantic. Pretty sure she's on the hit list along with Asstoll. What about Joanne? I hope she's okay. I should check on her.*

"Atoll is your priority," said Donnie, reading Jimmy's thoughts. Just then, another agent entered.

"There's been a shooting at the Wallins," said the agent.

"Who?" asked Jimmy and Donnie in unison.

"Unclear. It was the Tampa Police who did the shooting."

"Why didn't they wait?" Donnie asked the air as he and Jimmy rushed out.

Chapter 24

— • ⬤ • —

Carol sat rigidly with Jan on one side and Joanne on the other, all three with tears streaming down their faces. She stared at Jimmy, who was trying to explain what had happened, but all she could hear was, "blah, blah, blah."

"The bastards won," Carol said, her voice hoarse. Her eyes were swollen, and her chest ached from the accident. *I have to be strong. My baby needs me. I need them.*

"It can't be true," Jan murmured, swaying lightly back and forth in the harsh breeze of grief surrounding their chairs.

"It was just a mistake. She was in the wrong place at the wrong time, that's all," Jimmy said.

"Nobody would believe this shit. Too far-fetched, too stupid, too…" Joanne began.

"I should be dead," Jan whispered.

"Stop it, both of you! You, Mister Big Agent—where were you? Your buddies barged into MY HOME. THEY SHOT MY BABY GIRL. THEY KILLED MY FRIEND. My gentle, beautiful friend. Do you even know her name? Lisa Ann Kensington. SAY IT, SAY IT!" Carol shouted, standing and pointing a finger at Jimmy. Joanne stood and put an arm around Carol.

Carol shook her off and continued advancing toward Jimmy, "Why are you protecting them? Blue wall, isn't that what they call it? Protecting your buds while a killer is still …"

The door from the operating area opened and a doctor and nurse appeared. "Mrs. Wallin?" said the surgeon.

"My daughter?"

"She'll be fine. The bullet missed anything vital. Just soft tissue. She'll make a full recovery."

Carol's mind seemed to wake up. Boiling anger and grief had made it a numb weight. Now she tried to picture Kay smiling. *Stevie, oh god, Stevie. My brave girl tackled those cops. They wanted to arrest her. Stupid, stupid, stupid. Breathe. Kay needs you. You are strong.*

"Can I see her?" Carol asked.

"She's not awake yet, but John will take you to her so you can be there when she wakes," said the surgeon.

Carol turned to the nurse, who gently took her arm and led her toward the recovery area.

***

Jimmy placed his hand on the closest wall and took a deep breath, then turned toward Jan and Joanne, who leaned against the wall across from him. Noticing Joanne's knees giving way, he rushed to her, catching her just before her head hit the floor. Jan slid down the wall and crawled over to help.

"You okay? Can you hold her while I get a nurse?" Jimmy said to Jan's nodding head. He ran to the nurse's station.

Mrs. Wallin is right. All of the police were trying to protect the fuck up. And it was that. Yup, stupid. Despite the orders, they rushed in with their guns, saw Tony's gun, and fired. Lisa Ann Kensington, Lisa Ann Kensington. She was right; I didn't know her name. Why had she jumped in the way? "Damn, damn," Jimmy muttered as the nurse ignored him. "Excuse me, the lady down the hall has fainted. Can you come with me now?"

"Pardon?" said the nurse.

"Come with me, please. Someone's fainted," Jimmy repeated.

"Well, why didn't you say so?" the nurse replied.

"I… never mind. This way," said Jimmy, leading the nurse down the hall and around the corner in front of the operating room waiting area.

She'll be fine. Jimmy thought. He watched as the nurse checked on Joanne, called for another nurse, and then placed Joanne in a wheelchair despite her protests.

"Agent Perez?" someone behind him called.

"Yes," said Jimmy, turning to see Martin.

"Sorry, Martin. I know Donnie said not to dawdle here, but, well, you can see," said Jimmy. His stomach churned, knowing he wasn't where he was supposed to be.

"Donnie wants you back with Atoll. He's pissed. Get a description of Mr. K, like yesterday. I know you have a relationship with these people, but catching this guy is more important. You get that, right? What are you even doing here?" Martin demanded.

"I got a call from a friend at the Tampa Police. They sent someone to relieve me so I could be here. Is Sal with you?" Jimmy asked.

"Tampa Police? Are you serious? This isn't where you're needed. Get the information we need. Sal's waiting downstairs. Donnie thinks he might be able to help with Atoll. Double-team him," Martin replied.

"Yes, he could. Sal can be one scary dude when he wants to be. He's a great actor, too," said Jimmy.

"And you're still here," said Martin.

"On my way, you'll…"

"I'll handle the ladies. You get us something useful. Now!" shouted Martin as he started walking toward Joanne, who was now getting out of the wheelchair.

"Got it," Jimmy said as he headed to the elevator. *Damn it. Pull it together, Perez. Letting Asstol stew might work for us. Sal could be just the catalyst we need.*

"Hey, Partner," said Jimmy to Sal's back. As Sal turned, Jimmy continued, "You've got a look. What's going on? I'm in trouble for leaving Atoll, I know. I asked him about Toco. He didn't flinch. He did know who he was but didn't seem bothered. That's good, right? We've ruled out a suspect."

"Since when did you become a whiny ass detective? This lady, whatever you're feeling for her, isn't your problem. Donnie knows you two were involved. You are spinning out of control. Gotta tell ya, I'm losing respect, Jimmy."

"You're right. I'm back. Really. Let's work, Atoll. How do you want to handle this?" asked Jimmy.

Jimmy listened intently, mentally kicking himself. They decided Sal would take the lead, get tough, and then step out to grab food, leaving Jimmy to work the good-guy power trip leverage angle. *This has got to work. I may have gotten people hurt and blown my career. We must get this guy.*

Jimmy and Sal each went to the safe house. It wasn't that far from the hospital, in an older neighborhood from the 1940s. The unremarkable house was a three-bedroom with a living room in front, a kitchen in the back, and a single bathroom. *Two doors to cover.* After escorting the police guy out and letting Sal in, Jimmy locked the doors.

"So what have you got for me?" Sal asked as Jimmy checked the windows, doors, and rooms.

"I don't know anything," Atoll muttered.

"Fine, suit yourself. We all know you're in this up to your fake hairpiece. It's just a matter of organizing the evidence. Note, I said, organize, not gather," Sal said.

"You have nothing, or you would have arrested me," said Atoll.

"Well, we are a little more cautious about charging lawyers. Your time will come. Another death has happened," Sal said, dropping onto the couch before getting up. "I'm hungry. You are good here with Mr. Atoll, Agent Perez?" asked Sal as he headed to the door.

"What? Who?" Atoll stammered as Jimmy and Sal ignored him.

"I'm hungry. How about you, Jimmy?" Sal said.

"Tony, right? It was Tony," said Atoll.

"I haven't eaten much today," said Sal.

"I asked you a question," said Atoll.

"Did you say something, Mr. Atoll?' asked Sal.

"Who was killed? I knew he'd come back to clean up. Suppose it could be Eddy, but he's dangerous too. This place better be secure. You and your cop friends probably have so many leaks I'm toast. You're responsible for protecting me," Atoll sputtered.

"Did you ask if someone came back? Who came back? Someone to be concerned about? Why do you think Eddy is dangerous? What about Tony? Maybe it's one of them. Should we protect you from them?" Sal asked.

"It's not them, you fool. And Tony's dead. Right. You must tell me. Where's Eddy?"

"I'm going for some food," Sal said, signaling Jimmy to take over.

"Are you worried about someone?" Jimmy asked.

"I'm his lawyer," Atoll replied.

"You mean Ed Wallin's son?" asked Jimmy.

"If you have him in custody, you must tell me. I'm his lawyer, so tell me. You can't believe anything he'd say. Is it Tony? Is he dead?"

"Why do you think Tony's dead?" asked Jimmy.

"You said… Oh, I see, it's Eddy. I can tell from your change in posture and your eyes. You're just fishing. You think you're clever, Agent Perez? Remember, I interview and cross-examine, too. I may not be a criminal lawyer, but a corporate lawyer knows how to manipulate information just like you are trying to do," Atoll retorted.

"You think I'm manipulating you? As you said, I'm not that clever. But I am curious—why do you think it's Eddy? Would it change things if it were?" Jimmy asked.

Atoll started pacing while Jimmy sat quietly as if he had all the time in the world. *I have him worried, but is he worried enough?* Jimmy just let him pace, even pretending to nap on the couch. When Sal's car returned, Jimmy rose slowly, went to the front window, and moved the curtain twice—their agreed-upon signal.

"Do you see something? Is there someone out there? You should have an agent on the perimeter," Atoll said, visibly nervous.

Just then, there was muffled scuffling outside. Jimmy turned and flattened himself against the wall near the window. "Get down, you fool. If you have something to tell me, now would be a good time. I can't protect you if I don't know what I'm looking for. What does this guy look like? Describe him."

A shadow moved outside the front door, and Atoll ducked behind the couch. Sal opened the door. Jimmy just shook his head and tried not to laugh. Sal had McDonald's bags and purposely looked disheveled and wobbly.

"Hope you're not too hungry. Not much open this time of night. Where's our guest?" Sal asked as Jimmy signaled to Atoll, who was peeking over the back of the couch.

"We thought someone was outside," said Atoll.

"That was me. Dropped a bag. Hope you like Mickey D's. Time to get home to the wife, Jimmy. I'll stay with our esteemed guest," said Sal, heading to the kitchen.

"You can't leave me with this Neanderthal. He's Italian, you know that. He's probably in with organized crime. And he looks drunk," Atoll hissed in a loud whisper.

"No reason to stay. If I can't negotiate a deal, I might as well get some sleep. It's been a long day," said Jimmy, heading toward the door.

"Okay, listen. I'm not admitting anything, but I may be able to give you a description. I may have seen this, shall we say, person of interest. You must stay. I'll give you the best description I can. I want immunity from any type of prosecution. I want that in writing first," Atoll insisted.

"I'm listening, Mr. Atoll. To be honest, I'm tired, and I don't think your information will help much. We have other witnesses—from the hospital and one from near Roger Barnes' home. Oh yeah, as I recall, you were seen with this person both times," Jimmy replied.

Sal went over to the table, picked up a legal pad, shook it, and set it down. "As far as I'm concerned, you're culpable. It's just a matter of time. We'll get you, or he will—I don't care either way. So, if you have something to say, say it. Write it down or don't. For all I know, he could be in custody already," Sal said, heading to the kitchen.

Atoll moved to the dining table, picked up a pen, and exaggeratedly dusted off the chair with his hand, then sat down. Jimmy turned his back and sat on the couch. There was scuffling in the backyard.

Atoll's eyes widened. "Did you hear that?"

Jimmy ignored him.

"This is what I know."

Jimmy stood, shook his head, and pointed to the legal pad.

"I have information. Donnie, the FBI Agent in Charge, said you could make deals. I want a deal. Did you hear something outside again?" said Atoll.

"A deal for what? Write it down now, or I just walk out the door," said Jimmy as he turned away, knowing that Sal had slipped outside to mess with Atoll. Jimmy fought back a smirk.

"Fine," Atoll muttered, starting to write.

Jimmy could hear Sal re-enter and get on the phone in the kitchen. He was exhausted. *Finally, the bastard came through. I might keep my job after all.*

Chapter 25

Joanne shook off Martin's hand. "I'm fine. Where's Stevie? Jimmy? Benny? Is Jan okay?"

"Everyone is fine. Mrs. Wallin is with her daughter. Agent Perez is doing his job. Stevie is in the waiting room down the hall. How about you? Make sure you're okay before you start running around. You're still part of the task force, so keep your head straight. Jesus, what a cluster, you know?" said Martin.

"Benny?

"He's with Stevie. Satisfied?"

"What bug crawled up your ass? I'm just asking. Sorry about fainting, but I needed food. I haven't eaten since yesterday afternoon. I'm fine now," said Joanne replied, waving half a sandwich in Martin's face.

"Well, I'll tell you, we're going nuts trying to find our Mr. K, and Jimmy was supposed to get info from Atoll, but he was too worried about you to do his job!"

"And that is my fault, how?" Joanne said, getting up and moving toward the door. "I'm going to check on Stevie unless I'm under arrest because someone checked on me. And why are you staying with me?"

"I'm doing my job."

"Shouldn't you be searching for Tony, Eddy, or Mr. K? Speaking of that. Did Tony get away?" asked Joanne.

"He's on the list of people to catch. Trust me, we'll get him."

"He's only guilty of being scared, trying to protect his wife, and, well, stock fraud. And you guys come in shooting!"

"It wasn't us. He knocked out an agent and had a gun. I'm not arguing with you about this—you know it was a fuck up," said Martin.

Joanne knew he was right. She felt so tired and still hungry, now even angrier. She looked at Martin like she was seeing him for the first time. He had dark circles under his eyes, and his cheeks were drawn. "You look like hell."

"Let's stop fighting each other and figure out how we can catch the killer and not lose anyone else." Martin's beeper went off. "Gotta call in and check with the guy outside ICU. Maybe Perez got the description we need. You ready to continue?"

"I'm good," said Joanne, faking a smile.

"You're assigned to the Wallins with Benny. Carol may have seen Mr. K, so see if you can… Okay, I see that look, but we need information. I know she's upset, but it's more important to stop this madman before he disappears again. He's cleaning the house, so stay on your toes," Martin said as he headed toward the ICU.

"Go, go, I'm fine," said Joanne. "I'll find Carol and see what she remembers." *Damn, why did Jimmy come looking for me? He knows better. I don't think Carol saw the guy. Okay, Jersey girl. You're tough, so pull yourself together.*

Joanne walked down the hall toward intensive care. *Too much time spent in hospitals. Time for life to turn around. This madman is clever. Damn, Carol's husband. Good thing he's dead; I'd like to strangle the guy. Oh, good lord, someone already did; pull it together.*

Joanne stopped, scanning the few chairs in the waiting area, then backed up to look into each family waiting room and the kitchen area. Her instincts told her something, but she couldn't pin it down.

"Someone's watching me," she whispered, startled when she realized she'd said it out loud. She put her back against a clear wall and just let her senses take over. *What was it? A sound? A smell? It was a smell. Something she smelled in her house. And shoes showing somewhere? No, a shoe poking out. Small, white.* Standing still back still against the wall. *Safety in numbers. What about Carol? It's okay. He can't get into ICU, I hope. Damn, where's Stevie? Martin said, a waiting room. What waiting room? Think, were any doors closed? No. Okay. Where did you see the shoes..shoe?*

Keeping her back to the wall, Joanne moved to the nearest doorway, did a quick check inside, and then pressed back to the wall. The kitchen was further down the hall, across from her. *Wait, that's where I saw the shoe. To my right, as I entered—yes, a white semicircle, like a sneaker, sticking out from behind the drink machine. Hmm, best call the feds or find Bennie. Let's not get stupid.*

Her mind made up, Joanne turned and hurried to the nurse's station. She knew she wouldn't help Stevie by jumping into anything on her own. "I need your phone," she said to the nurse, who was busy with paperwork.

"There is a public phone by the water fountain to your left," said the nurse without looking up.

"This is an emergency. I am working with the FBI, and someone is in danger. Please, just give me the phone," Joanne said.

"Yeah, and I am the First Lady," the nurse said, still focused on her tasks.

Joanne grabbed the closest phone and started dialing, but just then, the elevator doors opened, and Benny and Stevie stepped out. Joanne dropped the phone and rushed to hug Stevie tightly.

"Wow, Aunt Jo, missed you too. Everything okay? Any news? Kay is doing well, right? They were about to move her to ICU from recovery," said Stevie.

"Oh, right. Your mom was with her in recovery. Did you see them leave?" Joanne asked.

"I saw them go about thirty minutes ago. Benny and I decided to grab something from the cafeteria. You should probably do that as well. When was the last time you ate? I'm going to switch with Mom and make her get something," Stevie said.

"No, she should stay with Kay. You should go there as well. Benny, wait by the ICU entrance," Joanne instructed.

"What's going on?" Benny asked.

"He's here. I can feel it," said Joanne.

"Who?" asked Stevie.

"Too long of a story right now," said Joanne, grabbing the phone again. The nurse rose with one hand on her hip and the other reaching for the phone.

Benny pulled out a wallet with an official-looking badge. "If you don't mind, we need to make a call," he said to the nurse.

Joanne dialed Donnie's number. Nothing happened.

"You have to dial 9," said the nurse.

Joanne redialed. "Donnie, I think he's here at the hospital, outside ICU. Benny and Stevie are with me… Uh-huh. Okay." She hung up. "He's sending an agent and told us to wait here."

"Did you see Martin?" Benny asked.

"He was going to check on everyone in ICU and make some calls. Oh, here he comes," Joanne said as she spotted Martin coming down the hall between the ICU and the Cardiac Unit.

"Ms. LaNina and Mrs. Wallin are in ICU, and everything seems in order. What's with the look?" Martin asked Joanne.

"I think he's in the kitchen on the left, around the side of the drink machine," Joanne replied.

"Mr. K? We need to let Donnie know. When did you see him?" said Martin.

"I already called him. He's sending someone. I only saw his shoe—maybe 10 or 20 minutes ago," said Joanne.

"He's probably waiting for the coast to clear. You check the rooms on the right. I got left," said Martin to Benny.

"Where's the kitchen?" asked Benny.

"Middle left," Joanne said as she grabbed Stevie's hand.

"Let's do this," said Martin as he and Benny headed toward the kitchen.

Chapter 26

—————————— • ● • ——————————

Holding Stevie's hand, Joanne was mesmerized by the movements of Benny and Martin as they proceeded down the hallway. Would it be too much to hope they could catch Mr. K now and end part of this nightmare?

She was sure she had seen a white sneaker hiding behind the soda machine. Then there was that smell—citrusy and spicy, oddly out of place in the hospital corridor. Joanne tried to breathe normally as she watched the two men searching the rooms on either side of the hall. All she needed was popcorn. It felt like being in a slasher movie when you know there's trouble coming. *Please get him.*

Worry enveloped her again. *How do I protect Stevie? Everyone? I keep smelling his smell. What am I sensing? Is he still here?*

A sudden noise behind them made Joanne and Stevie whirl around. Someone popped up from behind a nurse who now had a piece of tubing wrapped around her neck.

"Let her go," shouted Stevie and Joanne. Joanne held Stevie's shoulder tightly, terrified the girl would do something that would get her hurt. Stevie broke free and ran toward the opening of the nurse's station.

"Stevie, stop!" shouted Joanne

Joanne followed.

The nurse was shoved toward them and fell onto Stevie while Joanne was shoved aside.

"Benny, Martin," she shouted as Mr. K sprinted toward the opening elevator. Joanne ran as well. Sliding to a stop she glared as Mr. K. slipped in and turned toward her as the elevator doors were closing.

Joanne froze, looking at the elevator.

"His grin—the bastard was grinning at me," Joanne muttered, her voice shaking. "Those eyes, creepy dead eyes... and two different colors."

"Stay put. We'll head down," Benny instructed as Martin came up beside him.

"He grinned," Joanne repeated, the image still burning in her mind. Benny stepped into the next elevator, holding the door for Martin. She lightly touched his hand as he released the button, silently mouthing, *Be careful.* Joanne took a deep breath. She walked back to Stevie, who was holding the struggling nurse on the floor behind the nurse's station.

"OMG, who is this monster? Aunt Jo. Tell me!" Stevie asked, eyes wide with terror.

"A madman," Joanne said, her voice hollow. She fought to pull herself together, feeling a new surge of determination. She heard Stevie's calm, clear voice as she spoke to the nurse and then to her.

"Aunt Jo, get a doctor or nurse."

Joanne raced toward the ICU. As she rounded the corner, she remembered the hidden elevator meant for patient transport just across from the ICU entrance. Spotting a group of used oxygen tanks, she grabbed one and stood by the elevator. "Come on on Mr. K, make my day," Joanne said to the closed doors. All her instincts told her he was coming back. *Can I hit him hard enough? Jesus, I am such a fool. Why can't you show up now? Jimmy, huh?* As the doors slid open. Joanne's breath caught, but instead of Mr. K, a hospital employee emerged, staring at her in disbelief. "What the hell are you doing?" he demanded.

"Oh, this?" Joanne glanced at the oxygen tank clutched in her hands. "I don't know. Being stupid, I guess." She snapped back to urgency. "We need security up here and a doctor for an injured nurse by the cardiac station. There's a killer on the loose. Quickly, NOW!"

She watched as the orderly ran into the ICU to make the call. Joanne lowered the tank from her defensive position. *Just go be with Stevie or Carol, idiot. You're not helping anyone standing here.*

The elevator behind her opened again, and she spun around, half-expecting Mr. K's sinister grin. Instead, it was Benny.

"Did you see where he went?" Joanne asked.

"No, but I see you had the same idea about this elevator," Benny replied, his eyes landing on the oxygen tank in her grip. "I wasn't sure he left the hospital. He could've gone down one floor and circled back. Planning on using that?"

"Screw you," Joanne shot back. "I don't have a gun, remember? I'm going to check on Stevie and the nurse. Are you staying here? We need security at this door. Where's Martin?"

"He's searching. I don't think they're going to find him. From what I can remember, he was wearing scrubs but he's a chameleon. Be careful!" Benny called as Joanne hurried toward Stevie.

She paused, turning to face Benny; Joanne saw the elevator open again. A Security guard stepped out of one elevator and then quickly backed in as the doors closed. Moments later, the second elevator opened, and Benny lunged inside. Joanne only heard him shout, "It's him!"

Running back, she frantically jabbed at the elevator button, yelling, "Security!" to the empty hallway.

***

Jimmy felt a rush of anticipation as he entered the hospital. Donnie had been pleased with the detailed description. He loved leaving Atoll at FBI headquarters after he had worked with the sketch artist. *Boy was Asstol pissed. What a total narcissist.* Now, with copies of the sketch in hand, Jimmy was ready to catch this killer. *So, this guy has small feet, large hands, two different colored eyes, and a red birthmark on the left side of his face up by his hairline, running across his forehead to the middle in kind of a circle or a noose.*

Lost in thought, he almost collided with someone running by. *Geez, that guy was in a hurry. Dayna telling me over the phone she was leaving for good has me spinning. Guess I never gave her the time to tell me in person. Pull it together, Señor Imbécil; I'm losing it. Wait, that guy had a red mark. Didn't he?*

Jimmy turned and ran back outside, but there was no one in sight. Back inside, he did a quick search of the lobby area. There was only one old man with a walker near the exit door. Dropping his tense shoulders, he slumped over to the information desk. Donnie had said he should coordinate with the agent there.

"One more look," he muttered to himself as he headed out again. Only the same old man was walking slowly to the parking lot, but that's all.

"Damn, where'd he go?" Jimmy said as he stepped back inside, only to be met by Martin.

"I think I just saw him leave. He almost ran me down."

"Where?" asked Martin.

"Out this door, but he's gone now. Only an old guy with the walker. I swear, I'm starting to see him everywhere since I've been working with Atoll on this for hours."

"Let's look anyway. This bastard is slippery. He attacked a nurse near the cardiac unit, then managed to change clothes and take the elevator up to the ICU," said Martin.

Benny appeared beside them, out of breath. "Did you tell him the guy came to the ICU floor dressed as a security guard about twenty minutes ago? He saw me and disappeared. I checked two floors already. Where are we on the search?"

Jimmy handed Martin and Benny the sketch. "Is this the guy? I think he's dressed in scrubs now. Let's take another look outside," Jimmy said, absorbing the story about the nurse and their ongoing search.

"I only got a brief look. I did notice his eyes. One was light blue, the other brown. Weird," Benny said.

"That's him. Let's take another look outside," Jimmy said, motioning that he would go left toward the old man while Martin went right and Benny straight ahead.

About a foot away from where he'd last seen the old guy, he spotted a foot—an old man's foot.

"Over here!" Jimmy called as he looked down at the twisted body of the old man. "*He's a goner. His head is almost twisted off.* Sick bastard. Poor ole' guy never had a chance. What an idiot I am. Ya know, there's probably a Doc strangled somewhere along with a security guard and probably another hospital visitor," Jimmy said, feeling frustrated.

"We need to update Donnie and get protection organized for your 'special' friend and the Wallins. I need a cell phone, not just a beeper. Damn cheap FBI," Martin muttered as Benny joined them, staring at the old man.

"I'd better get upstairs to the ladies. He could still double back. Slippery, clever, and deadly. Not a good combination for us," Benny said.

"I'll stay with the old guy until they load him up. You want the FDLE, Tampa police, or FBI forensics here? I'll protect the scene if you think it's worth it?" Jimmy asked Martin.

"Sorry to be cold, but I want everyone to be looking for this killer. I'll get some of our people over here, but I doubt we'll find much. Buckman and another agent are by the information desk. I'll have one of them stay with the body. I don't want to involve the Tampa Police guys right now," Martin replied.

Jimmy knew Martin was right, but he couldn't shake the feeling that they were being watched. He wanted to be the one to catch this killer.

"Jimmy, I need you to deliver those sketches to everyone. Buckman can tell you where our guys are in the hospital while I update Donnie. Give all hospital personnel the sketch as well and make sure they know how dangerous this guy is," Martin instructed.

"I can do more than that," Jimmy said, frustrated.

"Just do what you're told for now. Is that too much to ask?" Martin replied as he headed back inside.

Jimmy stood there for a moment, clenching and unclenching his fists. He could just drop the large envelope with the sketches at the information desk. Fighting his anger at being reduced to handing out flyers, he took a deep breath and decided to follow orders.

You did this to yourself. Just do as you're told, he thought. *Can't believe Dayna is leaving me for that other guy. I deserve it. She tried, I tried... sort of. Oh, shit. Keep your eyes open. Think with the brain in your head. Do what you do best. Find what's missing. Organize! First, your thoughts, then your life.* "Yeah, right," Jimmy muttered to himself as he headed toward the information desk to hand out the flyers.

Chapter 27

———— • ● • ————

arol was exhausted. She felt like her teeth might fall out, her eyes were burning, and her stomach and jaw ached from being clenched. The residue of anger, worry, and grief pulled at her insides. *Damn them. Kay looks so small and fragile. I bet Joanne knows what's happening. Pull yourself together. Kay is fine. Stevie will continue to be the rock. Joanne, hmmm, what was Joanne? Damn strong women, yes. Was she still her friend? Was she going to hurt or help? Ahh, that's the rub. No, no, she is my friend first. Can I trust that? Can I trust Joanne?*

"How is she?" Joanne asked from the doorway.

"What? Oh, hi. Kay's good. She's just resting, still drugged," Carol replied, feeling heat rise to her cheeks like a child caught thinking dirty thoughts.

Psychically, Joanne asked: "You're wondering if I'm on your side. I love you and the girls. I told you I was investigating stock and fraud issues that might hurt your family. I could say it's just my job. I guess that's an empty excuse. Just know that I will do everything within my power to protect you and the girls. I won't be able to protect Tony or Eddy, though. I'm sorry."

"Come here, you," Carol said, rising to wrap Joanne in a hug. Her taller frame almost swallowed Joanne's petite form.

"Mom?" Kay's voice came out weakly.

"I'm here, darling. You're safe. You're going to be fine. Just rest," Carol said as she and Joanne turned their attention to Kay. Looking at Joanne again, Carol asked, "We will be fine, right?" But before Joanne could answer, Carol changed the subject. "Kay, sweetie, how about some ice chips? They might feel nice on your lips."

"I'll get them," Joanne said, immediately stepping out.

"Was that Aunt JoJo?" Kay asked.

"Yes, sweetie. She's gone to get you some ice chips. How ya' feeling? Are you in pain?"

"Just foggy and uncomfortable. Is Tony here?"

"Just rest, pumpkin. Don't talk too much. Let me or the nurse know if you need anything. You're going to be fine. The doctor will be here this evening. Go on, close your eyes, and rest. I'm here," Carol said as Kay drifted back to sleep.

Alone with her thoughts again, Carol's stomach clenched hard. *Something was very wrong, but what? It's not just Tony or Eddy. Gotta get Joanne to tell me everything. I can't protect my babes against something when I don't know what's happening. Ed, I wish you were here, but wait... this is all because of you, isn't it? Your gambling got us into this mess. I could hate you. You got my baby hurt and Lisa killed. How could Tony have been so stupid bringing a gun into the house?*

"Here's the chips. This spongy Q-tip thingy will help moisten her lips. Guess you know that. Sorry," Joanne said. "I'm going to get Stevie and bring her in here. The nurse said we can all stay in the room, but we need to keep quiet. Where's your mom?"

"I know you will understand, but no one else in the world could. She booked a flight thinking I was trying to get her killed. She and that devil dog are probably back in New Jersey by now."

"Even I don't understand that shit. Oh Carol, I'm so sorry. You must feel so alone and abandoned."

"Honestly, this is better. I can't deal with her right now, not with everything going on. Speaking of that..." Carol grabbed Joanne's arm and moved them outside Kay's room. "What is going on? Please, Joanne, tell me everything. I'm strong enough to handle it. Not knowing is killing me. Please!"

"You're right. Okay, grab a small chair from the room, and I'll get another. This could take some time, and we both need to sit."

Carol knew Joanne was gathering her thoughts. It was her way. She was always fast on her feet and quick to mouth off but not when it came to something serious. She wanted to be prepared. *I need to be prepared too*, Carol thought. She walked over to the nurse's station just as pandemonium broke out near the entrance, the automatic doors opening and closing in rhythm with the struggle. Someone was attacking Joanne's partner, Benny.

"I'll call the cops!" shouted one of the nurses.

Joanne rounded the corner, a chair in hand. Holding it like she was approaching a growling lion, she slipped through the pulsing doors and jabbed at Mr. K. He released the IV tubing from around Benny's neck. An elevator opened, and Mr. K turned, ran, and jumped in.

***

"Bastard," Joanne muttered, trying to wedge the chair into the closing elevator. She was too late. Benny lay on the floor, gasping for breath. A doctor and nurse arrived, and after a quick examination, the nurse dashed into the ICU and returned with a neck brace.

"Please say he's okay?" Joanne begged.

"He will be," the doctor replied as he and the nurse carefully put the neck brace on Benny.

Joanne silently recited the Lord's Prayer. "Is there anything I can do?" she asked.

"Get some orderlies or more nurses. We need a backboard," the doctor said. Joanne hurried into the ICU, instructed a nurse, and returned to Benny. The big lug looked so helpless.

The elevator opened again, and Joanne turned. She was relieved to see Jimmy. "Oh God, Jimmy, he got Benny," she said.

She watched as Jimmy assessed the situation. She wanted a hug but knew that was a bad idea. They watched as the medical team got the backboard under Benny and placed him on a gurney. Both spotted Benny's gun lying on the floor.

Joanne picked it up. "Let's go get this bastard."

"You're not going anywhere with that," Jimmy said. "Give it to me. I'll call Martin and the team. This guy's a chameleon. He's not that tall. How'd he get the drop on Benny? Damn! Go stay with Benny. I'll make the calls."

Reluctantly, Joanne handed the gun to Jimmy and went into the ICU, where Benny was being settled. Carol stood outside. They held hands when Joanne came within reach.

"Tell me," Carol said softly.

This can't be happening, Joanne thought. *Carol's family, her accountant, her friend Lisa, and now Benny. I've never really wanted to kill anyone, but I could kill Mr. K. You're not even human, you grinning bastard.* Swallowing hard, she faced Carol. "Do you want to sit?"

"Just tell me," Carol insisted.

"Okay, here's what I know. Parts of this we've talked about. Tony is in big trouble for attacking the agent and for Lisa's subsequent death. While the cops did fuck up, his actions and having a gun will be seen by the prosecutor as cause and effect," Joanne said, pausing to study Carol and let that piece sink in.

"As you have surmised, we have a murderer at large. We are calling him Mr. K. He's clever, he's dangerous. He's after everyone at this point. His MO, as you may imagine, is hanging and strangling. No one has ever been this close to him or known this much about him."

"Did he kill Ed? He came into my ICU room, didn't he?" Carol asked.

"We don't know for sure. He's incredibly elusive. He's suspected of over twenty murders internationally, all by strangling or hanging. The current theory is that these are directed and paid by one gang or another," Joanne explained.

"Mafia?" Carol's voice shook.

"That's one possibility. Political motives are also suspected."

"Oh my God, where's Stevie?" Carol's panic rose.

"Let me ask Jimmy. Wait here," Joanne said. Her hands and knees were shaking. She paused, gritting her teeth. She saw Jimmy on the phone. He held up a finger, signaling for her to wait as he listened. She used the moment to slow her breathing and steady her nerves.

"What ya' need?" Jimmy asked as he hung up the phone.

"Where's Stevie?" Joanne demanded.

"She's at the front desk with an FBI agent named Buckman. I'll go get her and bring her here. They'll lock down the ICU when I leave and only open it when I return. The administrator will be declaring a partial lockdown of the facility so we can control access and exits. I'm to stay in the ICU once I secure Stevie. Stay here. Don't wander anywhere. Got that?" Jimmy said.

"Okay. Can I have the gun? I was trained at Quantico," Joanne said.

"Oh, sure, that's a great idea with everyone on oxygen. No!" Jimmy snapped.

"Fine, hurry back," Joanne said, watching as the nurse locked the doors. Jimmy tested them from the outside and gave her a thumbs-up.

Carol is going to be freaked about Roger. She's strong. She'll adapt. Who's that lady crying on her shoulder? Time to let Carol know everything.

"Joanne, this is Donna, Roger's wife. I can't believe he's gone."

"I need to get back to my son. I can't believe he was hit by a car. Oh hell, I was so distracted. I didn't see him run into the street. Oh, Carol, what am I going to do without Roger? He was my rock. Oh, sorry to ask you that. Your world is crumbling too."

"I understand. You're strong. We'll all survive somehow. And little Rogie will be fine. Hold on to that. I wish I could do more," Carol said as she watched Donna walk away.

Carol turned to Joanne, her face angry. "Did you know? Of course, you did."

"I was about to tell you about Roger when everything fell apart. You were in a coma when it happened. I didn't know nightmares could last so long. What a frugal mess," Joanne said, using their childhood code word for a curse.

Carol managed a small smile. "You got that right—a frugal mess."

Joanne squeezed her hand. "Frugal, frugal, frugal."

Chapter 28

* ● *

"I can't believe you're going to the house," said Stevie as they left the hotel where they'd been living for the past two weeks.

"I need stability, Kay needs stability. I want to go home. Kay can't stay alone in her house since they arrested Tony. It's too depressing," said Carol as they got into Stevie's car.

"It's a crime scene. That's depressing, too," Stevie replied.

"I've had the place cleaned and painted. It will be fine. Kay has agreed. Jan packed up some of her things and arranged the guest room. She even brought over a few of the little unicorns Kay likes so much. She's stronger than you think."

"She's focused on getting Tony released. Not sure that's the best idea."

"I talked with Joanne and his lawyer. His release isn't going to happen, but the idea does give Kay hope. She knows the reality but chooses to hold onto the hope."

"Kay does think that way. We've even discussed that Tony might not be good for her. She's not my baby sister anymore. But she still needs us."

"Ya' know, I have another guest room—my upstairs office. I cleared it and moved my stuff to Ed's office. We could all be together. What ya think?" said Carol as Stevie maneuvered her Olds into a parking space at the hospital. *Give her time, MOM. Let her decide.* Silently, she thought, following Stevie into the hospital.

"I'll consider it," said Stevie as they got into the elevator to pick up Kay. Carol saw Joanne standing outside Kay's room.

After hugs, Carol gestured for Stevie to go into the room while she pulled Joanne aside. "So? Did we catch the bastard?"

"I wish. No such luck. They think he has already escaped by boat out of Miami to the islands. We may have to live without knowing," said Joanne.

"Frugal that. I want him dead."

"Me too. We're working on it. Your Mr. Atoll has been charged by both the locals and the feds. They're fighting over him. Tony's cases will be tried separately. His lawyer lobbied for that. Atoll is squealing like a pig, but they are not cutting him much slack. He might get some leniency for what he knows, but both the local and federal prosecutors are done getting screwed by the mafia and friends," said Joanne.

"He should be hanged, too."

"I agree. Let's focus on the good news: Kay has healed well. She's going to your place, right? Ya' know my place isn't that big, but you're both welcome."

"Thanks, but we need to get back to normal including my house. I went there yesterday to make sure everything was set. Jan's been a trouper, stocking up on groceries and keeping an eye on repairs. I'm a lucky girl to have such great friends. I know you're doing everything you can to protect us. I accept that Tony made his own bad choices. Kay knows that, too. So don't be a stranger."

They turned as Stevie rolled Kay out of the room. *My girls. I am lucky.*

"There is another long talk we need to have. I've listened to all the tapes. Ed was not as bad as he could have been, but he was in deep with some bad characters," said Joanne softly as Stevie distracted Kay with reading a Get-Well card.

"Let's make time. I appreciate that you're willing to disclose everything. I am sure you're fighting the authorities on this. I also appreciate that you've somehow completely cleared me and the girls," said Carol as her eyes changed focus from Joanne to Kay.

"I wish the fight was over. I am on your side, my friend. Go take care of your family. I'll call you tonight to set a time to meet for that talk. And please, stay alert to any possible dangers. As you know, there are monsters at large," whispered Joanne as Kay wheeled up.

"Frugal that—no one hurts my girls," said Carol, smiling at Kay, straightening up, and leading the procession homeward.

***

After kissing and hugging goodbye to everyone, Joanne stood alone, reflecting. *Am I the good friend I pretend to be? I feel responsible. Maybe if I'd told Carol more, she'd been able to protect herself and her children.* "Stop, this helps no one," she muttered She went to check on Benny once more before leaving. He was doing well, with only a slight change in his voice that no one would notice.

"What's up, partner? Can't be without me?" Benny croaked as she entered.

"Oh, shut up, you fool. You're getting out tomorrow, right? You staying at your aunt's or going back to that tiny rental apartment? You could come stay with me if you want."

"My apartment's just fine. I'm closing on my condo in two weeks. My car's still in the parking lot here, and Sal insists on driving me home. I'm sure my aunt is the one who insisted. It's kind of nice being around family, especially now that my mom and sister are gone."

"I get that. Tampa's feeling like home."

"I'm getting too old for this shit. I have enough saved up. I'm tired of chasing the next idiot. Right now, everyone is still spooked since they haven't caught their Mr. K."

"About that. Do you think he's gone?" asked Joanne.

"Martin thinks the guy wants to silence anyone who might have seen him. At this point, that's a lot of people. He'd target Carol, Mr. Atoll for sure, Tony, Eddy, and me. And you and lover boy are on the list."

"Don't call him that."

"Sensitive, aren't we? Me thinks she protestith…"

"Shut up. You don't want to hurt your voice," Joanne said, sitting in a side chair.

"You're not responsible for anything that happened. You know that this cluster-fuck has plenty of guilty parties to go around."

"I know you're right, but, well, I like being responsible," Joanne said, standing and putting a kiss on Benny's forehead. "You sure you don't want to stay with me for a few days? I make excellent lasagna."

"I need to go home and get some needed rest. Hospitals don't ever let you rest. Seriously though, what is happening with you and Agent James Perez?"

"We're friends now. Good friends, no benefits. I think he and Sal feel like outsiders. The Tampa police and FDLE are mad at them, though they didn't do anything wrong. The FBI's mad at them too, for reasons nobody understands," Joanne said, sitting back down.

Benny sat straight up and croaked, "You're friggin' kidding me. What about the Tampa police's actions?"

"They are pointing the finger at Sal since he was the liaison. Jimmy and Sal worry they'll be scapegoats in this mess. The Governor needs someone to blame, and the FBI rarely takes responsibility."

"You got that right. Look at poor Toco."

"Sal said he's still hanging around?"

"He came in here one night late—about 2 a.m.—mumbling, 'You good, you good.' He was gone before I fully woke up. I told Sal and he said not to worry."

"I don't know. The guy gives me the creeps. Listen, I gotta go. I'll bring lasagna and beer tomorrow night, and we can plan our next steps. We still have to file reports with the SEC and FBI to complete."

Sal settled back in his bed. Joanne straightened out his blankets.

"I got some papers and notes from Carol on Ed's company that will make us look good and thorough. With all the blame flying around, I want us to still get our pay and get out of this crap," Joanne said, giving Benny's forehead another kiss.

"Keep us smelling pretty."

Walking to her car, Joanne felt a prickling sense of being watched. Even the tiny hairs on her arms raised in warning. She jumped into her car, locked the doors, and quickly called Jimmy. "Where are you? I think I'm being watched."

Chapter 29

Joanne opened her favorite cheap Chianti, a Fiasco, and, after a long slug straight from the bottle, took out all the ingredients for her mother's famous lasagna. The straw-covered bottle added the perfect accent to her cooking atmosphere. Her mom always poured a cup of Chianti into her sauce; Joanne put at least one cup into herself as well. *God, I miss you. Okay, guide my hands Moms and my creation will heal like chicken soup. I'll make you proud.*

As she chopped and stirred, Joanne found herself reviewing options. Benny was healing, but he was not the same. He could retire now—he had his Marine pension and enough savings from living carefully. He could afford the condo he was buying.

The pay from the SEC is not quite enough for me to get a house. That's what I want. A home for myself. I can be close to Carol and the girls. The guy that owns this one said he might let me rent with the option to buy, but without work or someone to do the stuff Benny did, I don't know. I could trust Benny. I can teach stocks analysis to pay the basics but without the contracts, I can make it from paycheck to paycheck. I do have investments. No mind, Lasagna will fix everything.

Two hours went by. Working diligently on each part, noodles, sauce, layering, grating cheeses, mixing, and baking. Busy packing up pans to share, she hardly noticed the time—or the noise out back. Then her senses warned her along with an instinctive sudden arrhythmia.

Putting her sauce-covered hand to her chest, she stood still and held her breath, listening. *Could it be that crazy Toco or Mr. K; it's a cat probably. Her heartbeat continued tapping out her anxiety.* For some reason, she dropped down to the floor, moving on her hands and knees toward where she thought her purse and cell phone were. Groping along the couch, she found her bag. But just as she reached for her phone, the lights went out.

***

"I'm not sure I want to do your check-in with your Jersey Girl. I'll wait in the office or head home. You can call if you need me. Not that what I think should matter. You've all but ruined your career and your marriage," Sal muttered as he shuffled papers on his desk next to Jimmy's.

"Sal, stop busting my balls. My marriage issue wasn't all my fault. Dayna decided it was over."

"Oh, you've re-written the rules, and two wrongs do make a right now?" Sal scoffed.

"If you want to head home, I understand," Jimmy replied.

Jimmy knew Sal was upset with him. But they were partners; they needed information from everyone they could contact. The prosecuting attorneys asked that it not be formal right now. Yet, fact-checking was important. Jimmy kept busy with paperwork, giving Sal time to cool off. Some trust had clearly broken between them.

"No one's home, so I might as well tag along—if you two don't need privacy."

"I've got it under control, and so does she. We are good friends, no benefits. We do need to check on her and the Wallins. You're right; I was stupid for getting involved. But that's over now. Can you try to trust me?" Jimmy asked. He didn't expect an answer as they headed to his SUV.

An uncomfortable silence filled the space between them. They left downtown and headed toward Hyde Park, Jimmy's old danger zone. He missed the excitement but not the guilt. He could feel the anger pulsing off Sal. *It's not only me. He's pissed because the FBI seems to be targeting us. Even his old buddies like Donnie have turned cold. Bastards. Don't want to admit to their part in Mr. K's escape and the death of innocents. Sal's wife was smart enough to go to her sister's place in Ft. Lauderdale since Sal was in a mood.*

It was six p.m. on a Saturday, and Bayshore Boulevard was empty except for the walkers and joggers along Tampa Bay. Jimmy's SUV practically drove itself, pulling into Joanne's alley like it was second nature.

"The lights are out. Let's head to the Wallins," Sal suggested as they stopped.

"Something's not right. She said she was making lasagna and would have some for us to take home. You go up the right side to the front; I'll take the back and the left. There's a porch along that runs down the left and back. I'll try to get in from there while you take the front," Jimmy said, exiting the car.

Both followed the prescribed course. Jimmy thought he saw a shadow running as he reached the left porch. Too worried about Joanne to pursue, he opened the screen door and tried the sliding door. "Joanne, it's me. You okay?"

"Jimmy, thank God!" Joanne said, rushing over as Sal entered from the front.

"We're back here. I saw someone run across the street," said Jimmy.

"I didn't see anyone. I'll check the electric box. Could've been Toco. I think he likes watching her," Sal said as he headed back out.

"Great, I'm watched by a perv," Joanne muttered.

Jimmy's stomach lurched as he turned back and noticed a dark stain on Joanne's shirt. "Don't worry. We'll take you to the hospital. Please, sit down."

"This is tomato sauce, you idiot," Joanne laughed just as the lights flickered back on.

Sal came through the screen door. "Someone cut the electricity off. You'll have to report it to Florida Power and Light so they can put their straps back on the cut-off box. Something smells amazing here. I assume all that red on your chest is sauce, or you'd be lying on the ground," he smirked.

"Well, big brave Jimbo was about to haul me to the ER," Joanne teased. But her smile faded as a thought struck her. "Do you think Mr. K is still around? Why would anyone want to hurt me? What is it they think I know? Oh shit, what about Carol and the girls?" She hurried to grab her bag and headed toward the bedroom. "We need to get to their place. Can you do another check-around?"

Jimmy reached for Joanne's landline to call the police. "The line's dead," he told Sal.

"She's right; we need to get over to the Wallins. Use your cell phone, or we can use my car phone. We need to move now. Joanne, what's taking you so long? Where the hell are you?" asked Jimmy as he walked into the living room.

"Sorry, just needed to pee and change my shirt," Joanne replied, rushing back into the kitchen. She packed the lasagna pans and a few bottles of chianti that were on the counter.

Both Jimmy and Sal stood watching and shaking their heads in tandem.

"Don't call those stupid Tampa cops. They might shoot someone again. At the very least, they'll scare Kay. She's just gotten home after they shot her," Joanne reminded them.

Jimmy and Sal double-checked that everything was locked up, as Joanne called Carol to tell her they were on their way.

"Carol's been through enough. We can't let anything happen to her or the family," Joanne said, her voice firm.

"We need to call for backup," Sal insisted as they made their way to the Wallins. With a nod from Jimmy, he dialed from the car.

"Not the Tampa cops!" Joanne protested.

"Listen, it's only if we need help. I'm calling over to FDLE. Technically, we should call Tampa, but you're right, it is not a good situation with them right now. I'm alerting my Captain. Call me if the coast is clear. The captain will decide who will be back up," said Sal.

Sal explained things briefly to the captain during the five-minute drive. Sal got out on the side street and signaled that he would go around the front. Jimmy maneuvered his SUV lights out behind Carol's house. Putting his finger to his lips, both he and Joanne listened and studied the house. The lights were on in the kitchen, and no lights upstairs.

"Be careful. We still haven't found Wallin's son Eddy. He could be as dangerous as Mr. K. at this point. He knows he's in trouble and might need money since everybody is looking for him, and he wouldn't have access to his account," whispered Jimmy. *Don't do anything brave either,* he thought. He touched Joanne's shoulder, urging her to stay safe.

***

Joanne gave him a thumbs up and opened to get out. *Well, if he's around he probably saw the light when the car doors opened. Real sneaky. Shit!* Walking as quietly as possible, she approached the door to the dark lanai. "Carol?" she whispered to a shadow figure near the lounge chairs.

"Oh, thank goodness it's you," Carol replied, clutching a potted plant in one hand. "I heard the car and picked up this plant as a weapon. Silly, right? I knew you were coming, but I didn't want to take any chances."

"We're being cautious. You can put down the frugal plant, Carol. Everything's fine," Joanne said, half-smiling.

"That's fucking plant not a 'frugal' plant now. I've grown up these past few weeks," Carol joked, her smile shaky.

"I've got to call Sal so he doesn't call the calvary. Everything good inside? Were you able to check around?"

When Joanne finished assuring Sal that all was well, they both went to the car and collected the food. Once deposited in the kitchen, she walked over to Carol with her arms wide open. Giving her a big hug, she said, "It's gonna be okay. I've got lots of lasagna. You know it's better than chicken soup."

"I know. But we didn't catch Mr. K, as you call him. Tony's situation isn't good. Lord knows what's happening with Eddy."

"The boys are looking around, so one foot then the other, girl. You're not the hysterical type. That's my job. I'll get the wine."

Joanne relaxed as Jimmy came around the corner and gave her a thumbs-up. Carol was standing still, holding a wine glass, when she returned with the lasagna bag in one hand, and two bottles of wine clutched to her chest.

"Hey you, open the screen door. I've got refreshments," Joanne called, seeing Carol's face relax as she let them in. They opened the wine and set the food on the counter.

"Was that your doorbell? It's probably Sal. Go let him in. I'll put the lasagna in the oven. Let's eat and drink," Joanne said.

"Sounds perfect," Carol replied, turning to Jimmy. "I have some questions, Detective."

"So do I," Jimmy replied with a half-smile.

"Don't know the question, but lasagna's the answer," interjected Joanne. *Please, we need one night without a tragedy. It's family time, damn it.*

Chapter 30

---·●·---

Carol was glad Joanne had come over. She was even grateful that the two policemen showed up. It was comforting to have Sal check outside. The front doorbell startled her. *That must be him ringing at the front door*, she thought. "Stevie, can you answer that? It's probably Jimmy's partner, Sal."

She watched as Kay, Joanne, and Jimmy busied themselves in the kitchen.

"Let's use the good China and make this a celebration," Kay said, pulling a pork roast out of the oven. Jimmy opened a bottle of chianti, and Joanne unwrapped one lasagna pan to let the top melt and crisp while Carol put a second in the refrigerator.

"Do you want me to make a salad?" asked Kay.

"Dressing might interfere with some good wine drinking," teased Joanne.

Carol watched as everyone moved around the kitchen in a kind of dance—a family dance. She liked Jimmy; he had checked on her often in the past month. She could tell from the things Joanne said that they were close. His partner, Sal, seemed like a family guy as well. Kay seemed to be handling things well, even though she'd been estranged from Tony since he was out on bail. *I need to talk to Kay about that*, Carol thought. *She's been through so much. She's stronger than I gave her credit for.*

"I've got some nice cheeses in the fridge, as well as salami, prosciutto, and olives. We can nibble on that while the lasagna is warming," said Carol, snapping back to the task.

"I'll set the table. Should I use the dishes in the dining room cabinet?" asked Jimmy. He froze as he started to move from the kitchen to the dining room, his hand instinctively going to his gun.

"I wouldn't do that unless you want Stevie to get hurt," Carol heard Eddy say from the living room.

As if propelled by a tornado, Carol grabbed Kay, her purse, and rushed out the pantry door before Eddy could notice. Joanne grabbed a knife, concealing it, and then followed Carol and Kay.

"We can't call the police," begged Kay as Carol pulled her across the back of the yard.

"We'll call the FBI. Their guy instructed me to call if we saw Eddy or any of the crazy guys they're looking for," said Carol firmly.

You will not hurt my babies. Carol instructed Kay to get her cell phone out of her purse and call Donnie Castillo's number. *This time, they'd better not fuck it up. She could take Kay away, but that would leave Stevie. Her car was blocked anyway. Joanne's Jimmy has a gun. Does that make things better or worse? Where's that other policeman Sal Carducci?*

***

"We don't want anyone to get hurt. What can I do to help you, Eddy?" asked Jimmy, hoping to de-escalate the situation. He carefully surveyed the area he could see. A sliver of light from the streetlamp outside the front door told him the front door wasn't fully closed. Eddie's gun was small but still deadly.

"Where's Kay? Where's Carol?" demanded Eddy.

"Carol and Kay just left to get some bread. What do you need from her? Maybe I can help," said Jimmy.

"She always keeps cash around. I need it."

"Okay, we can get that. Maybe Stevie knows. But she's scared right now. Please lower your gun, and she can go get any money that's here," suggested Jimmy.

Stevie said slowly and deliberately, "Eddy, it's in the office."

"Take me to the cash, now!" demanded Eddy.

"Easy, Eddy. No one needs to get hurt. I'm sure Stevie is willing to help you. We all are," said Jimmy, noticing Eddy's grip on Stevie was tightening.

"Since when are the fucking police willing to help me? If anything happens, it's on you. I know you're a cop. Where's your partner? You've been chasing me day and night. You went after my stupid Dad."

Stevie stood very still. Jimmy could see her breathing slowly, gaining control of her emotions. Now, he just had to keep Eddy from hurting her.

"It's hard to have an addict in the family. It was a compulsion—he had to gamble," said Jimmy, focusing intently on Eddy. He wanted to look around more but knew that would spook him.

"I couldn't believe Dad lost all that money, the money we borrowed from the wrong people. Mom was right about him. We had to do what we did. The guy was our only choice. Now he's after me. Everyone's after me," rambled Eddy.

Jimmy's training taught him to empathize and stay calm. "You were desperate. Your Dad put you in a bad position, and you had to handle things." He noticed the sliver of light behind Eddy shift and then return to steady luminescence. *Someone came in the front door. Maybe it's Sal. Just keep him calm.*

"Okay, Eddy, we'll let Stevie go get your money. I'll back up into the kitchen and stay out of your way. You can wait there in the living room. Does that work for you?" asked Jimmy.

"You think I'm stupid? Give me your gun."

"No need for guns. I'll just put it down. See? No problem," Jimmy said, removing his gun from the holster and placing it on the floor, hoping Eddy didn't see him quickly remove the clip.

"Kick it over here."

Jimmy gently kicked the gun; it slid about six feet into the dining room but was still about 10 feet from Eddy.

"Now, you get me the money, and don't get cute, or someone's going to get hurt," warned Eddy.

"No problem. I'll get it. I'm moving toward the office now," said Jimmy, taking a route around the other side of the table rather than near the gun.

Eddy backed up, his gun still aimed at Stevie but no longer pressed to her temple. Jimmy watched him back out of the living room up the small step and toward the stairs. Stevie pointed to the office on the other side of the dining and living room. With his hands raised, palms out, Jimmy walked backward toward the office, catching a glimpse of movement behind the large rubber plant by the stairs.

Got my ankle gun, but he's got too tight of a hold on Stevie. Can't take the chance.

"Tell him where," Eddy demanded.

"Left bottom desk drawer, under the hanging files," said Stevie.

"Thanks, Stevie. I'll bring it right to you." *Good girl. Nice and calm.*

"Nothing funny."

Keeping his hands raised, Jimmy backed into the office, turned on the light, and opened the drawer. He reached under the files, found an envelope, and removed it. "Got it, coming right out," he said, quickly pocketing his ankle gun. He exited with the envelope in his raised hand.

Eddy's eyes were fixed on the envelope, his grip on Stevie loosening. *Just a little more, girl. Slowly, slowly.*

Suddenly, a figure jumped up and struck Eddy on the head. The gun fell, Stevie screamed, and Toco ran out the door, yelling, "Get ambulance for Sally Sal, hurry," and then slammed the front door behind him.

Jimmy heard noises outside the front door. He secured Eddy's gun and Eddy, who was still out. Stevie stood there, wide-eyed.

"Be careful, Stevie. Step aside," Jimmy said as he raised his gun. Stevie stepped back. There was a scuffle, then a thud at the front door. He lowered his gun and cracked open the door.

"Got ya, you SOB!" Carol yelled, holding a broken rake handle. Jimmy looked down and saw Toco lying on the bottom step. "Wow, you're strong; I've got him now," said Jimmy as he pulled more quick ties out of his back pocket.

"I think that's Sal lying near the corner of the house," Carol added.

Jimmy secured Toco, then called for backup while running over to Sal.

"What the hell?" Joanne asked, arriving at the scene.

"Jimmy's gone to take care of Sal. Kay's hiding in my car with the doors locked. I called the FBI," Carol explained in a breathless rush.

Ten tense minutes flew by but too slowly for Jimmy. Sal was still unconscious. There was a rope in Sal's hand. He couldn't tell if he'd been choked, but he was breathing. Just as Jimmy was about to call again, three black SUVs and an ambulance arrived.

"Over here; you may need another bus or two," yelled Jimmy. He then directed the ambulance. When he was sure Sal was safe, he spoke with Donnie. Meanwhile, three FBI agents stepped over Toco.

They entered the house, squeezing around Stevie and Joanne. Three others spread out around the property.

"Where's Kay?" Jimmy asked Carol.

"Locked in my car," Carol replied.

Jimmy spoke with an agent standing guard, and he and Carol went to the back to let Kay know it was safe.

"Something's burning!" yelled an agent from inside.

"There goes dinner. Well, we still have wine," Joanne joked, heading back inside.

"Try not to laugh too much," Jimmy said, watching her grin.

The hand gesture was subtle, but Jimmy understood. *Even with all this, she's the tough Jersey Girl. Damn, these women are something special.*

***

Joanne took a big swig of chianti. Everyone was putting on brave faces, and hers would be reinforced with wine. *Drinking from the bottle could become a habit. Uh-oh, ruined this batch of lasagna. Good thing I brought extra. What a frugal mess. Yup, Carol's right. We've officially graduated to a fucking mess.*

They'd all answered questions for hours. The killer had slipped away again. Stevie was fussing in the fridge as Carol, Kay, and

Jimmy came in through the lanai door with an FBI agent on their heels.

"We'll check the rest of the house inside and out again to make sure it's secure before we leave," said the agent as he headed out of the kitchen.

"How's Sal?" Joanne asked.

"I thought he'd only been choked. During the struggle with Mr. K, he was thrown down. He hit his head on a rock. He woke up just when the ambulance arrived. Said he almost got our elusive Mister K. He's disappointed but he'll be fine," said Jimmy.

Kay looks pale and shaky. Lasagna. Everyone needs lasagna. "Come over here, my Kick um Kay. Aunt JoJo's got a big hug," Joanne said.

Without hesitation, Kay melted into her arms. "The men I trusted weren't who I thought they were. My sympathy for Eddy and Tony has run its course, and I am done babying my dear husband," Kay said, tears spilling down her cheeks.

Joanne admired the strength in Kay's voice. *This little lady has grown up. Unfortunately, the hard way.* "You got that right. Bizarre as it is, I'm starving. How about you all?"

Stevie came into the kitchen and put her arms around Kay's shoulder. Joanne saw her concerned look.

"We can let the cops do their thing and enjoy our feast. They can't question us with full mouths," said Joanne, trying to lighten the mood.

"I agree. Let's finish setting the table and eat. Oh dear, is that the lasagna all burnt? I like the crispy parts, but that might be too much," Stevie observed, looking at the pan on the counter.

"No problem, the second batch will be ready in 15. Let's put the finishing touches on the antipasto and set the table with the good china. Sound okay, Carol?" asked Joanne.

"You're right. Time to eat," said Carol while she grabbed a water glass, holding it almost steady as she extended her arm to Joanne.

Filling it with Chianti, Joanne smiled at Carol and the two girls. *God, I love this family.*

Chapter 31

———— • ⬤ • ————

At Sal's bedside, Jimmy tried to figure out his next steps. Sal would recover, just like Benny had. And, like Benny, he planned to quit. *Can't believe Mr. K got away again. And, as usual, the FBI managed to blame Sal and me for the* chaos. *Benny was only ten years younger than Sal, even though he was technically Sal's nephew. Weird. Sal's right; he stayed way past his time. He thought the FDLE was going to be an easy way to get to sixty-two. Not so easy.*

Jimmy's attention was drawn to Sal's movements. The brain bleed and subsequent stroke from his head injury had kept him hospitalized. For the last month, Jimmy had either been working to wrap up the convoluted case or sitting here by Sal's bedside.

It was time to make some decisions about his own future. *Should I leave the FDLE, too? Joanne had suggested he work with her. Could they work together? He wasn't so sure. The initial heightened passion had worn off. She thinks 10 years is too much of a gap. In fact, it was probably only nine. Men do it all the time. She's in good shape, too.* He knew he was thinking with the wrong brain. Sal stirred again like a quiet conscience.

Okay, let's weigh the pros and cons.

My skills fit. Military security, forensic accounting, psychology, investigative experience.

Her skills fit back. Stocks and bonds, business connections, business acumen, FBI training, investigative experience.

Both of them could take on side investigations to support the day-to-day. They could also teach if they needed extra income. Plus, they had enough savings to help get them started.

Joanne even had some international banking experience with Barclay's, Deutsche Bank, and J.P. Morgan. He had some international investigative experience through Interpol, from when he helped integrate the worldwide fingerprint identification system. Joanne was fluent in Italian, and Jimmy in Spanish and Italian.

A good fit if my correct brain was engaged. This might be the best move.

***

Joanne hesitated at the door to Sal's room. She could see Jimmy sitting there, deep in thought. *Is he considering my offer?* She wondered. She hoped so. Benny had decided he needed a life outside the FDLE. He was good at so many things. She knew he'd miss the rush of being on the chase, that thrill of knowing you're close to a breakthrough. But he wouldn't miss the near-death experiences. He'd had enough of those.

She believed she and Jimmy could work together. The sexual tension could work in their favor or against them. What if she dated someone? Would he get jealous? What if he did? Would it come between them? *I guess it would be like living in Florida. You know there could be a hurricane. You need to be prepared.* Still smiling, she walked into Sal's room.

"How's the patient?"

"I'm fine," Sal croaked.

"Here, take some water," Jimmy said, holding out a cup.

"Where's Marie?" asked Sal.

"I sent her to get some food."

"Good. How's everyone else doing? I'm furious that bastard got the drop on me. If my head hadn't hit that rock, I would've had him. I'm surprised he didn't finish me off."

"I think all the confusion scared him off. And, of course, the feds are blaming us again."

"Toco was released from the hospital yesterday. Cleaned up and on medication, he's not a bad-looking guy. He and I had a long talk.

He still has a crush on you, Jersey girl. Of course, he talked a lot about you, too, Sal. Said you two had a conversation," Jimmy added.

"Not your business," Sal muttered.

Joanne noticed the slight tension between Jimmy and Sal. She felt a pang of guilt, knowing she had caused a rift between them. *I hope Mr. K has left for good this time.* Her 'no benefits' relationship with Jimmy had started with the dissection of Ed and Atoll's tapes, and it had paid off. Satisfaction replaced her guilt as she remembered how she and Jimmy had traced the money and proved Charles Atoll's fraud. They'd recovered the money he stashed. The SEC was satisfied, too, so it had all worked out. *We do make a good team.*

"So, is this your new partner?" Sal asked, catching Joanne by surprise. Her heart almost stopped as she looked at Jimmy, waiting for his answer.

"Yes. Yes, she is," he replied. "Now it's time for you to get the hell out of the hospital and stop leaving me with all the paperwork."

Joanne took a deep breath and decided to address the situation head-on. Sal was an important part of Jimmy's life and was close to Benny. "How do you feel about that?" she asked Sal directly.

"At first, I was pissed at both of you acting like horny teens. But you do work well together, and I am retiring. More importantly, can you make a living at this? Benny said he's ready to slow down, so you do need some muscle. And, much as I hate to admit it, Jimbo here is intelligent muscle."

Joanne looked from Sal to Jimmy. *What could she say? Her finances would be tight. If they could pick up a job within the next two months, they could make it. If not, it would be hard.* "It will be a tough first year financially the next," she admitted. "But I'm confident a job will come along soon. My reputation is solid, even with the flak the FBI is trying to throw. My clients were satisfied. To tell the truth, with Jimmy's educational and investigative credentials, our resumes are strong."

The smile on Sal's face was like a massage. As Joanne's shoulders relaxed, she looked at Jimmy. "We're doing this, right?"

"Go get us some work, woman."

Chapter 32

———— • ● • ————

Carol's decision to sell her home finally felt right. Too much had happened here. *There was that apartment in a building off Swan that was for sale. An apartment facing Tampa Bay would be lovely.* Could she live in an apartment? She certainly didn't need a three thousand square foot house. *Maybe a smaller house that is still in the Tampa Hyde Park area.*

A sound from the back of the house made her jump. She peered out from the lanai and spotted the culprit—a squirrel. Since they hadn't caught Mr. K, she was easily startled. Joanne had assured her he had left the area, but still… Maybe focusing on a new business and selling the house is the best way forward. She tried to relax in a lounge chair, enjoying the mild evening. The Florida humidity had finally subsided.

The ringing phone brought her to her feet. She hurried to the kitchen and grabbed the receiver. "Hello? Hello? Damn, missed it."

Walking around the kitchen, she took stock of her belongings. So much stuff. She'd have to let go of many things to live in an apartment. An ache in her chest reminded her that her grief over losing Ed, Roger, and Lisa was not over. They'd never determined if Ed's death was murder or suicide. *They say not to make big changes when you are grieving. Will I ever stop grieving? It was time to plan something new. My whole family is grieving.*

Poor Kay must sell her home. Her divorce from Tony is imminent. Maybe I could buy a place where we all could live. Hold on, Cowgirl. Your children are grown women who need their own space. Still, it would be nice if the girls could live together.

Carol continued her inner dialogue while making herself a sandwich. These musings had been her constant companion in recent months. The girls had already told her to sell, and they'd turned down any offers of help. Kay had enrolled in college to renew her teaching certificate. Stevie was doing well with her medical coding business and had even hired a team. She'd also met a lovely doctor.

The ringing phone interrupted her thoughts.

"Joanne! So nice to hear your voice. Did I miss your call earlier? Sorry about that. Were you able to settle everything with the SEC? Oh good. Glad you finally got fully paid," Carol said, listening as Joanne updated her on her business. She was so happy for Joanne.

Jimmy seemed like a great fit for her business. Actually, she thought it was a shame it was strictly business between Joanne and Jimmy. *Well, time will tell.*

"Yes, I'd love it if you came over. I want you to take a critical look at the house—time to sell. I know you told me. I'm ready to sell. I know you've been telling me this for a while. I'm finally ready. How about seven tonight? And bring Jimmy. I have a business proposal for both of you."

Their friendship had picked up as if it had never drifted. Although the grief over Lisa wasn't gone, Joanne had managed to join Carol and Jan, building a new sisterhood. Now Carol was ready to move forward.

Carol had seen an emerging technology at a tech show in 1999. It was called Bluetooth. Some very talented programmers and engineers she knew had approached her to invest in their development of Bluetooth technology beyond voice to all forms of communication, even music and gaming. She hoped Joanne and Jimmy would do some hard investigating of their business. They were poised to take it public. Joanne could help with that. Jimmy's expertise in forensic accounting could ensure there was no funny business. On the accounting side, she was lost without Roger Barnes. *So many losses.*

The day passed quickly as Carol puttered around the house, eventually sitting down to type up her proposal for Joanne and Jimmy. She knew it was formal to draft a plan and contract before even discussing it, but organizing her ideas was as much for herself as it was for them. *After all, this is about new technology.*

The doorbell chimed as Carol finished arranging a tray of fruit, cheese, and vegetables.

Hugs completed, Carol ushered them through the living room into the office. "I thought we would do business before pleasure."

While Jimmy borrowed a notepad to make notes, Joanne highlighted sections of the proposal as she reviewed it.

"This looks like a great opportunity," Jimmy said. "I read about the Bluetooth Special Interest Group that was formed recently. One article credited Hedy Lamarr with laying the groundwork for initial technology."

"I knew she was more than just a pretty face. You two are the technology buffs here. I can help with taking this public. Your timeline is ambitious, but with technology, it's best to move quickly," said Joanne.

"To be honest, this is exactly what we need to get our business on its feet. I want to get away from hard-core criminals, and this would be perfect," Jimmy added.

"As we've seen in the past few months, though, white-collar criminals can have some nasty types as well," Joanne said.

They all nodded in agreement.

"Speaking of that, any news? Is everyone sure your Mr. K has left the country?" asked Carol.

"Sorry, but we're not sure about anything," Jimmy replied. "There was a reported sighting in the Bahamas, and now they think he may have gone to Taiwan. They don't have an extradition treaty with us, but who knows."

"No matter. I need to focus on something new. So, what do you think of this idea? The company needs funding and experienced management. I have both. I'd like you two to get things rolling as we take it public," Carol said.

"This is making me hungry," teased Joanne.

Carol laughed as they made their way to the kitchen. After snacking and sipping some wine, they returned to the office.

"Joanne, I'm hoping you have a connection with a reputable underwriter. I'd like you to help select one, and then both you and Jimmy would oversee the SEC review," Carol said as everyone settled into their chairs. She waited as Joanne and Jimmy went over the proposal one more time.

"Hard to refuse. The money you're offering is fair, though I may need to adjust the figures a bit. Are you comfortable with that? I don't want anything to get in the way of our friendship."

"I've worked with friends before, and I know we can navigate the agreement and the relationship. You'd both be doing me a favor. Having two people I trust on the team would be a huge relief," Carol replied.

Carol noticed Joanne working through her mental list of pros and cons while Jimmy was visibly enthusiastic. She could tell he was fully on board; the technology excited him as much as it did her.

"Are you prepared for all this with everything that's happened? You and the kids are finally able to breathe again. Are you sure this isn't too much, too soon?"

"I am sure. So many changes and losses. But as T.S. Eliot said, 'Only those who risk going too far can possibly find out how far they can go.'"

About the Author

Susa Capo has spent years crafting stories that capture life's messy, complex truths. With a unique perspective and an ability to portray raw human emotions, she uses life's pains and pleasures as the foundation for profound storytelling. Enough Rope reflects this voice—a gritty, unfiltered exploration of relationships, loss, and resilience.

Susa Capo's stories cut to the bone, weaving truth from the messiness of life with a voice that dares to be unfiltered and deeply human. Enough Rope is not just a book; it's an invitation to face the rawest parts of ourselves and find strength in the unvarnished reality of being.

Known for writing with a deep sense of empathy and realism, Capo invites readers to see themselves in characters facing the hardest of choices, delivering a story that lingers long after the last page.

www.ingramcontent.com/pod-product-compliance
Lightning Source LLC
Chambersburg PA
CBHW071235300726
48975CB00002B/423